A RIVER OF ROYAL BLOOD

AMANDA JOY

putnam

G. P. PUTNAM'S SONS

G. P. Putnam's Sons
An imprint of Penguin Random House LLC, New York

Copyright © 2019 by Amanda Saulsberry
Map illustration copyright © 2019 by Cheryl Thuesday
Map hand-lettering copyright © 2019 by Amanda Saulsberry
Penguin supports copyright. Copyright fuels creativity, encourages diverse voices,
promotes free speech, and creates a vibrant culture. Thank you for buying an authorized
edition of this book and for complying with copyright laws by not reproducing, scanning,
or distributing any part of it in any form without permission. You are supporting writers
and allowing Penguin to continue to publish books for every reader.

G. P. Putnam's Sons is a registered trademark of Penguin Random House LLC.

Visit us online at penguinrandomhouse.com

Library of Congress Cataloging-in-Publication Data
Names: Joy, Amanda.
Title: A river of royal blood / Amanda Joy.
Description: New York: G. P. Putnam's Sons, [2019] | Summary: Seventeen-year-old
Eva must harness the magick inside her to defeat her older sister, Isadore, as well as
other forces, and win the crown in the Queendom of Myre—or die trying.
Identifiers: LCCN 2019021262 (print) | LCCN 2019022309 (ebook)
| ISBN 9780525518587 (hardback)
Subjects: CYAC: Magic—Fiction. | Princesses—Fiction.
| Sisters—Fiction. | Fairies—Fiction. | Fantasy.
Classification: LCC PZ7.1.J8 Riv 2019 (print)
| LCC PZ7.1.J8 (ebook) | DDC [Fic]—dc23
LC record available at https://lccn.loc.gov/2019021262
LC ebook record available at https://lccn.loc.gov/2019022309

Printed in the United States of America
ISBN 9781984816528

1 3 5 7 9 10 8 6 4 2

Design by Suki Boynton
Text set in Fournier MT Pro

This is a work of fiction. Names, characters, places, and incidents either are the product
of the author's imagination or are used fictitiously, and any resemblance to actual persons,
living or dead, businesses, companies, events, or locales is entirely coincidental.

To Kiki and Madge, who never once stopped believing

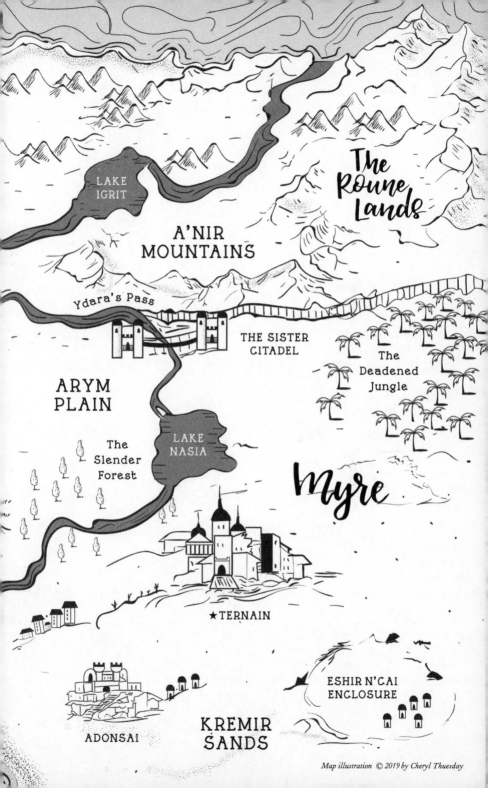

Map illustration © 2019 by Cheryl Thuesday

The Naming

ASIM HAD NEVER known a spell of Harkening to last this long.

It was his tenth morning venturing to the spellwork chamber at dawn to collect a sheet of parchment slipped under the door. So far they had been unmarked, which meant his Sorceryn brethren still had not determined the magick inside the Princess. Every day after learning there was no news, he would climb to the top of the Temple and send up a plume of blue smoke, conveying the message to the city.

Harkenings—the spells cast by Sorceryn to name the magick inside newborn human children—weren't usually cause for such ceremony. But in Myre, nothing was so closely followed as the birth, and subsequent naming, of a Princess.

Asim walked the dim halls of the Temple. Robed Sorceryn nodded grimly as he passed. They knew his task. He wondered if inside they were half holding their breath, as he was.

Today he would likely find the parchment slashed with black ink for death. A Harkening spell that lasted longer than five days was dangerous, but once the spell had begun, it could not be broken. After ten days, the chances of survival were exceedingly slim.

He rounded the last corner and stopped cold. The bronze doors of the Spellwork Chamber were thrown open and five Sorceryn stood in the hallway. One held a small, wild-haired thing, howling and swaddled in bright poppy cloth—the Princess.

They murmured the name of her magick in reverent voices, barely noticing his presence. He was, after all, just an apprentice.

Asim spun on his heel and headed to the aviary. He should have gone straight to the Temple's roof and lit the signal fire, but there was another task he must see to first. Head bowed, Asim moved through the halls quickly, lest anyone notice the delay. He crested the Temple's central staircase but stopped before he reached the top. Instead he took a sharp left and emerged in the musty room where the messenger ravens were housed. Already Asim could hear the bells of the Ivory Tower ringing to announce the end of the spell, meaning the apprentice sent to bring word to the Queen's Palace had already arrived. Asim was already minutes behind.

Myre's capital, Ternain, would soon descend into celebration. It was as everyone had hoped: a girl child, a Rival Heir born to fight for her seat upon the throne. For Queens ruled in Myre and killed for the right to do so. Weeks ago the Auguries had predicted a Blood Moon, an omen of great change, would rise tonight. At sundown people would fill the streets—fey, bloodkin, and human alike—chanting as the Sorceryn had.

Asim hastily affixed a message to a raven's leg and reached below his collar, fingering the tattoo inked upon his shoulder. He whispered a location into the bird's ear.

Once he felt the magick take hold, he sent the raven gliding out of a nearby window.

✦

The raven flew north. Day turned to night as it followed the Red River up through the mountains beyond Myre, until finally it came to a valley ringed with sheer cliffs, like a mouth full of broken teeth. The creature alighted on a black tent in the small camp assembled at the foot of the highest peak.

Drawn by the familiar scrape of talons against canvas, a horned woman with silver hair and a smooth, unlined face emerged. Shielding her face against snowfall, she scanned the white-capped peaks that encircled the valley, the snow glistening beneath a bleeding moon, and removed the small, hollow bone strapped to the raven's leg. It was about the size of a finger joint and sealed with blue wax; she tucked the message into the folds of her cotton skirt and returned to her tent.

The woman lit a candle and carried it to her bedroll before easing the strip of parchment from its tight roll. There were just three words: *Marrow and blood*.

She read the message three times, the words sinking into her skin like frost, and then held the paper to the flame. As it crumbled to ash, she began to plan the fall of a Queendom.

– I –
BLOOD MAGICK

Magick of marrow and blood, a rare gift, held most notably by the first human Queen of Myre and continued through her line. It is also the most fearsome. Despite a Court known to exalt the strength of its monarchs, the gruesome practices of this magick have made it a subject of whispers and, for its users, shame.

This is unsurprising. Power has always inspired fear.

—From *Killeen: The Cobalt Dagger of Myre*, by Kreshi Isomar

✦ CHAPTER 1 ✦

THE PASSAGE BENEATH my bedchamber was silent as a crypt, though as always, the Empress scorpions that nested in these forgotten tunnels started hissing disapproval the moment my feet touched the ground.

I crouched and checked the circle of cinnamon sticks and dried lavender I'd laid to deter the wicked beasts, and then knotted the hem of my skirt. If left hanging, the chime and rattle of its beading would echo through the passages, and although I'd never crossed paths with anyone here, I couldn't risk discovery.

I adjusted the belt knife in its soft leather holster at the small of my back. Whenever I shifted, nicks in the wooden handle scratched my skin, but it couldn't be helped. This knife was my only weapon plain enough to suit this disguise. In a floor-sweeping skirt and a top that bared my midriff but covered my arms and their tattoos, I could pass as a common human girl out for a night of revelry.

Flint struck stone inches from my face, sparks dancing through inky darkness. I jumped, a curse on my lips, but my hand fell from my knife. "I'd appreciate some warning next time."

"Just keeping you sharp," said the young man standing mere feet away.

Falun, second-in-command of my guard and my closest friend, towered over me in the cramped passage. He was long-limbed and graceful, though still not quite grown into his wide shoulders. Like many of the fey, who originally came from the North, Falun was fair-skinned and fine-haired. Even in the scant torchlight, his skin gleamed like mother-of-pearl. All the fey had a certain sameness—luminous skin, oversize eyes, pointed ears, and vibrant coloring—but Falun was among the most beautiful. His hair was streaked with apple red and dark gold, and the sharp line of his jaw emphasized his full-lipped smile.

Two nights ago, Falun had gone to my room at dawn to propose a journey to the kitchens and found me missing, my bed pushed aside, trapdoor hanging open. He knew I became restless at night, and instead of sounding the alarm, he'd waited until I returned. In exchange for such a kindness, I'd decided to bring him tonight, though I'd been very light on the details.

Falun held the torch to the passage wall, the dancing flames making his blue eyes flash silver as he inspected the words engraved on the stone. They were written in the khimaer language, the sinuous alphabet of the people who'd once ruled from this Palace. Nearly two hundred years ago, humans had wrested control of the Queendom from the khimaer, but signs of the previous rulers still lingered all over Myre.

Falun's eyebrows rose as he recognized the language. "How did you find this place?"

"When I was seven, Isadore and I found the trapdoor after her earring rolled under my bed." I didn't add that we'd found a similar hatch beneath hers and spent a year sleeping very little as we explored every inch of these passages at night.

I went to great lengths to avoid discussing my sister.

The tips of Falun's tapered ears went pink. "Isadore knows about this place? Don't you worry about seeing her?"

I snorted. "Why would my sister come here? There is nothing about the Palace that would make her want to leave."

"True enough." He swiped a hand across his face, but his grimace remained in place. "I'll regret this, won't I?"

"You won't, and you know it—why else would you have come?"

He leaned forward as if sharing a secret. "Actually I came to keep you out of trouble."

"And that works just as well." I grinned, even though I could protect myself. I snatched his torch and snuffed out the flames beneath my boot. "Follow me."

We ran through darkness so thick the only sign of Falun beside me was his hand in mine. After months of sneaking out through these passages, finding my escape route—and avoiding the scorpion nests—had become second nature. When Isadore and I were children, we'd stuck to the passages around our quarters, but when I returned to the capital ten months ago and began exploring again, I soon realized they tunneled through the grounds around the Queen's Palace, right up to its outer wall. The floors of the passages changed now from stone to tile to packed earth, a sure sign that we were close. After about a mile, we stopped at a steel ladder. Night air blew through an opening overhead.

I climbed to the top and emerged in an orchard with rows of flowering trees, though they didn't bloom during the scorching weeks of high summer, as it was now. Fresh air kissed my skin, heavy with damp heat. I breathed it in, my pulse a driving beat beneath my skin.

Almost, it hummed.

Falun joined me, following my gaze to a carved expanse of white stone.

The wall that marked my freedom.

I wasn't allowed outside it without a guard of at least twenty, per my mother's stipulations. Compared to my home for the previous three years—at Fort Asrodei, an army base in the highlands, where my father still lived—the Palace was cramped and held little of interest. Every room crawled with courtiers, the very last people I wanted encounter. Aside from training at the sparring grounds and attending Court every morning, I rarely left my rooms. These nightly excursions were my only escape.

We scaled the wall and dropped down into a vacant alley in the bloodkin sector.

Four races dwelled in Myre—human, fey, bloodkin, and khimaer. Of the four, only bloodkin, fey, and humans were allowed to live freely in the capital, and the city was divided evenly among them. Humans lived in the southern sector, fey in the east, and bloodkin in the north. The Red River was west of the city, where its red-brown waters were clogged with river ships and water markets.

Falun and I left the alley and emerged in a narrow avenue lined with abandoned flats and blood brothels. The men and women strolling beside us could've passed for human—the darkness hid the telling red tinge to their skin—but for the bloodletting knives at their belts, the scabbards marked with patterns to signify the wearer's trade. When bloodkin reached maturity at seventeen, they sustained themselves by drinking the blood of the living. The narrow blades weren't worn out of necessity—bloodkin largely used their fangs to feed—but were mandated by a law created so that humans who feared bloodkin could identify them at a distance.

The northern sector was a warren of streets so cramped you could barely tell them from the alleys. Most shops were shuttered and didn't look like they'd be reopening anytime soon. The Night Souk was buried within those tight streets. Because it was a smugglers' market, the peddlers set up their makeshift stalls at sunset and took them down by sunrise. When we arrived, business was still thriving, before fear of a visit from the City Guard sent many of the smugglers home early.

"Ya, ya," they cried. "Ho-chee-chee, ho-chee-chee! Best in Ternain!"

We passed towers of stoneware stacked haphazardly, vats filled with powder dyes, and burlap sacks of beans and spice pods. I stopped to exchange two coppers for a handful of spell-worked beads that wound through my curls with little effort and would fall out whenever I bade them. Clothiers hawked silks, stretching out their arms to measure the yardage and show off the vivid colors.

Gazes lingered on Falun as much as could be expected—he was, after all, lovely—and their eyes moved right over me, a plain human girl to all appearances. Exactly as I intended.

My minimal disguise worked for two reasons. No one expected a Princess in these streets, and so no one truly saw me. Knowing the young Princess was orange-eyed and wild-haired was different from connecting those features to a random girl in the market. My first nights outside the Queen's Palace, I thought if I let my cloak slip even once, someone would recognize me. But in the bloodkin sector, most had never seen any of the royal family up close. And even if they had, I'd been away for three years, and since my return, I'd rarely left the Palace. Few outside of it knew my face.

Still I was careful. I dropped my eyes to the ground whenever anyone met them, and kept my hands hidden unless haggling with a shop owner absolutely required it. If I had more ordinary magick, I wouldn't have bothered to hide my tattoos. Every human in Myre had magick inked onto their skin, but the white and red symbols—for marrow and blood—on my arms drew the eye.

Ahead of us, drums rolled like thunder. We'd finally reached the Patch, where bloodred tiles had been used to mend the broken paving stones of the sector's main thoroughfare. The tiles had taken on a different purpose soon after—a place to dance.

Gripping Falun's hand, I took off running toward the

sound, coming to an abrupt stop as we reached the press of bodies around the Patch.

Throngs of young fey glided through the street with flowers woven through lustrous hair and brass bells hanging from their wrists. *Glamour*, the fey ability to cast illusions over the world and themselves, made their glossy skin shine as bright as the moon. Beside them human girls in large groups held hands, swirls of silver paint on their tattooed arms glittering as they passed around tiny cups of *ouitʒa*, dark liquor made from the sugarcane that grew along the river.

Three-story *akelaes*—Myrean homes built around a central courtyard—painted in bright jewel tones filled the street, bougainvillea climbing terraces filled with candles as tall as my waist. Food carts were set up beneath the eaves, selling liquor and paper sheaths full of roasted nuts and boiled shellfish.

I collided with a bloodkin boy with flawless umber skin. He smiled, hands falling to my hips to steady me. He opened his mouth, but Falun's hand dropped onto my shoulder.

The boy frowned, but when he looked at Falun, his gaze warmed. "Are you new to the Patch?"

Falun's cheeks reddened, mouth hanging open as he sought an answer.

"We aren't new," I said, removing both of their hands.

"See you on the tiles," the boy called as I pushed farther into the crowd. Falun followed, glancing over his shoulder as the boy disappeared behind a group of human girls.

One handed Falun two cups and ran her fingers through his hair. He smiled and the girl's eyes went soft with wonder.

She didn't even blink as he plucked her hand away. The ouitza burned a path down my throat. Falun sipped his, wrinkled his nose, and gave the rest to me.

The gathering opened up and I caught sight of the Copper Steps, the fountain, where coins were dropped in nightly; by morning about half had been retrieved by those who desperately needed them. I explained the custom to Falun, and we kissed our coins, wishing blessings for whoever would find them.

After we tossed the coins into the fountain, Falun leaned down to my ear, yelling over the sound of the drums. "You told me there would be dancing?"

We inched around the lip of the fountain to the back, where the patch of crimson tiles began. We'd made it just in time for the next dance. The drumming was the call to the dance, a prelude of sorts. Already boys and girls were lined up across the tiles, arms held aloft, sweat coating their faces.

Musicians sat across from them. There were five young men beating on makeshift drums, a willowy man with a fiddle, and the singer, a tall, imposing bloodkin woman with a hawkish nose and beaded braids hanging down her back.

I let go of Falun's hand and stepped onto the tiles. "Watch first, and then join me."

There was only one dance done on these tiles at night: *chatara*, the dance of new lovers.

It started in your feet and you started the dance alone.

The drummers began with a simple beat, building it gradually. Our hips rocked side to side, keeping pace with the rhythm. We twirled, hips winding in figure eights until the singer began to howl.

Gooseflesh prickled my arms as I swept them down and raised them back up to the night sky. I tossed my head, watching the moon as I moved through the steps—switching my hips and kicking my feet into the air.

The singer's magick swept through the crowd, carried by the sound of her voice. Bloodkin called it the *thrall*, because with it, they could ensnare the mind until they controlled every emotion and sensation a person felt. This was partly the cause for the laws mandating bloodletting knives, so that no one could be enthralled unaware, so that people could guard their minds against attack. Even among bloodkin, the singer's was a rare gift. Most believed bloodkin projected the thrall with their eyes, but some could also use their voices.

I felt the magick heightening my emotions as I danced. The singer's thrall turned all our emotions into a shared experience. As we danced, we became one in our wanting, and the awareness of our bodies sharpened until it was dizzying. I felt sweat slide down our spines and the scrape and glide of fabrics I wasn't wearing.

The smell of salty blood, orange blossoms, and incense filled the air—the scent of the singer's magick. It pulsed through the air, pushing every movement farther. Curls clung to sweat-dampened cheeks as I arched back, twining my arms above my head. Each movement carried echo and premonition, of the girl just a beat ahead of me, of the boy just behind.

And when the singer's voice broke, the sharp edge was

like nails dragged slowly across my skin. We all crowed with her as partners joined us on the tiles.

I didn't expect Falun yet, so I jumped when warm hands circled my waist, soft and dry and hot against my skin.

It was the bloodkin boy from earlier, smiling sweetly, springy coils of hair falling into dark brown eyes. "Your friend won't join us?" He looked to where Falun stood at the edge of the tiles. His eyes were wide but unreadable.

"Not yet." Our limbs twined together as we moved in sync. He caught my wrist and spun me around. I fell flush against him, warm from the ouitza and his touch. "Though I think he will join sooner with your convincing."

"You think so?" His warm breath touched my cheek.

"I know so." I smiled, beckoning Falun forward.

He didn't move. But there was naked wonder in his gaze—mine had been just as wide the first time I laid eyes on this place. The bloodkin boy, whose name I still hadn't gotten and hoped never to, waved him over. Still Falun didn't move.

I stopped dancing and held out my hand, wishing I had brought him here sooner. After a long moment Falun stepped onto the tile and gave my hand a squeeze.

I left him with the bloodkin boy and found another partner. One who didn't seem to see me at all, and only wanted to dance.

Even out here, there were things I couldn't allow myself. Princesses bound for death couldn't have romantic entanglements. It would be too cruel, for them and for me.

We reveled in the music, stopping only to drink, eat, and trade partners. An hour passed before Falun and I danced together; I coaxed his stiff limbs into rhythm and showed him how the deadly grace inside him was useful for more than swinging a sword. The bloodkin boy stuck fast to Falun and I tried to ignore the twinge of longing in my chest when they kissed.

They disappeared into the throng together and another's arms wound about my waist. I turned to find a young human man, his skin a soft, warm brown. He was tall, with muscle-bound arms tattooed in white. Something about him nagged at me. I had to crane my neck to get a good look at his face. His nose was at least twice broken, the end jutting to the left, and his eyes were hazel. A dark, inviting color, and yet when they caught mine, unease swept through me.

I stepped out of his embrace. He was wearing a City Guard's blue uniform and his eyes were warm with lust. He spoke in a ragged voice: "Pretty little thing, aren't you?"

I bared my teeth at him, spitting out a curse as I backed away.

His gaze, once leering, sharpened. "You . . ."

I could have my knife out and pressed against his throat in the time it would take for him to draw his next breath. I would have, if not for the crowd dancing blithely around us.

Keeping the City Guard within my sight, I searched for Falun but found no sign of him, no flash of red hair, no fine-boned face. I caught a glimpse of the Guard's cruel smile before the singer screamed out one word: "Raid!"

Bodies slammed into me on every side and I could still feel the Guard's eyes burning a hole in my back. My stomach knotted as more City Guardsmen in dark blue uniforms spilled onto the Patch, cudgels and short swords in hand. Cries of fear and the sound of weapons striking flesh filled the air.

I pushed toward the Copper Steps, mouth dry. At least once a week, raids on the smugglers in the Night Souk spilled into the Patch. Public gatherings were against the law in Ternain after midnight. Most of the time, the Guardsmen only arrested those who couldn't afford a bribe, and I always kept my sigil ring on me in case I was caught. It wasn't the raid that scared me. It was the Guard.

For a moment, it had seemed like he recognized me, but then why hadn't he told the other Guards? Either way, I had to lose him in the crowd. I would run until I found Falun or reached the Palace wall, whichever came first.

I slammed into a woman's back and she fell to the ground. As I helped her to her feet, a hand curled around my elbow.

Heart pounding, I reached for my belt knife and the Guardsman nearly wrenched my arm out of its socket.

"Eva, it's *me*," Falun said. "We have to get back to the Palace. *Now.*"

His skin had lost its sheen and his usually pointed ears were rounded like a human's. His hair shifted color as I watched, from fiery red to muddy brown—glamour. Our fingers laced together and his magick slipped over my skin like a wash of scalding water. We ran.

⤙ CHAPTER 2 ⤚

THE DOORS OF the Throne Room were tall enough to admit a great many creatures—horned, winged, and the like—though only humans and fey passed through them now. Falun and I stood before them, awaiting our announcement to the Court. Their exquisite metalwork shone in the morning light, but it was the portraits lining the hall that always drew my eye. All eight of the human Queens seemed to glare down at me, eyes cold despite the smiles curving their lips.

As with every time I waited outside Court, the sight of Queen Raina made my jaw clench. The First wore a necklace of bones held together by fine golden chains, and the tattoos on her arms mirrored mine almost exactly—chains of white animal bones woven through the petals of crimson desert roses with leaves shaped like blades.

We shared the same magick—of marrow and blood.

She was known as the First because she was the first human Queen to sit on the Ivory Throne. In the past, the khimaer ruled Myre; their elders chose Queens from the most powerful daughters born to their noble tribes. Millennia passed under their peaceful rule, until two hundred years ago, when Raina the First led humans in a rebellion against the throne. She slaughtered thousands of khimaer to gain the throne, killing off all but a few of the tribes. When the rest rebelled a decade after the war, she forced every khimaer in the Queendom to move into two remote Enclosures, because she believed they would only rebel again if left free. In the generations since, little had changed. The only sure way for khimaer to escape the Enclosures now was to enlist in the Queen's Army.

During the Great War, she'd killed her sister for remaining loyal to the khimaer. It was after Raina's sororicide that the Rival Heir system was born.

Though Myre was the most powerful nation on the continent of Akhimar, there were two other nations on the continent and both were hostile. There was Dracol, the small, magick-less human Kingdom north of the A'Nir Mountains, and the Roune Lands, the lawless country more or less governed by bands of thieves with their own monarchs and courts.

Raina had led explorations of both lands, and extended Myre's boundaries by seizing control of the Mysoado Isles, which no other mainland Queen had done before, and she grew the nation's coffers by trading with the lands beyond Akhimar. Most humans believed that Raina was our greatest Queen. I didn't see it that way. The ballads written to honor the slaughter she'd led in the Great War made me sick.

Inheriting her magick was a curse. It made me a source of curiosity and dread for most people I met. It struck me as the worst kind of trick, having magick of marrow and blood. The Court said it wanted the strongest Queen possible, and yet the stories of Raina's magick were too chilling, too damning. She'd gone onto battlefields not just as a ruler, but a weapon.

They could not reconcile their next Queen having such violent power, though in truth they had nothing to fear from me. The Sorceryn had named my magick, and tattooed my skin, but they could not teach me how to wield it. The last time marrow and blood had appeared in the Killeen line was five generations ago. All records of its practices had been lost.

Falun gave my hand a squeeze, following my gaze to the portrait. Distaste flickered across his face.

Several hours had passed since the raid at the Patch, and though we'd snuck back into the Palace with little trouble, he was still ill at ease. I pitched my voice low: "You'd think we were facing a battalion of soldiers."

"I'd prefer that. At least we would have weapons in hand." He looped his arm through mine, not at all looking like he'd gone without sleep. He was resplendent in soldier white and a coppery braid more intricate than any I could manage hung to the middle of his back. "I'll relax once I'm convinced we aren't walking into another disaster."

"No luck there," I muttered, as more trouble surely waited beyond those doors.

When I turned thirteen, I'd journeyed to Asrodei to live with my father and to search the Queendom for someone who could instruct me in marrow and blood magick. During the three years I was away, a chasm had opened up between the Court and me. What interested my peers—rumors, wealth, and subtle political maneuvering—I found either exhausting or infuriating. If not for Falun, who'd spent those three years at Asrodei training to become a soldier in the Queen's Army, these trips to the Throne Room would have been more loathsome than I could stand. As it was, I had to resist the urge to return to my rooms and claim my monthly bleeding had struck.

The crier—a tall, narrow-boned man who bore an uncanny resemblance to a crow despite his white-and-blue livery—eyed us, his lips flattened like a beak. I resisted the urge to tap the diadem perched on my brow to hasten this process.

I smiled a wolf's smile, tongue sliding across my teeth. The corners of the Crow's mouth turned down in exaggerated annoyance. Well, the feeling was mutual and a welcome distraction from the dread beginning to pool in my stomach. I hated being announced. It would've been better to slip into the room unseen like a ghost. Or, better yet, not to have come at all.

He motioned for the guards at the door and folded back his shirtsleeves, revealing sinuous black-and-ocher tattoos. The doors swung open with a groan just as the Crow pressed his hands to his neck. Beneath his touch the skin reddened and the smell of burnt sugar and mint filled the doorway.

Though I didn't use my magick, I'd always been able to smell its use in others, each scent as distinct as the crier's magick of speed and sound.

"Her Highness Evalina Grace Killeen," his voice boomed, racing ahead of us into Court. "Attended by Lieutenant Falun Aramis of House Malfar."

Despite my earlier confidence, it was Falun who pulled me forward, slippered feet dragging across the marble tiles.

The Throne Room was a circular courtyard surrounded by a garden of stone pillars, each carved with a different legend from Myre's past, like that of Sikama, the prince who ate the sun, and that of Meya, the ebon horse who rode shadows. Mosaics on the walls depicted Myre's varied regions—glittering gold for the Kremir Sands, slate and white for the A'Nir Mountains, emerald for the jungles and ocher for the grasslands. High summer sunlight filled the courtyard. Already I'd begun to sweat, though I wasn't sure whether to attribute that to my nerves or the heat. Soon it would grow too warm and Mother would have one of the Court magick-workers cool the air.

The Ivory Throne was in the center of the room. Rising behind it was another, even larger portrait of Raina, so that the Court could always weigh the current Queen's legacy against hers.

The throne looked to be carved from the trunk of a massive tree, with vines curling over the arms and delicate rosettes curled up at the base. Atop it, my mother looked as if she was sitting in a lush, albeit frozen, garden. It suited her, icy and remote in a diaphanous white dress with piles of pale blond curls tumbling over her shoulders. Her hands rested on the arms of the throne, tattoos of crashing waves ending right below her elbows.

Queen Lilith, her magick of air and sea, maintained a cool expression. Back straight, shoulders rolled back; her delicate chin pointed up, she gave no reaction at my arrival.

Well, when I arrived late in a dress that didn't match House Killeen's sigil—the cobalt dagger—being ignored was not the worst reaction. Since she'd demanded my return to Ternain last year, our relationship had not progressed beyond our old dynamic of constant disappointment and long, thorny silences. I'd tried to numb myself to it, but pain still lanced through my chest when she ignored me for all the Court to see and whisper about later.

I clenched my fists at the sight of Lord Cassis at her side, whose traces of fey blood made him tall, lean, and unaccountably beautiful. His skin was dark brown, and his eyes and hair were the same shade of dark violet. One hand rested upon Mother's shoulder as he whispered into her ear, far too familiar. My parents had been estranged since I was nine, but the presence of her lover at Court still came as shock. It wasn't his existence that infuriated me; it was Mother flaunting him like a consort, when Papa was just a week's ride north.

Courtiers lounged about the room on low sapphire sofas; servants hovered near them with pitchers of chilled wine. Taking advantage of the heat, most of the women wore light kaftans or *kinsah*, gowns with detached bodices and long, silk skirts. The men fared worse, sweating in their *helbis*, knee-length coats embroidered with patterns in the colors of their House. Most turned to watch our entrance, their whispering voices choking the air. The sound of my teeth grinding soon joined the chorus.

"I know you'd rather be anywhere else right now," Falun murmured, "but at least try not to look pained."

I plastered on a fake smile and wiped sweating palms on the crimson silk of my kaftan. "Happy?" He nodded, displaying a far courtlier curve of the lips. "You should go find Jessypha."

"Are you quite sure you'd like to face them alone?" Falun said. "I can avoid my mother for one day."

I cut a look at him. Since Lady Malfar had been named to the Queen's Council, she never missed a day in Court, and if I had to see my mother, he had to see his.

"Oh, all right, if I must. You'll be fine?"

"I always am," I murmured softly.

He frowned at the lie, but before he could reply, I squared my shoulders and set off for the throne. We would find each other afterward, once our duties were met. In truth I didn't want anyone around when I spoke to my mother. The sooner I got this over with, the sooner we could escape this place.

I had taken ten steps at most before I heard her: laughter like a shower of broken glass and the smoky, knowing tone of her voice. My sister.

I walked toward the nearest pillar as I scanned the room. Most of the Court was gathered around the ring of columns closest to the throne, but a large group of young courtiers remained at a distance. They all stood gathered around one young woman, holding her own court.

I cursed such a fool mistake. I should have searched for my sister the moment I stepped into the room, and then kept far away. Isadore was two years older than me, and though we'd once been as close as sisters could be, when I returned to Ternain, she'd made it her business to torment me. Few of the younger members of Court were outside Isadore's influence.

Today would be especially infuriating to Isadore. A week ago an Auguri had come to Court to announce that a Blood Moon would rise tonight. The Auguries, women who read the sky's omens to map out Myre's future, rarely left the Temple they shared with their male counterparts, the Sorceryn. The omens triggered visions, which the Auguries then interpreted for the Queen. The details of the visions were sealed to the crown, and rarely shared with anyone else. The appearance of an Auguri at Court had filled the streets of Ternain with talk of the moon. The last time the city had seen such a marvel was nearly seventeen years ago.

In Auguri teachings, Blood Moons were portents of great change. The First had been named beneath one and so was I. And in my Harkening spell to learn my magick, the Sorceryn had named it marrow and blood, just like the First. Bets were set while I was still in swaddling, predicting I would become the True Heir, and eventual Queen. My mother had never given me any hint as to what the Auguries saw in my future, and almost seventeen years later, I'd fallen short of those early expectations. Isadore was the would-be Queen; I was only Princess Eva, my name said with disappointment.

All because I did not know how to use my magick—a weakness few in the Queendom could forgive. Soon after returning from Asrodei, my mother had asked for a demonstration of the magick I had learned while away. Before the entire Court, I was forced to admit that I couldn't use the one gift given to every person born on Myre's soil. Rumors of my inadequacy had spread through Ternain quickly.

Still, the Auguries' announcement reminded everyone that my nameday was just under two months away, on the last day of high summer, and their bloodlust had risen accordingly. A fight to the death between Rival Heirs was both a source of entertainment and a chance to increase the strength of Myre through a Queen whose power must intimidate our enemies. My mother had been the previous Queen's only daughter. It had been many years since the generation before hers, in which three sisters, triplets, had fought.

All of that was more than enough reason to avoid Isadore.

I continued forward, closing the distance between the courtiers and me. They'd drifted into my path and now the only thing to do was face my sister. I focused my gaze on the throne and Mother's spill of golden hair turning quicksilver as the sunlight hit it, but I wasn't truly seeing.

My skin began to itch and my heartbeat thumped in my fingertips, reminding me to breathe. Ten more steps and the courtiers surrounded me. Isadore's circle was tight and exclusive; all fifteen of her devoted sycophants were heirs to the most powerful Houses in Myre. I knew them all. We'd grown up together and had been close until I left.

I smiled and was pleased to find it held as their eyes swept from my slippered feet up to my diadem, sneers peeking out when polite expressions faltered. I bit my tongue, tasted blood, and smiled wider, deeper. Too quickly I found myself in the center of their circle. Dread rippled through me with such startling intensity that my hands shook.

My elder sister's dark gold hair was swept over one shoulder, falling in soft waves around the sharp angles of her face. Isadore and I only vaguely looked alike. She looked like a younger copy of Mother. They had the same eyes, deep-set and flashy green, and Isadore's hair was gold to Mother's light blond. They were both rail thin and shared the same slightly overlong but dignified noses. The main difference between them was Isadore's golden-brown skin—the combination of Mother's pale pink complexion and Papa's rich brown.

All I had of our mother was her heart-shaped mouth. The rest of me was of my father: his thick black curls, his broad face, full cheeks, and short, stocky form, which translated into some well-placed curves I was still getting used to. Only my eyes were my own: large, upturned, and a shocking blood orange. A coarse rumor, started when I returned to Ternain, had called them khimaer eyes. The rumor was quickly smothered by Mother, but it didn't matter. It was just another way they'd found to make me feel small and out of place, though they needn't have bothered. The main difference between me and everyone else at Court was that they used magick and I did not. There was nothing I could do to make up for that, so I'd stopped trying.

Isa's smile deepened as she cupped my cheek. I cupped hers, hoping my face didn't reflect the fear slowly filling me.

At Court it was customary to graze hands in greeting, but close family touched each other's faces, as a show of trust. Usually it was only a brief point of contact. Mother's fingers sweeping against my cheek, cold and stiff, was as familiar a feeling as anything. So was Papa's thumb sweeping over and pinching my one winking dimple. The first person to make contact was meant to first break it, but Isadore's hand settled into the contours of my cheek and didn't move, nails digging into my skin slightly.

She inclined her head and I gasped.

Magick rose from her skin, silk soft, yet vibrating like lightning.

Two things happened in quick succession:

First the young courtiers swayed toward her like flowers seeking the sun. I searched for alarm in their expressions, but all I could find were empty smiles. They should have been offended, disgusted she would use magick so casually to bend them to her will, but her magick of persuasion had them in its grip. There was nothing but blankness behind their eyes.

Yet no haze fell over my mind. I recognized the cloyingly sweet scent of Isadore's persuasion magick; she'd been using it since she was a child, bending my will to hers by accident before she learned to do it on purpose. She could convince a person to do almost anything, but this time she didn't even try.

Second, Katro bent close, his cheek grazing mine. "Hello, Evalina. Are you well?"

The words hadn't come from Isadore's mouth, but they were spoken in her voice, each one furled and predatory like the spine of a jungle cat. I staggered into the courtier behind me. I twisted, an apology on my lips, but he only stared blankly.

The floor tilted beneath me.

How? I'd never seen this particular trick before, her treating people like puppets.

Her smile dropped and so did the magick. If Isadore's spine wasn't always ramrod straight, I wouldn't have noticed, but she sagged. Though she'd controlled that courtier, it had cost her.

"Breathe, Evalina," Isadore whispered, this time from her own lips. Her voice oozed with faux concern, so patronizing it would have been appropriate directed at a six-year-old in the midst of a tantrum. In truth I was on the verge of one. Only imagining the Court's reaction kept me from sprinting from the Throne Room as fast as I could.

I forced myself to speak. "Isadore. Are you well?"

"I am quite well actually." She lifted her chin, lowering only her eyes as she spoke. "And you?"

"I am." The lie rolled smoothly from my lips. I wanted to slap that simper off her face; she knew I hated that look, hated craning my neck to meet her gaze. "It is a lovely day. I hope it won't grow any warmer. I'd hoped to ride along the river today."

"Lovely," she echoed, glancing down at her lacquered nails. "We plan to visit the pools later, once it cools a bit."

"Well." The moment hung. I wouldn't have considered going to the pools, lest Isadore subject me to more conversation with her speaking from other people's mouths. And yet I longed for her to at least offer an invitation.

Foolish that it stung.

"Will I see you tonight?" Her expression softened, eyes wide and green as the underside of a sand beetle's wings. "Mother is hosting a dinner to celebrate the Blood Moon."

Hope pulled me under like a drug. I could see what would happen: When I approached the throne, Mother would fold me into her arms. She would say the dinner would be hosted in my honor. She would tell me she loved me before the Court. She would repair our fractured family.

Except our mother would never do any of those things. She wouldn't tell the Court she loved me, because she didn't. And she certainly wouldn't fix us, when she was the one who created the first cracks that left us shattered now.

The taste of caramel and oranges drizzled with honey bloomed on my tongue. Too sweet to be real, so thick I could drown in it. This was Isadore's magick of persuasion, poisoning my thoughts.

I knew only one way to resist Isadore's magick once I was under its spell: pain.

"Remember, I know your tricks." I held up my hands, wet with blood from ten perfect half-moon cuts. "And the answer to your question is no. I have other plans tonight. Now if you'll excuse me . . ."

Isadore looked past me, her smile deepening. "And what are those plans, sister?"

To slip my chains and dance beneath a blood-drenched moon.

Anger and exhaustion warred within me until I felt nothing at all. In the months since my return, Isadore had done everything in her power to intimidate me at Court. Usually it worked, but today I was too tired, my nerves still raw from last night.

"That's enough, Isadore," I snapped, and for once the anger in my voice gave her pause. "I'm Rival Heir just like you. You may pretend that I'm less, but that won't change the truth, sister."

"Who's pretending?" she said. "Your magick is feeble and useless. You haven't the loyalty of the Court. You are *less. You left.*"

I tried not to flinch at the memories that dredged up. *Because of you,* I wanted to say, but instead whispered, "Stop it."

"Why should I?"

"Your friends may let you use your magick on them, but what about the rest of the Court? If they find out that you use magick to earn their loyalty—"

"I don't need anything to earn their loyalty. This is just practice."

"If Papa knew, if Mama—"

"Papa isn't here and Mother doesn't care. All that matters to her is power and I have it. She'd probably encourage you to use your magick as well if it wouldn't result in you accidentally killing everyone in some mad accident."

Air hissed out of my mouth, her words like a punch to the gut. A memory flashed through my mind, but I smothered it. "You know I can't use my magick."

She inclined her head. "That's exactly why you should have stayed away. You don't belong here and, lucky for me, you never will."

I looked into her eyes, hoping to find some sense of shame, or even pleasure. But she wasn't savoring the taste of this small cruelty—her eyes were flat with truth. If I had any question as to whether saying such things cost her anything, the answer was clear.

The bitter part was that the same sentiment crossed my mind every day. I didn't belong here. I didn't even want to belong here. If I'd been allowed to stay away from the capital, to let my nameday pass without mention, I would have done so, but the law was very clear.

All daughters born to the Queen will become Rival Heirs. As Raina the First slew her sister, so shall a Princess in each generation sacrifice her kin in a show of strength. The victor will become the True Heir to be crowned the following year.

This was our birthright: to kill and become Queen, or die.

It became more obvious with every passing day which of

us would live out the rest of her life perched on the Ivory Throne.

I wanted to run, to feel my feet slap the cool marble floors, to pull out every pin forcing my hair into submission, and to wrench the jeweled bangles from my wrists. But instead I moved on, searching for Falun's bright head. I couldn't help but look at Mother. I had her attention now. Her eyes tracked me across the room, studying me, lips curled into a vacant frown. The barest smile crossed her face. Her contempt washed over me, cold and familiar.

Damn Isa. Damn this place.

If I were meant for this—being Princess and one day Queen—I would have had the strength to stay. I would have swallowed it all back and marched toward my mother.

But no.

For today, one conversation with Isadore had been more than enough.

I startled as Falun's hand settled against the small of my back, and I let him guide me from the room. The crier, lips pressed into thin disapproval, wouldn't meet my gaze.

No tears escaped until the doors slammed shut behind us. I held to that victory hours later, eyes finally dry, alone in my room.

→ CHAPTER 3 ←

"OUT WITH IT." Mirabel stabbed her knife into one of the petite hens she had brought for lunch. With her other hand, she pulled the hem of her skirt over her lizard feet. In the soft afternoon light, her scales shifted between teal and jade.

She was half khimaer; the slight gazelle horns spiraling back from her brow marked her as much as her feet. Physically, humans, bloodkin, and fey were mostly the same, besides a few minor differences, like the bloodkins' fangs and the fey's pointed ears. The khimaer, on the other hand, were graced with horns, and shared physical attributes with animals—wings, tails, talons, and the like.

Outside my bedchamber, Mirabel wore long skirts. Luckily her feet were easy enough to hide; had she possessed more obvious animal aspects, she wouldn't have been allowed inside the Queen's Palace, let alone around me. It was the Queen's unspoken policy to hire only khimaer with mixed blood to work in the Palace.

An hour ago, I came back from Court to find her in my

sitting room meeting with two young men. One was blood-kin and brown-skinned with fangs that seemed too large for his mouth, and the other, a human with sea-green tattoos. They'd gaped at me, stammering greetings as Mira hustled them out the door with instructions not to be seen near my rooms.

Last year, when we returned to the capital, Mirabel had created a network of spies—*ghosts*, we called them—because knowledge was power. If secrets were coins, she always said, they would be gold.

She didn't look like much of a spymaster. Her round, beautiful face was cut with deep lines from decades of frowning and laughing. In a cotton blouse and bright-patterned skirt and with not one hair out of place in her iron-gray bun, she could have been my grandmother, but for her horns.

I rarely saw our spies; recognizing a face I had no business knowing could endanger them. Even Mira rarely met with them in person.

I'd been ready to ask her to leave with them before she shoved a tray of food under my nose. Only then did I notice I was starving. Mirabel always remembered such things. When I forgot to eat, she was there to bring me a meat pie or spiced *mazi* fruit.

I folded flatbread smeared with chili paste around a slice of the hen and I groaned as smoky heat filled my mouth.

"I received word from the King. As the two of you discussed before we left Asrodei, he's increasing the number of soldiers in your guard leading up to your nameday. The first should arrive within the week."

I gave a noncommittal grunt. Another thing I didn't

want, someone new to follow me around the Palace. How I regretted agreeing to add more soldiers to the guard. If I'd known that returning to Ternain would mean I wouldn't be left alone unless to sleep, I might not have agreed to it. But it was necessary; contests of Rival Heirs were dangerous leading up to the challenge. Though the Entwining spell ensured that only we could strike the killing blow, heirs had been kidnapped before. Kidnapped and starved until they were too delirious with hunger to win a fight.

"Eva," Mirabel pressed, gaze soft as she awaited an answer. "What happened at Court?"

I set my food aside, appetite lost. "I don't want to discuss it, Mira."

This seemed just the opening she intended. "I'll talk, then, if you'll allow that. This morning you woke on your own. I usually have to drag you out of bed before Court, but not today."

"I couldn't sleep." That was close enough to the truth anyway. "I thought you'd be pleased I was up early."

"I was until you came back hours before I was expecting you. Tell me what happened." She brushed her fingertips across my cheek, wiping away a rogue tear.

This tenderness was so unlike her. Though Mirabel was once my nursemaid, now her duties varied between adviser, spymaster, and near-mother all in one. And just like my real mother, she wasn't one for comfort.

She solved military dilemmas for my father when she was bored and favored jeweled hairpins that doubled as blades. She complained about my recklessness as she mended tears in my clothing, and taught me ciphers and how to survive if stranded in the desert. She wasn't good at softness and neither was I. I never cried in front of her. I never cried in front of anyone—or at all—if I could help it.

The black leather-bound book where she kept all her golden secrets sat beside her on the floor of my bedchamber. She opened it and held up a white card. "A courier came by while you were at Court. Your mother sent an invitation to a dinner she's hosting for the Blood Moon, which . . . surprised me."

I snorted as I plucked it from Mira's hand. I traced the illustration of a crimson moon on the back of the card. Mother must have sent it before I'd stormed out of the Throne Room. "Lovely. Shall we pick out something to wear? It's much too late to have a dress made, which I'm sure was her intention, but I must have something to suit the occasion. Red for the Blood Moon? Cobalt for House Killeen? Perhaps sea-foam for my mother, the Storm Queen? Honestly," I added, "the red should be for Killeen or for the throne, for all the blood spilled in its name."

Mirabel cringed but said nothing.

I filled her silence. "I can't go back there. I have less than two months left and I don't want to spend those weeks at Court."

"Your mother won't like that."

"Whatever punishment she devises is sure to be better than being dissected like a moth under glass at Court. That's hardly a way to spend the last days of my life."

"Stop with that foolishness. You'll live well beyond your nameday."

"How, Mirabel?" I snapped. "You must have at least one ghost at Court. Haven't they told you about Isadore? One flex of her will and she won't even have to kill me herself. I'll be burying the knife inside my own chest."

Her chestnut skin went ashen. Maybe the image flashed behind her eyes the way it flashed behind mine. My body broken, battered, and all that I was, gone from it. Forever.

"You are not going to die. You're going to sit on the Ivory Throne and change this Queendom."

"I wish you were right. I can't even change how the Court sees me. How can I change anything else?"

"You certainly won't if you don't at least go to Court and try."

"Today Isadore admitted she uses her magick to turn courtiers against me, and that Mama"—I gritted my teeth— "Mother encourages it. What do you suppose I try against that?"

She waved a hand in dismissal. "Your father will find something soon. We must remain hopeful. There are still stones left to turn. North near the border, or the Isles. The Deadened Jungle, even. Any place where old magicks are known to return."

The magick Mirabel and my father so wanted me to learn was not like Isadore's, nor like my mother's. Magick of marrow and blood was a killing power. How could she want me to embrace that? I refused to let the crown turn me into a murderer.

Better to die than be like every other Queen.

I ignored the spike of panic in my chest. "Just accept that there is no one to teach me."

Searching would yield nothing, just as it had for the last three years. My magick was a relic from another age. Papa would never find someone to teach me. Anyone who might've known about marrow and blood magick was long dead.

I used to count that failing as a gift, since I couldn't be forced to learn, but as my nameday drew closer and closer, all I felt was numb. It was clear that I was helpless against my sister. Why worry when my fate was inescapable? I wouldn't be the first Princess to die, nor the last.

Mirabel's claws rasped against the floor as she stood and gripped my hands tight. Her beringed fingers were tough, sturdy. These hands fed me, clothed me, and combed my hair. They had held me every day since my first nameday nearly seventeen years ago. I knew the feel of them well.

"I will not give up, and I won't allow you to either. I'll remind you every chance I get, even if you don't want to hear it: you deserve to live, you deserve to fight, and you deserve to survive. The throne, all its glory and bitterness, is your birthright. Don't let your sister convince you you're worth anything less." She pressed a kiss to my cheek and swept from the room.

I tried to see the truth in Mirabel's words, but I knew better. I didn't deserve the crown. I didn't even want it, and against Isadore I had no way to win.

The first, and only, time I used magick, I was just shy of my ninth nameday.

For human Myreans, the ninth nameday was second only to the seventeenth in importance. It marked the time when we could be tattooed by the Sorceryn and given access to our magick. Though unbridled magick often spilled out of children before their ninth year, it couldn't be learned until our arms wore a lace of ink, each design articulating a different ability.

Though I remembered several days of feasting for Isadore's ninth, I waited and waited only to find no celebration was planned for mine. My first clue to understanding why came during Court a week before my nameday.

I sat on the dais, Isadore and I arranged on a large pillow at Mother's feet, like we always were back then at Court. She liked to keep us close enough to scold when we misbehaved. Lady Feransa, Mistress of Trade on the Queen's Council, mounted the dais to speak with the Queen. After a brief conversation, Mother dismissed her, and on her way down the dais, Feransa spoke to my sister first, asking after Isa's lessons with the Sorceryn. Then Lady Feransa turned to me and pinched my cheek, before taking my hands in hers.

Her kohl-rimmed eyes focused on the portrait of Raina behind the throne. "You must be a brave girl," she murmured shakily, "to be gifted with such savage magick, Your Highness."

My gaze followed hers. The First had golden-brown skin and amber eyes lit with rage, and wore a gold sleeveless gown, dotted with red rosettes, showing off the tattoos that stretched from fingertips to shoulder.

Trying not to feel the sting of Lady Feransa's words, I couldn't look away. I would know soon if my tattoos were to be the same.

Isadore saved me from having to answer when she spoke

in a tight, quiet voice: "Yes, my sister is brave, as all Princesses are known to be, but she is not savage."

At just eleven, Isa had a commanding way about her and a glare that shined with cruelty.

She smiled in triumph as the Mistress of Trade sputtered an apology, backing away until she reached the foot of the dais. My eyes welled with tears as Lady Feransa took one last glance at the portrait of Raina. My thoughts spun through memories of times my magick had been mentioned at Court, finding that same fearful expression, and I finally understood. The Court wasn't celebrating my ninth because they were frightened by it.

Frightened by *me*.

When Feransa was well away, Isa pulled up her sleeve and showed me a tattoo of a bright green serpent coiled around her wrist. I knew it was one of her persuasion tattoos, because the tattoos for her light magick were all pale yellow.

"Once you're tattooed," she promised, jade eyes burning with a fire to match Raina's, "you can chase away anyone who bothers you. Until then, I'll protect you."

Two nights later, she kept that promise.

It was late enough that we should have been fast asleep, sharing a fort draped with silk, curled together on a heap of pillows. Instead we'd crept through the passages from Isa's room to the kitchens, collecting sticky buns and candied almonds to nibble on during our journey through the passages. Isa decided we should go to Mother's dressing room to try out her jewels and gowns without someone chasing us away from all the finery.

But when we arrived in her dressing room, Mama was still awake on the other side of the door, the lamplight from her bedchamber spilling under the doorway. Whispering excitedly, for this was a thrilling and dangerous development, I suggested we stay, while Isa proposed a climb to the glass menagerie on the roof. I deferred to Isa, as I always did then, and we would have left had I not heard Papa's voice. It was a curious discovery, for neither of us had ever seen Papa near Mama's rooms. We crept closer to the door leading to her bedchamber, our fingers laced together.

I could hardly make out anything, but one word stood out: my name.

I rushed forward, untangling my hand from Isa's, but she pulled me back. "Eva," she said, so loud I thought she wanted to get caught. "What are they saying?"

"They're talking about me." I pressed my ear to the door.

Not one to let me hear anything she couldn't, Isa shouldered me aside. She grinned, listening with me now.

Mama's voice was pitched high with agitation. "She is too young. We need to wait, Lei. I know you believe she's ready, but—"

Papa cut her off, tone sharp. "Lily, waiting is too dangerous."

"Her magick is what's dangerous, Lei." I pressed my lips together to stifle a gasp. "You know the history better than I do. Eva could hurt someone—"

"I understand your fear, but that magick is hers, Lily. It is who she is." Papa's voice softened. "Even you cannot keep her from it."

The pit of nerves in my stomach hardened. Lady Feransa's

words echoed in my head. *Savage magick,* she'd said. I thought of Raina's tattoos, with bloodred roses, blades, and bones; how could I do anything but hurt someone? I wanted to run, but I couldn't turn away. I pressed even closer, wishing I could slip right through the door and see.

"I can keep her from whatever I damn well please, Lei."

"Do not press this. This is interference, Lily. I won't take it, not this early. You may favor Isa all you like, but this is sabotage."

"I won't let her endanger my Isadore." All the sweets we'd eaten threatened to bubble up as my stomach churned. My magick was why Mama preferred Isa—because she thought I'd hurt someone. But even if I could, I wondered, why would I hurt my sister? Back then I didn't know our fate as Rival Heirs and wouldn't learn the truth for years. "I won't have her learning this . . . this barbaric power. I won't."

"You know nothing of this so-called barbaric power," Papa said. "That is why you fear it."

"I've spoken with the Sorceryn." The sly calm in her voice was so different from the anger seconds ago. Even knowing she couldn't see me, I didn't dare breathe. "They say—"

Isa yanked me back and I missed Mother's next words. "We should go, Eva."

I needed to hear the rest. Maybe Mama was right. I needed to understand so that I wouldn't hurt Isa. Fear and desperation warred within me as I shoved her away, Raina's red-and-white tattoos vivid in my mind's eye.

Isa was two years older than me, taller and stronger, and always won any tussles between us. Still she fell to the floor and a soft cry escaped her.

Then a strange thing happened. My thoughts circled back, realizing that my hand had felt hot when it connected with Isa's chest. Isa's flesh had given under my fingertips with a dull pop, sinking in like a piece of overripe fruit.

I rushed toward her. "Are you all right?"

She'd fallen, curled in on herself, and didn't respond to my words. I crouched and reached for her. She flinched as my fingers brushed her shoulder and gave me a bewildered look. My mind flashed to the kitten with the twisted leg we had found last month. He'd twitched away from our every touch. Even after we led him up to my room and gave him a cup of cream, he never lost that suspicion. Like he knew somebody would hurt him again. Like it was only a matter of time.

Tears slid down my face.

I didn't understand what I'd done, but with Mother's words about endangering Isadore ringing in my head, I knew this power was *wrong*.

Isadore stood and tried to cover my mouth. There was a bruise on one of her arms, so dark it looked like a splotch of spilled paint or the petal of a purple flower.

"Hush, Eva." She said it over and over. When the door swung open, hitting her in the back and causing her to stumble to the floor and cry out in pain *again*, she kept repeating it. "Eva, don't tell them. Not about anything. Don't say a word."

I only wept harder, unable to speak around the force of my tears. Isa ignored all of their questions. She spoke only once, coolly requesting a healer.

After that, Mama glared at Papa, hovering protectively over Isadore. "Leave us."

My cries took on a hysterical edge as my father scooped me into his arms. I didn't want to be separated from Isadore, because soon Mama would know what I'd done. And I was sure she would never let me be around my sister again.

Over the sound of my hiccupping, I heard Isa say again and again, "Hush, Eva. Don't tell them anything. Don't say a word."

And so I never did.

Instead I decided. This was my magick, wicked, savage, and wrong, and I wanted no part of it.

After Mira left, I passed the evening alone, reading a book of myths from the Isles instead of accepting my mother's invitation. My nerves couldn't handle seeing her or anyone else from Court tonight.

When night dropped inky curtains of starlight, I slid from my bed. Remembering the City Guard from last night, I hid an extra knife in my boot, and opened the trapdoor. Falun waited below. I took off before he could say a word, lest he mention the disaster at Court.

We stopped on the stoop of an abandoned building in a familiar alleyway on the edge of the Patch. Not wanting a repeat of last night, we agreed to meet there at the end of the night if we were separated. Falun said he'd only come along to stop me from going out alone, though I was certain the young bloodkin had at least some small part in him not hauling me back to my room. With the Blood Moon, there would be no raids tonight. Omen sightings and festival nights were the only times the laws against late-night gatherings became void.

Falun was quiet on the way out; maybe he wanted to talk about Court. Maybe his mother had said something that upset him, but he'd had to worry about me instead. I should have asked, I would have, but I didn't want to mention Court out there. Not when we were free.

"You haven't looked at it once," Falun said.

He was wrong. I'd glanced at the moon twice. The first time it was just a glance, but the second, I truly took it in. A rich, bloodied moon hung in the sky, bruised with black shadows and bathing the night with a strange, rosy glow. It was so close if I climbed one of the taller flats around us, I would've sworn I could touch the edge.

But after that I didn't let my eyes linger at the wonder of it. The Blood Moon had betrayed me once before, heaping its legendary expectations upon my infant shoulders. "The moon means nothing to me tonight. I'm just a girl, remember?"

He must've caught something in my voice. "Is that why you come here? To leave your titles behind?"

I shrugged, unable to meet his pitying gaze. "I come here to pretend that I'm free from the throne for just a little while." To pretend that the moon's omens didn't matter. That my title didn't matter, at least for this short time.

I pulled him along, and made a promise to myself: Princess no more.

The silence between us was broken only when Falun asked how I'd originally found the Patch.

My secret forays outside the Palace began seven months ago, at the beginning of Far Winter, when I was still settling into life here. I wanted to know the city I was supposed to rule one day. I had always loved the night, but Ternain taught me its true magick: transformation. I could be whomever I wanted at night, as long as I was careful.

It took several weeks of wandering through the city to find the Patch, and two more weeks of slipping through its crowds to find my place in it.

I'd been wrapped in a cloak, afraid someone would recognize me, when I'd stumbled upon a crowd of people gathered around the tiles. I slid through the press of bodies and found the crowd watching a pair of dancers. My feet were rooted to the ground as I watched a bloodkin boy and girl circling each other.

They were beautiful, as is anyone who is sweating in the moonlight; in their skin, all worries seemed forgotten. Waist-length braids spun around her lithe body, and long coils of hair sprung proudly from his brow all the while they moved, barely a hand's-width apart.

They were one in the dance.

Hips rolled and feet slapped the ground as they twined around each other, two moons in the same orbit. Perfectly in sync.

Chatara wasn't dancing, not as I'd always known it. Yes, there was music and, yes, there was movement, but the intimacy of it made me blush the first time I watched. At Court we had nothing to match its intensity.

I found I couldn't look away.

Eventually their song ended. Everyone rushed onto the tiles when the drumming started. I stood frozen. During the dance a fire was lit under my skin. Every other night

I'd been looking, seeing all the sectors of Ternain up close, but tonight I wanted to be a part of it. There weren't just bloodkin crowded onto the tiles, there were fey, long rope-like braids woven around their wrists, and humans, tattoos scrawled on their arms.

I wanted to lose myself among them. I wanted—*wanted*.

Since returning to Ternain, it was the first time I had wanted anything but to be left alone.

As I stared, the dancing boy caught my eyes. A slow smile curved his lips, and a tremor snaked down my back. *Oh.*

Warmth bloomed in my cheeks as he motioned for me to join him. My gaze drifted to his open shirt and broad, sweat-damp chest. I stepped forward before I remembered myself. Remembered who I was; much as I wanted to be someone else, I hadn't yet learned to pretend. I didn't know how to smile and join him, much as I wanted to. I didn't know how to lose myself in the embrace of someone so beautiful. At least not yet.

I rushed back to the Palace, but I returned the next night, clad in a scrap of a shirt and a long, clinging skirt instead, determined to learn.

In the months since, the Patch had become my only true solace. When all the things I despised in my life piled up, I could come here to forget them for a few hours.

Tonight, as always, the streets smelled of honey, liquor, and, since it was the Patch, blood.

Because of the moon, it was more packed than last night. Falun jostled a human boy nursing a cup of palm beer while a copper-haired bloodkin girl laid a tarnished bloodletting knife against his wrist. Clearly surprised to see bloodkin feeding in public, Falun murmured an apology. The boy blushed, but the girl kissed both of us on the cheek.

We reached the tiles in the midst of a round of chatara, so we waited. I saw Falun spot the boy from last night—a hot flush rose in his cheeks—but he stayed by my side.

I pushed him onto the tiles. "Go."

After that dance ended, I stepped onto the tiles alone.

When the music started, my thoughts were usually carried away, and there was only my body and eventually whichever boy would join me.

But tonight peace wouldn't come.

I couldn't help but look to the moon, and as soon as I did, it was like someone placed a brick on my chest. The moon only reminded me of all the things I had come here to forget. Like Court, this wasn't my place either. I was as weak and forgettable here as anywhere else and a small voice whispered it was no one's fault but mine.

The wrongness of it thrummed beneath my skin, discordant and harsh against the sound of the chatara drums.

Only when a boy with a vaguely familiar face joined me, his hands coming around my waist to spin me to and fro, could I sink into the heat of his touch and the rush of being no more than a girl dancing with a boy.

The truth—that this was as false as the facade I wore in the Queen's Palace—was too thorny and painful to touch.

I threw my mind and body into the music, drank a few welcome sips of ouitza, and let the heat of him leak into me, forcing everything else away.

Princess no more, I swore. Just an ordinary girl dancing in the Patch, not the ill-suited Rival Heir. *Princess no more*.

Those words went on echoing in my head even after I stopped dancing. Hours later, I ended up where my night began, letting the moonlight wash over me while I waited for Falun on the stoop. I strung together a song beneath my breath; I barely knew what it was about. Just a boy, a girl, and a boat where the Red River met the Silvern Sea.

Air stirred beside me. "Fal," I said, "would you ever be with someone common? Not for a night, but forever? Jessypha wouldn't like it, but—"

When the blade kissed my neck, the rest of the words died on my lips.

Princess no more.

I laughed even as ice slid through my veins. Blunt fingers ran through my curls, jerking my head back, and the dagger bit into my skin until hot blood dripped down my neck. My eyes rolled up to find a man staring at me, a fixed smile on his face.

"I need to get a good look at you," a rough voice grated. A hand replaced the knife, smearing the blood down my neck and chest in a sickening caress. "Wouldn't want to kill the wrong Princess."

The words echoed in my head, distorted by panic. *Kill the . . . kill the wrong Princess?*

All the air punched out of my chest as I stared at him. I sucked in a breath and did the only thing I could think of: I screamed.

➤➤ CHAPTER 4 ◄◄

THE ASSASSIN GRINNED as he slapped me hard across the face, clicking his tongue in disapproval. "Now, we can't have any of that. I won't have our time together cut short."

A tremor rolled through me as pain flared in my jaw. I tried to pull away, but his grip on my neck wouldn't budge.

I recognized his crooked nose, that smile that didn't touch his eyes. The man I'd thought was a City Guard was apparently an assassin in a stolen uniform. The realization made me cold down to my bones. How could I have failed to see what was so obvious now? The cold of the grave lingered behind those muddy brown eyes.

"I was hoping you would put up a fight, little Princess." He stroked my cheek with his thumb. "How disappointing."

I bit his hand and foul blood flooded my mouth. He cursed as I scrambled away. I spat out his blood and stood, drawing my belt knife. I was thankful that he hadn't bothered to disarm me. Such hubris would be to my advantage.

The assassin pulled a short sword from a scabbard strapped to his back. I recognized the blackened steel forged in the Deadened Jungle, folded and re-formed a hundred times to make it unbreakable. Soldiers in the Queen's Army carried the same. "So you do have teeth. I worried after our encounter last night."

"Why not just kill me yesterday? Why follow me again tonight?" It would have been easy for him to slip a knife between my ribs last night. Or just moments ago when he'd first approached. He could've slit my throat and been far away from here by now.

"My patron prefers discretion," he said, staring hungrily at the ebon blade. "And I prefer a slow death to a quick one. Don't you?"

Fear dragged wicked claws down my back, but my fury kept it at bay. I refused to die in this forgotten street, discarded like trash. He would regret not killing me when he had the chance.

The assassin darted forward with chilling speed, our blades ringing with discordant music. I gritted my teeth, arms burning with the effort of holding back his blows. With his reach, and much longer blade, it would be over soon if I didn't disarm him quickly.

I slashed at his sword arm, but he dodged with sinuous fluidity, opening a shallow wound on my wrist. I backed away, knife still raised but wavering as I fought the pain. The assassin didn't let me get far. He pressed forward, swinging his blade almost lazily. I feinted, and when he dodged, I slammed the hilt into his wrist. The assassin's eyes widened as his sword fell.

I kicked it away, smiling.

"Don't think you've won just yet, Princess," he whispered. Soft golden light began to emanate from his body. I squinted against the brightness, cursing my mistake. I had forgotten to watch for his magick.

He rushed me, smelling of storm clouds and the scorch of lightning. Beams of light exploded from his body, as if he wasn't calling magick, but was made of it.

He sent us both crashing to the ground. I dug my knife into his shoulder a moment before my head struck the paving stones with a sickening crack. My belt knife hissed against the ground as it left my hand, disappearing in the shadowed alley. The assassin straddled me. He didn't seem to notice the blood soaking his collar as he gripped my neck, choking me.

I clawed at his hands, my vision tunneling until his face was all I could see.

With darkness gathering, the Blood Moon like a halo behind him, I suddenly smelled magick. The bitter scent of bloodberries and ripe plums perfumed the air as long-dormant power swelled within me.

The wound on my wrist still spurted blood and every tattoo it touched became warm.

The assassin sensed the change, his grip tightening as he leered over me. "You will not save yourself. You'll die here alone. After I dispose of your body and kill your companion, everyone will believe you've run away again."

No.

I couldn't die and leave Falun to face him. I would not die. The dark lake in my mind began to churn and froth as my magick came to life. As much as I dreaded this, I had always known my power lived deep in those waters, like a torpid beast waiting for me to call it to shore. So when the lake offered its magick, writhing and red as a sunset, I took it.

My hands became painfully hot, my tattoos glowing scarlet. Somehow I sensed his pulse, discordant beside mine. With the last of my strength, I pressed my hand to the wound I'd given him earlier on his collarbone, sticky with drying blood, and thought, *More.*

Bleed, I wished. *Die.*

Beneath my fingers, the wound . . . widened. Hot blood sprayed from the assassin's neck.

His eyes met mine. There was a flash of accusation and wonder, and then he was gone.

His blood washed down my body, leaving a burning path with every tattoo it touched, stirring more magick than I'd ever felt before.

The edges of my mind pulled taut like animal skin over a drum. I drew each hand through the warm coating and the pressure mounted even further. My ears popped, pulse echoing like thunder.

This was my magick, of marrow and blood.

If that power cut his neck, this would have cleaved all the flesh from his bones. Revulsion rolled through me as I upended the contents of my stomach.

I shuddered, pushing his body off me, and crawled until I wasn't touching that spreading pool of blood. I knew I needed to get up, find Falun, and return to the Palace, but fatigue made me feel like I was wading through mud. Head swimming, I drew my knees to my chest. I could still see the assassin's eyes as darkness dragged me under.

How could you? they seemed to say, but it wasn't the assassin's voice I heard.

It was mine.

⤙ CHAPTER 5 ⤚

I WOKE TO the rasp of a blade being tended.

I sat up, head throbbing, and pulled back the silken canopy around my bed. At my desk, Falun ran his broadsword over a whetstone, face hidden by a tangle of waist-length scarlet hair. Mirabel stood near the door, handing an old woman in a gold healer's tabard a bowl of pink-tinged water. Strips of wet linen hung over the edge, spotted with blood. She slipped a few coins into the healer's wizened hand and shut the door behind her.

Only then did I notice the fresh bandages covering my left wrist up to my palm. I flexed my fingers, marveling at the slight twinge of pain.

At least there wouldn't be any lasting outward effect from last night, but inside everything had changed. Even though the assassin needed killing, that didn't stop the oily slide of guilt in my stomach.

A man was dead by my hand.

Shivering, I wrapped a blanket around me and left my bed.

"You're awake," Mirabel said, an unusual eagerness in her gaze. "The healer said you'd sleep for hours yet."

"Er, good morning." I looked at Falun, hoping he would give some indication as to what happened last night.

He set aside his sword and tucked his hair behind the elegant points of his ears. He shook his head slightly, as if dispelling an unsettling thought, and gestured to the covered lacquer trays on the desk without meeting my eyes.

My skin prickled. Was this awkwardness because they knew what I'd done? "I suppose I should explain what happened, then."

"Yes, you should," Mirabel said, still eyeing me curiously. She sat down at the desk across from Falun, who pulled up another seat and offered it to me. It was a wide mahogany affair, large enough for the three of us to share.

It could've been any other afternoon when we sat here drinking cup after cup of tea as we worked. Mirabel thumbed through her book, scrawling notes in a cipher. Falun, finished honing his sword, now oiled it. And yet, unlike any of those other times, I could feel wariness rolling off them. They wondered how I'd survived.

"The night before last, a man in a City Guard's uniform stopped me while I was dancing. The Guardsmen often arrest people when they raid the Patch. I managed to slip away from him and didn't think much of it." I shrugged. "I didn't know he was an assassin until he found me in the alley where Falun and I planned to meet last night."

"If I'd stayed by your side, you would've been safe," Falun said. His skin was ashen, expression grim.

Mirabel grunted in agreement and I shot her a glare. "I

am safe. Thanks to you, I woke up here, and not in the city dungeons."

Or, more likely, in the cells buried deep in the belly of the Palace. Mother would want me shackled before she could swoop in and rescue me, only to lock me in my bedchamber for the next two months, not for killing a man but for disobeying her by leaving the Palace.

"When I found you, I thought I was too late," he said, fists clenched upon the table. "You were covered in blood, but your pulse was strong, so I carried you back here and found Mirabel."

Thank magick for that. I trusted any healer Mira sent for wouldn't let word of my injuries travel. "And what . . . of the body?"

"The Captain and the rest of the guard went to collect it," Falun said, glancing toward the door. "They returned just a few minutes before you woke."

It turned out most of my guard were stationed on the other side of the door, awaiting news of my health. I could've done without everyone knowing I'd nearly died. If I knew them well—and after three years at Asrodei, I did—now they'd all want a part in protecting me over the next few weeks. Protecting me—and pummeling me on the sparring grounds for the sake of my training.

Falun stepped out of the room, and when he returned, Captain Anali Vala strode in behind him, her salt-white cornrows swinging. She was khimaer, with white ram's horns framing a delicate heart-shaped face, and her skin was a cool dark brown, so rich it showed no flaws. Hand resting on the sword pommel at her hip, she walked as if no one could bar her path. She was petite, but with strong shoulders, and if need be, she could probably incapacitate all three of us with little trouble.

Anali was the first person my father introduced me to when I moved to Asrodei. She'd been given charge over my combat training, so we'd spent hundreds of hours together. When it was time for me to return to Ternain, I'd asked her to become the Captain of my guard.

At the sight of me, she pressed a hand to her heart and bowed her head. "Your Highness."

"Did you find it?"

She grimaced. "I'm sorry, Eva. We found the alley that matched Lieutenant Malfar's description, but the body was already gone. Someone tried to wash away the blood, but there were signs they'd dragged the body away. We followed the trail until it disappeared in the human sector."

"Gods damn it," I swore.

"That about sums up the situation. I think we can assume whoever contracted him had the body removed. I left a few of the guards in the bloodkin sector. If we're lucky, they'll find something."

"If not, I will," Mirabel said. "Though first, I must send word to the King. If Princess Isadore is behind this, your father is the only one who can do something about it. Unless"—she arched an eyebrow—"you'd prefer to leave it up to the Queen."

"Of course not." Mother would defend Isa's innocence even if we did find proof. I'd learned that lesson before I ran away almost four years ago. "But I don't think this was my sister." Isadore wanted the spectacle of challenging me

53

before the Court and didn't consider me a threat. Killing a Rival Heir before her nameday was treason, punishable by death. "Why would she risk herself to kill me now, when she'll have the opportunity in just two short months?"

"True, but we can't rule out anyone yet," Mirabel argued. "Your sister has more to gain from your death than anyone else."

Silence fell at her words. The rattle of porcelain soon filled it as Falun poured tea. I took the first cup, but even the scalding liquid couldn't warm the frost spreading inside me. This was just the beginning. Whoever sent the assassin would try again and again until I was dead.

Could Isadore have ordered my death? Was there so little love left in her? She'd been so smug at Court yesterday, so certain I was worthless as Rival Heir. What would make her want to kill me now?

"There's one other thing, Eva." Mirabel marked something in her book and closed it. The fervor in her eyes returned as she stared me down. "You haven't told us how you survived."

"I killed him," I whispered, clasping the blanket tight around my shoulders.

Mirabel leaned forward. "How, child?"

I put down my teacup and drew in a steadying breath. I'd accepted that I would have to tell them. Even so, it was difficult to speak the words. "I . . . used magick."

Time seemed to slow as the sword slipped from Falun's hands, ringing as it struck the marble floor. He barely noticed, worry smoothing from his face as he reached for my hand. "Brilliant, Eva."

Mirabel rapped her knuckles against the desk, biting back a smile. "Finally, as I knew you would."

Captain Anali gave no visible reaction beyond a slight widening of her eyes.

"I knew," Falun continued, "when I saw the body, that you must've found a way."

Bile rose in my stomach. I swallowed, gripping the edge of the table. "What do you mean?"

"You were unarmed when I found you, but the wound on the man's neck was neat. It could only have come from a blade or . . ."

My magick.

I searched their faces for fear or disgust. Falun and Anali must've seen all that blood in the alley, and I'd spilled it without a weapon. They simply blinked back at me, relieved. "How? How can you be so happy?"

"Why wouldn't we be?" Falun asked. "You're alive and you used magick. You can win now."

"Win?" It didn't feel like victory when I killed the assassin. All I felt was horror and relief sharp enough to cut myself upon. "I can't win. I barely survived last night."

The only thing that had saved me was that the assassin wanted to toy with me.

"Eva," Falun began gently, "this was only the first time. You'll get stronger, much stronger."

"Right, so I can become an even better monster."

"Nonsense," Mirabel said. "Magick is magick—it cannot change you."

True, magick couldn't alter your nature; it was merely a reflection of it. And with magick of marrow and blood, I was indeed wicked. The first time I used magick to hurt Isadore had made that clear. Only Isadore, Papa, and my mother knew about that night, but I was sure that once Mirabel, Falun, and Anali saw me wield this power, they would agree.

I crossed my arms, trying hard to keep a tremor from my voice. "The last Queen with my magick killed her sister and set off a war. I already have to kill my sister. Has it never occurred to you that the Blood Moon rose because I might follow in Raina's footsteps?"

Falun surprised me by laughing. "That is absurd. No matter what the moon intends—if moons can have intentions—if you don't want to follow Raina's path, you need only study it and choose differently. What war would you start anyway?"

My mind whispered an answer, that it would take a war to right the wrongs of the past, but I kept silent.

He was right. I knew little about Raina, because I chose to avoid learning about her. She was the deeper darkness sewn onto my shadow, dogging me with every step. I'd worried I would relate to her if I knew more, but ignorance left me open to making the same mistakes.

Suddenly I knew what I needed to do today. "You aren't going to like this, but I need to go out into Ternain."

"Why?" Anali asked. "We don't know when there will be another attempt on your life. Killers once denied usually try again, Princess."

"And you've already missed Court," Mirabel added. "You'll try your mother's patience leaving the Palace today."

It was a risk worth taking while someone was trying to kill me. If anything held the secrets to controlling my magick, it was Raina's past. Though there was a library inside the

Queen's Palace, the best place to dig through history was on the other side of Ternain.

I needed to visit the Temple.

I changed quickly into a saffron dress with skirts divided for riding and retrieved the pine box shoved into a shadowy corner of the highest shelf in my dressing room. It was about the size of my hand and carved with flowering trees, with a sturdy brass lock on the front. I'd lost the key years ago, but found that a hairpin worked just as well. I worked it into the lock, my shoulders relaxing when it clicked open.

An old gift from my father, the box had been one of the few things I brought when I ran from Ternain. There were four treasures inside: two flat orange rocks with fissures of white, the skull of a small bird, and a gold necklace with a pendant shaped like a snake's open mouth, a lapis stone gripped between its fangs.

I'd gotten the charm visiting a village a few miles outside of Asrodei. The old woman selling it had promised me it would ward off my enemies. Unsurprisingly it didn't work—charms rarely did—but when I focused through the stone, I could smell magick even when it wasn't being used. If I cast my awareness in a wide net, I would sense the approach of anyone unfamiliar. It would be of little use at the Temple today, where magick was constantly taught, but I couldn't leave my rooms without it again.

Had I worn it last night, it would've given me warning.

I slipped the charm over my wrist just as a knock sounded.

Looping the chain until it was snug, I called for the person to enter. I expected Mirabel, but Captain Anali opened the door instead.

Earlier she'd said little in response to the news about my magick, but that wasn't unexpected. When we'd first met, her silences vexed me. I chattered to fill them during our training, hoping that something would pique her interest or bring a smile. Now I knew better. She was always listening, but wouldn't share her feelings until she was ready. She never spoke in anger or without careful consideration.

"I sent the guard to prepare our horses," she said, leaning against the cabinet where my real jewels were kept. "How do you feel?"

I felt like a teapot with the dregs stuck to the bottom, empty. "I'm fine. You needn't worry. The healer sorted my wounds." Even the bruise around my neck had been healed.

She nodded. "Ah, that's good to hear. My first time, I vomited on the poor bastard. Luckily he was already dead, but it was not my finest performance."

"Your first time killing someone?"

"I wasn't much older than you. It was my first week in the Queen's Army, and no one was interested in having a *beast* in their midst. I was in the barracks sleeping when he tried to knife me. Didn't have a weapon, so my shadows did the trick." She lifted a hand; shadows like velvety black flames danced around her fingers before sinking back into her skin. "Choked the life out of him before I realized what was happening. Had your father not protected me, they would've hanged me."

Anali always said she had had a rough time when she first

enlisted, but I never knew about these attacks. They were the worst kind of vile, but the sort of foulness Myre was built upon. Humans thrived here not because of our accomplishments, but because of what we'd stolen from the khimaer. We'd shown through the Enclosures that khimaer lived and died according to what humans decreed. Of course these men had decided they had a right to Anali's life.

For most humans, khimaer were the monsters that lurked in the night, never mind that Raina had conquered and caged them centuries ago. Guilt and fear turned so easily to hatred.

If I became Queen, which was doubtful at this point, I hoped to change much of that. My father believed Myre would eventually fall if we didn't integrate the khimaer back into the Queendom, and he'd chosen Mirabel as my nurse-maid and introduced me to Captain Anali so they could guide me. My mother was considered a revolutionary simply for letting khimaer join the Queen's Army, but freedom that could cost your life was just enslavement under a different name. Whether Myre fell or not, the Enclosures had to be abolished. I couldn't allow them to go on like the Queens who came before me had done.

It would be worth ruling, if only to change those two things.

I met the Captain's soot-gray eyes. "I'm sorry, Anali."

She waved a dismissive hand. "It isn't your sin to carry."

I fingered the hidden pocket at my hip where I'd stashed a knife. "Did you regret it?"

"For weeks I dreamed about knocking him out instead. Not because I cared about his life. This was a man so full of hate that he would attack a fellow soldier. I didn't believe he deserved to be etched in my memory." Her laugh was a bitter thing. "It wasn't a week before the next attack came and I hesitated, searching for a way we could both live.

"That was a mistake." She undid the first two buttons on her white jacket and pointed to a puckered inch-long scar on her collarbone. A few inches higher and she would have died.

"How often . . . how many soldiers attacked you?"

She took her time buttoning the jacket back up. I caught a flash of white-and-black feathers curling around the nape of her neck, quickly hidden beneath the fabric. "In my first year, seven. I remember all of their faces. Sometimes I wish I could forget, but it's right that I carry their deaths. Killing should never be simple, nor easily washed away."

"How do you live with it?"

"I accept it." She shrugged. "You will have guilt, Eva. But you won't regret being alive to feel that guilt."

"I don't regret his death," I said, and blushed when she arched an eyebrow. "I *shouldn't* regret it. He wanted to kill me. It may have been a job, but . . . He wanted to kill me." I shuddered at the memory of the sadistic pleasure in his eyes when he spoke of a slow death. "It's just, I don't want to be a killer, Anali. I wish I'd at least done it with my knife."

The justice the assassin had deserved was a hangman's noose. Not my magick ripping blood from his neck.

"Why?"

"You've heard the stories, Anali. You know what this magick is capable of."

She nodded solemnly. "You know what we believe." Khimaer believed that magick was neither good nor bad. It was a gift of the land, given to everyone in the Queendom. "We decide how to use our gifts. You shouldn't be ashamed to use magick to protect yourself, no matter how violent or powerful it is."

"I can't just stop feeling something so easily, Anali."

"I know, but you have to decide what you fear more— your magick, or being killed."

With that, she left my dressing room.

Days ago, I would have had trouble answering that question, but after seeing my death in the assassin's eyes, I knew no fear of my magick could compare to the fear of death. Even if I had to become the wicked girl of my nightmares, a maelstrom of marrow and blood, I would do whatever it took to stay alive.

⟶⟶ CHAPTER 6 ⟵⟵

I SAT ASTRIDE Bird, my palomino mare, as the Temple came into view.

Perched on a hill in the heart of the human sector, the white sandstone pyramid was the highest point in the capital besides the Queen's Palace. Steps painted in alternating shades of gold and blue led up to an opening at its zenith. A lush garden surrounded the Temple, with rows of palm trees and cacti, and bright crane flowers and orchids that couldn't have bloomed in this heat without magickal assistance. Two obelisks stood at the base of the steps. One was carved with the symbols of Sorceryn tattooing, and the other depicted the Auguries' domain: stars, the moon, and other heavenly bodies.

The Sorceryn, men who dedicated their lives to the study of magick, dwelled in the bottom half of the Temple. Their feminine counterpart, the Auguries, lived in its upper reaches, mapping the omens and interpreting their visions. They also kept the largest library in Akhimar.

Beneath my riding glove the lapis pendant pressed painfully into my palm. I hadn't bothered to use it as we rode here, since the guard kept a close eye on everyone we passed, but now I couldn't help but test myself. Dozens of patrons walked up and down the steps, young parents with children in tow, students with parchment tubes on their shoulders, and Sorceryn gliding up and down those stairs in diaphanous robes. I focused on the cool weight of the stone and drew in a deep breath.

The smells of a hundred different magicks swirled around me. Ginger and smoke came from the boy with fiery tattoos on his palms, the ink only half done. A young girl with a pen nib caught between her lips smelled of juniper and hazelnuts. The Sorceryn smelled of winter stew, layered with different flavors, the scents impossible to pick apart. The competing scents threatened to give me a headache, so I relaxed as we drew rein at the steps.

Captain Anali and I dismounted as a Sorceryn approached. He was tall and solemn-faced, with pinched features and golden-brown skin gone thin with age. His shaved head glowed in the afternoon sun.

"Your Highness, my name is Jorin. I am honored by your presence," the Sorceryn said. I caught a warm smile before he bowed.

For a spell-worker, he wasn't very powerful. Sorceryn acquired magick throughout their lives and inked the symbols of those new magicks until they ran out of skin. Tattoos often covered their ears and scalp, leaving only their faces unmarked, but Jorin's only peeked out from his collar.

"And I by yours, Brother Jorin," I replied, in a voice I

hoped sounded sincere. Though they had failed me, I tried to respect the spell-workers. More than a century had passed between Queen Raina's birth and my own; it wasn't their fault that the Sorceryn of the past had been negligent in their records.

"We had hoped you would visit our halls sooner when you returned to the Capital." There was a hopeful light in the Sorceryn's eyes, and in his voice, a searching. Like everyone else in Ternain, he wondered if the rumors of my inability were still true.

"My duties at Court take up much of my time." I fought to keep my voice light. That was the only way to escape conversations like this one unscathed.

"Many of my brethren were dismayed to learn the King's search yielded little fruit."

Of course they were. What good was a Rival Heir without magick?

"As was I." I smiled. "But I have not come today to discuss my magick. I would ask for your escort to the library."

Jorin bobbed his head in agreement. I knew the look in his eyes—disappointment, regret, and cringing pity. He was seeing my death.

Just as I'd seen it in the assassin's eyes last night.

Anali counted out five guards including herself and Falun. Jorin gestured and three hostlers approached to take our horses to the stables behind the Temple. I stuffed my gloves into my saddlebags but kept the pendant hidden in my fist.

Sweat trickled down my back as we mounted the steps. We reached the top, all but Jorin winded from the ascent, and he led us through an unadorned archway into a wide ante-chamber, tiled from floor to ceiling in pale gold. There were doors on opposite sides of the room, one marked with a fist and the other with a crescent moon.

Each door in the Temple was adorned with one of the symbols, the fist indicating rooms where the Sorceryn worked, and the moon signifying the Auguries' chambers.

We took the second, and walked through stone hallways lit by floating orbs of blue-white magickal light. The sight of them reminded me of the assassin's light magick, my stomach turning as I smelled his blood again.

We stopped before two oversize doors, the wood inlaid with silver depicting the full cycle of the moon. At a flick of Brother Jorin's wrist, a gust of wind blew the doors open. "Welcome to the Auguri library."

We were greeted first by words inscribed onto the shell-pink marble floor: *May the pages of our books number vast as the stars, so that we can know the world as we have learned the skies.*

The library was exactly as I remembered. Its main room was an immense circular chamber, with three mez-zanine floors where the majority of the library's collection was stored. Hanging ferns covered the upper balconies and there were small potted trees placed throughout the room. Sunlight streamed through a glass ceiling, illuminating the scholars seated at a row of long tables. Perhaps their books held more interest than I did, or they were intimidated by soldiers. Either way, none stirred at my appearance.

The only flutter of movement was at the back of the room, and soon a human girl in a rumpled blue tunic and trousers was skidding to a stop before us. She looked no older than fourteen, with a cloud of dense black curls and chestnut skin. Hazel eyes took up most of her round face and there was a tattoo of a yellow sun in the center of her forehead.

Sarou, library clerk and the Auguries' only apprentice, was a peculiarity. When we first met, I was less than half my current age. She looked just the same now as she did then, all sharp elbows and ink stains, her eyes innocent as a child's until she started recounting ancient history with the confidence of someone who'd lived it.

We first met when I was on a trip to the library with my father. I was seven when Isadore began her lessons with the Sorceryn. Most mornings, Papa would bring us both to the Temple together. We would drop Isa off in the chambers below, and go to the library until she was done. While Papa studied old maps, I tried to count the rooms of the library. Dozens of smaller rooms were connected to its central chamber, hidden in those upper floors, but I could never get an accurate count. My father always intercepted me before I could venture far. Then, one afternoon, I found Sarou sitting on top of a bookshelf, a leather-bound book open on her lap. She'd jumped down and promptly told me the number of rooms—twenty-eight—before shooing me away. But when she turned her back, I followed her, asking about the library and the sun inked above her eyes.

In every visit after, I sought her out, always with more questions than she was willing to answer. I was ten before I realized that as I grew taller, Sarou was ever the same.

All Auguries and Sorceryn were unusually long-lived for humans, but whatever had caused Sarou to cease aging entirely, she wouldn't say. Nor would she explain how exactly the Auguries' visions worked, or if they were guided by magick. Whenever I asked about them or the Blood Moon, she'd replied, *You will learn our secrets when you become Queen, and not a moment before.*

I wondered if she would say the same if I told her the likelihood of that had greatly diminished.

Sarou bent at the waist and smiled as if no time had passed at all. "Hello, Lady Eva."

She straightened from her bow and I was surprised—and annoyed—to see we were of an even height now. Sarou was quite tall for the age she appeared and I'd gotten none of my mother's statuesque figure.

"Hello, Sarou. Are any of the Sisters about?"

"They are busy"—she shrugged—"interpreting the omen from last night's sky."

And why, I wanted to know, aren't you with them? But that was not a question Sarou would answer.

"The Blood Moon?" I asked. In a way, I was pleased. Whenever we visited the library when I was a child, my father had insisted we call on at least one of the Auguries. Like Sarou, they all had tattoos above their eyes—of the sun, the moon, or a cluster of stars, sometimes even the far-off worlds they had named, like three-ringed Clyastis or Juni of the six moons—and their gazes were always far away. Those looks seemed cultivated to add to their air of mystery. When I could, I avoided all but Sarou, fearing they would have another omen to drop upon my shoulders.

Another part of me—the part that would live forever in that alley remembering the assassin's flesh giving way—wanted to see the Auguries now. I needed to know if their visions held more for me than the running of blood and the rending of flesh.

Sarou smiled obliquely. "And others. There is much more to the sky than one red moon. There are hundreds of omens, and thousands more across the tremendous sky beyond our sight. Eclipses of the moon and sun, stars falling, worlds we can only glimpse once a year."

"And will you still refuse to tell me of them? Or why there is a sun on your head, and not the moon?" I already knew all of this.

"If you've come back to the Temple just to ask questions I will not answer, I will return to my work." She glanced over her shoulder at the large desk at the back of the library. The table itself was clear, but several towers of books around it were as tall as a man.

I told Sarou what I needed and she brought us to a small room—with shelves built into the walls and three round tables, each equipped with a brass lamp, an hourglass, an inkwell and pen, and a roll of parchment—to wait while she searched. I might've gone with her, but only Sarou knew the library's complete system of organization. Having five soldiers and a Princess in tow would only delay her.

Anali and three other guards sat down at a table, but Falun stayed by my side as I walked to the opposite side of the room. There were private study chambers like this all over the library, but I knew this one. Sarou had likely chosen it on purpose.

My father had once favored it. He liked to spread his work across all three tables, pen resting behind one ear, with an inkwell and a sheet of parchment in hand as he walked back and forth, taking notes. *Every good General*, he would tell me, *should be an even greater scholar. We learn first from the battles of the past and apply the lessons they taught to conflicts we engage in today.*

I crouched, feeling around under one of the bookshelves until my fingers scraped against two words etched into the wood. I sank to the floor, tracing them as I slipped into a memory.

Isadore lay on her back, golden hair spread out behind her like fine silk. She had a ruby earring in one hand and was using the post to etch words into the shelf. I settled down beside her. Isa clasped my hand and followed the sloping lines of our names. *Now even if no one writes a book about us, we'll still be here forever.*

She'd sat up then and approached the table where our father worked, bent over a manuscript bound in twine. *Cast us an illusion, Father.*

He pushed back the pages and waited, an eyebrow arched. Isadore rolled her eyes, but laid her cheek on his shoulder and asked again, more politely. *Please, Papa.*

Very well, he said, brows drawn down in mock seriousness. *What do you propose? A ball at the Palace? A hunt for a desert krakai? A menagerie floating on the sea?*

But even as he spoke, the illusion had already shimmered around us. Books floated off the shelves, rustling like a flock of birds as they took to the air. Their spines cracked open and words marched right off their pages in ribbons of black ink. We raced around the room trying to catch the words before they drifted away.

Falun's hand on my shoulder drew me back to the present.

I was sprawled out just as Isa had been in the memory, my eyes wet. When I closed them, I could still see words woven through the air, and Isadore climbing up shelves to capture them.

"Are you well, Eva?" Falun asked, tugging at the braid hanging over his shoulder.

Captain Anali and the rest of the guards were watching me, their expressions wary. My face warmed as Falun helped me to my feet. "I'm fine."

"Perhaps we should go for a walk while we wait for your friend to return?"

"Yes." I didn't want to be stuck in there with my memories. I looked to Anali and the hourglass. More than half its red sand had fallen to the bottom. "We'll be back before the hour is up. I know this place well."

"Very well," Anali agreed, though her eyes were concerned. "Any longer and I'll assume I need to mount a search."

Falun and I wandered back to the main chamber of the library and climbed the steps to the upper mezzanine. Here it seemed the rows of shelves went on forever, and silence pressed in on all sides. Unlike the flawless pink marble below, the black-and-white tiles on the floor were scuffed and in need of repair, several having cracked beneath the weight of the shelves.

"Are you going to tell me what happened?" Falun asked as we roamed the stacks. He kept a hand on the pommel of his sword, completely out of place among the dusty shelves.

"We used to come here all the time with my father when Isa had her lessons." I shrugged.

"Ah," Falun said. "Bad memories, then?"

"Not exactly." The memories were warm and golden, but the present made every remembrance bitter. "I'm still not used to being in Ternain. Wherever I go, I remember when everything was . . . less complicated."

"Yesterday at Court my mother asked me to come home," Falun said, his jaw tightening. "She knows that I cannot. Your nameday is barely seven weeks away. After last night, I can't risk being gone."

Falun's mother, Lady Jessypha, was the head of House Malfar. The family split their time between the capital and their large estates just a two-day ride south. Most of their wealth came from the fruit orchards on their land, and a roving herd of sheep, which produced the best wool in Akhimar.

"I'm sure the Captain can spare you for a week or two," I said. Though Mira and Anali as my only company for that long was a tiresome possibility, Falun had younger twin brothers and an elder sister he'd seen only once since returning to Ternain with me. He ought to see them before it became even more dangerous to be around me. I envied those uncomplicated relationships—his fierce protectiveness of the twins, his equal amounts of admiration and exasperation for his sister, Erina. It was a reminder of just how different our worlds were. Even if I lived to have children, my daughters could never have such closeness, at least not for long.

"When I was young, it seemed that my father was always away, but last time I went home, I saw him everywhere. Singing to the trees, herding sheep he called by name, dancing with my mother at the hearth." We stopped at the end of the aisle. Falun stared at the floor, frowning slightly.

A little more than three years ago, just months after I moved to Asrodei, Falun's father had been killed in a skirmish with raiders near the Dracolan border. When his body was recovered, I rode south with my father for General Malfar's burial. The following month, Lady Jessypha sent Falun north to begin his training at Asrodei, to follow his father's path in the Queen's Army.

"I'm sorry, Fal."

He shook his head. "Don't be. Erina says that having only a few memories makes them burn even brighter. And I will see them in a few more turns of the moon. They'll be coming to your nameday ball."

Yes, though there would be no celebration if I could not survive these next months.

We lapsed into silence and turned back toward the room where Anali and the guards waited. I'd intended to spend the rest of the day at the Temple, but now I hoped to take Sarou's recommendations and leave quickly. Thinking of the young Auguri again, I reached for the lapis charm on my wrist. Sarou spent all her time here. She wouldn't tell me of the omens, but maybe I could discern something of her magick by sniffing it out. The library must have reeked of Auguri magick and the scents our powers carried often hinted at their nature.

I inhaled, but Falun's was the only magick I sensed— sweet cherry wine, sour oranges, and mint. Glamour always smelled of wine or liquor. I tried again and caught a faint earthy musk. I couldn't explain exactly how I knew it wasn't Sarou, except that it just didn't feel like her. Something about the scent gave me pause and prickled the back of my neck. I drew in a deeper breath this time.

We turned a corner and the scent vanished. I circled back until it grew stronger and was laced with the iron tang of blood. I made to continue forward, but Falun stepped in front of me. "What are you doing? Anali will worry."

I held up the pendant. Recognition settled over his face. He'd seen me use it before in Asrodei, though he was skeptical then. *Magick has no aroma,* he'd said, but had eaten those words when I guessed the magick of the Fort's soldiers as we walked its halls.

"Can't you smell that?" But of course he couldn't. The fey had sharper senses than humans, but they couldn't smell magick. "It's almost like . . ." I trailed off, trying to place it. "It smells of fear."

Falun held up a hand, cheeks red with frustration. "Just to confirm, the magick reeks of fear and you want to follow it?"

In answer, I took his hand and we proceeded forward on a winding path through the stacks until we came to a plain wooden door. The scent was so strong here it made my teeth ache.

Falun pressed his ear the door, brow wrinkling. "There is someone inside."

We entered the room. Copper lamps, like miniature suns, bathed the small room in pinpricks of warm light, casting patterns in shadows on the walls. Bookshelves fitted with rolling ladders stretched to the ceiling. A marble-topped table took up most of the space, filled with a strange assortment of items. There was an hourglass turned on its side, a hunk of uncut quartz, three golden eagle feathers, a potted fern—though how it could grow in this sunless, still room was beyond me—and an aged sword. The hilt was dented and spotted with rust; the leather on the scabbard looked as if it had been left to age in the sun for a century. All it would've taken was a strong wind to blow it to dust. A set of worn saddlebags had been shoved haphazardly beneath the table.

Other than that, the room was empty.

I looked to Falun, a question on my lips, but he stepped in front of me and pointed across the room. A figure clothed in midnight stepped out from a shadow beside one of the rolling ladders. My skin prickled as I caught the scent of that musky, wild magick again.

The figure looked up, his grin sly enough to make me sweat. "How lovely it is to have . . . visitors."

⤛ CHAPTER 7 ⤜

I OPENED MY mouth, but no words came to mind. I couldn't figure out how to stop staring.

He was fey and didn't look a year over twenty-five. His hair was as blond as Falun's was red—more the idea of blondness than a single shade. White, honey, pure gold, and ash all blended into a sheet hanging to mid-thigh, framing his body like an animal pelt. Sun to Falun's moon, the man's warm skin shone with flecks of copper and gold. His bone structure held the same sharpness I had come to expect in any of the fey, but was cast more finely than most. There was elegance in the dark sweep of his eyebrows, seduction in the upturned corners of his lips, danger in the dark hollows of his cheeks.

He was clad all in black, with tight leather breeches tucked into soft boots, and a knee-length slim-cut coat of the same fabric, with gold embroidery along its lapel. The collar of his undershirt hung open, revealing a glimpse of toned golden skin. A tuft of pale hair curled on his chest. More than ten rings were worn on each of his hands, some made from metal and precious stones, but most were bone jewelry.

Just like Raina.

He smiled, displaying bright white teeth. His canines were long and sharp, giving him a wolfish appearance. I resisted the urges both to lean backward and to inch forward.

More than attractive—the man was arresting.

He glided toward us, fingers skimming over the edge of a bookshelf, and stopped at the table. His walk was that of a leopard, all deadly grace and indolence.

Of course, his magick smelled of fear. This was a man who knew how to stoke terror.

"Did the little Auguri send you here?" His gaze roved over Falun before settling on me.

Was he another library oddity? Like Sarou, his apparent age didn't match his bearing, but he couldn't have been trapped within the halls of this place for very long. That golden skin knew the sun. I lifted my chin. "No, why would Sarou have a reason to send me here?"

"Who can know the motivations of those who commune with futures and fates?" The man shrugged, but his eyes were keen. "How did you come to this room, then?"

As if his words were a spell, my answer was out of my mouth before I could consider their wisdom. "I followed the scent of your magick."

The man's eyes widened a fraction before he leaned back, perched on the edge of the table with his jaw balanced on his palm. "How terribly interesting of you. Will you tell me your name?"

Falun gripped my hand and the slight twinge of pain

chased away my desire to respond. "If you think I will let you ensorcell her mind, old one, you are mistaken." Falun's voice crackled with quiet anger.

"I'm sure you can tell that I have laid no magick upon her. The girl only responds to my . . . natural charm," the man drawled. "You'll remember you are the ones who came to my door. I do not mean you any harm."

I looked to Falun, who nodded, his expression grim. The man was telling the truth, but it was not reassuring to know he'd had such an effect on me without magick. "Who are you?"

He arched a pale eyebrow. "Why don't you guess?"

Old one, Falun had called him.

I had a suspicion. It was barely within the realm of possibility. And yet when Falun and I exchanged glances, I was sure we were thinking the same name. My thoughts raced, seeking any other explanation. "If you want a guess, give me a clue."

"Very well." The blond fey grinned.

A warm wind tore through the room, tossing books from their shelves. His skin glowed like he'd swallowed a spoonful of the sun as he tossed back his head and howled. Beside me Falun stiffened, choking on a gasp.

The wind smelled of blood, old and fresh, and carried the sound of wolves, paws pounding on a forest floor, biting at the ankles of their prey. Most profoundly, it held terror. I tried to tell him to end it—my head ached at the pressure of his magick—but suddenly apparitions of massive wolves appeared around the table. A silvery mountain wolf with a scarred maw and pale gray eyes laid her nose against my arm. I rubbed her head, fingers combing through the thick fur behind her ears, and a contented growl vibrated in her throat. Across the room, another wolf, this one so black it ate up the light, lifted its head and howled. All the rest echoed his song.

I sang slowly, "Baccha, Baccha, Lord of the Hunt, wielder of death, kills when he must."

"Baccha, Baccha, Hound of Death, smiles as he severs your head from your neck," Falun said, finishing the tune.

A shudder ran through me. An old song for an old legend, an old myth. It truly was him. But how could it be? All of the Godlings—ancient fey and khimaer whose magick was so powerful that they lived for several centuries—were long dead. Wild magick like his had died out after the Great War.

Back when khimaer Queens ruled, Lord Baccha had led a group of fey and khimaer mercenary magick-workers who called themselves the Wild Hunt. Legend said they'd roamed Akhimar, killing, carousing, and committing a number of atrocities until their leader was tamed by the Queen and made to do her bidding. The story said she had yoked his will to hers with his blood. After, he and the Wild Hunt became enforcers of the Queen's laws, hunting criminals across the realm and often executing them.

Baccha snapped his fingers again, and the wolves, as well as the nimbus of light surrounding him, disappeared. He sank into the nearest chair and propped booted feet up on the table. "*Finally*. It's been exhausting having to introduce myself. Can you imagine it? 'I am Eva Killeen. You know the one—the Princess fated to kill or be killed, the one with lovely, fearsome magick'? Gods, how tedious."

I shifted uncomfortably. "You could have indicated that you'd recognized me, Lord Hunter."

"And you, my little Huntress, might've done the same." He gestured for us to join him.

"How do you know who I am?" I asked, sliding into a chair beside Falun.

"I heard about you almost as soon as I returned to the capital. You match the descriptions of the younger Princess, and there is a soldier by your side. I'm glad to find those most unfortunate rumors are untrue."

I frowned, thinking I had misheard him. "What?"

He cocked his head, confused. "You must realize that your ability to sense power that way is a gift of blood magick. As they say, all magick lies in the blood. I've only known one other who could do the same."

I flushed as I considered his words. I'd heard that adage during one of my few lessons with the Sorceryn but had never been sure how exactly it connected to my magick.

Raina's name floated unspoken between us, dangling like bait. The other he spoke of must have been her. I couldn't remember any of the tales written about the Hunter that involved the First, but then, legends and history were slippery things. Baccha's most popular ballads all took place before the Great War, but he'd lived through her reign. The bone jewels around his neck looked just like Raina's, so they must have been connected. I was sure of it, but I wasn't going to take the bait until I was sure of him.

He could be another fey with strong glamour masquerading as the Hunter. That made more sense than finding him holed up in the Temple.

I took a deep breath. "There is a line in every song I've heard about you. They add it even if the song isn't written in Khimaeran. *Al'aedin colish coleen, al codish volduva.*"

" 'The world is wild with untamed things,' " Baccha translated, his eyes twinkling with pleasure.

"I've heard tales that the khimaer Queen who tamed you left her mark upon your skin."

He grimaced. "Must I prove myself to you once more? And what of you? Will you show me your magick to prove yourself?"

I held up a hand. "What more proof do I need with this on my skin?"

The Hunter made a great show of extending his wrist. He had a sinuous faint white scar. I shivered and asked the question that had stuck fast in my mind since he appeared. "Did you know Queen Raina? I've never known a fey to work marrow magick, but your jewelry looks just like the necklace she wears in her portraits."

He sighed. "Yes, I knew her. I wasn't born with blood or marrow magick, but I learned it from Raina."

I fought to smother the desperate edge in my voice. "Will you teach me, then? By your words, I know you must have heard that I cannot use magick. The Sorceryn do not know enough of the past to instruct me."

"I sympathize with your difficulty, but I've no time to become embroiled in a contest of Rival Heirs. I am only passing through Ternain on my way to the Isles."

"Why aren't you on a boat now, then? Why hide in the library?" I remembered the saddlebags under the table. "Are you sleeping here?"

"That is my concern," Baccha said. There was danger in his voice now, a warning.

I did not heed it. My father had searched for years for someone to instruct me in the ways of marrow and blood magick. Lord Baccha was my only chance at commanding my powers. The good fortune that had carried me to this room would not strike again.

I refused to accept anything less than his acceptance.

"Of course it is, Hunter. I don't want to intrude on your affairs, but you should consider that my mother would not find such an answer satisfactory . . . None of the stories speak of releasing you from your service. If she hears of your return, she may ask you to resume your duties to the crown." Beneath his tan, Baccha paled. "Unless I convince her that your time is better spent elsewhere."

"You offer . . . protection from the Queen's attention?"

"I'm sure my mother will agree that teaching me is a duty worthy of someone such as you, Lord Hunter." I spoke in my Court voice, all its sharpness hidden beneath layers of gossamer and charm. All the while my heart beat at triple its normal pace. "All that I ask is that you extend your visit two short months. On my nameday at the end of high summer, you'll be free to leave Ternain."

"I could be persuaded to stay longer than I anticipated, but before we finalize this plan of yours, Princess, you should know that I can only teach you in the manner that I was taught. We must achieve *coalescence* and combine our magick."

Before I could ask exactly what that entailed, Falun protested. "That cost is too high, Eva. Coalescence would tether your magick to his. He would have full access to your magick."

Baccha looked at Falun through thick eyelashes. "And she to mine, love. What is the problem?"

A rosy flush swept over Falun's cheeks as he turned to me. "May I speak with you *alone?*"

I practically hauled Falun to the front of the chamber. "What are you doing? I nearly had him."

"I don't like this," Falun whispered. "Coalescence is a fey technique. We used to do it in times of war to increase our power. I've never heard of a human and a fey using coalescence together. I assumed it only worked with fey because our magick is compatible. Who knows what the effects of combining your powers with Lord Baccha's could be? Even between fey the results can be strange."

"Strange, how?"

"They say it bonds people for life, even after their magick has been detached."

That was just the sort of vaguely ominous warning I couldn't afford to worry about. Besides, I could use a connection to Baccha. He would impress the Court, and my mother, and could potentially help me gain more fey allies. Just as long as I kept him on a tight leash, which, considering earlier, would be no simple feat.

"What other choice do I have? He knows how to use my magick, Fal. And he's *Baccha*. How can I say no to that? Even if he doesn't agree, I have half a mind to call down every soldier stationed in Ternain to capture him."

"I know." Falun's hands flexed, inching toward his sword. "But he's dangerous, Eva."

Of course he was. "Then what do you suggest?"

"Take lessons with him, but don't trust him until we know more. I'll keep an eye on him as much as I can."

Baccha was practically beaming when we returned. "Have you resolved your quarrel?"

I folded my arms. "I have one last question for you, Baccha. Why did you return to Myre? Why now, after hundreds of years?"

"Because an old friend asked."

"Who?" Falun demanded.

"An old woman who doesn't like young men poking into her business," he replied smoothly. "I'm allowed some secrets, aren't I, Princess?"

Sure he was, until we could uncover them. "Very well. Please, Lord Baccha, will you help me?"

"Until the summer ends," he agreed. All his earlier mischief disappeared as he looked into my eyes. "Though don't mistake me, Princess. The threat of the Queen's interest does not worry me. I could disappear from this room without harming either of you, and you would never see me again. But having to avoid every soldier in the Queendom would delay my plans even more than waiting out the months till your nameday."

Thanking the Gods for empty threats and Baccha's sharp ears, I stood and gripped the table to steady myself. I was light-headed and wanted to let out a shout. I felt so much— exhilaration, shock, joy—over the absurdity of what I'd just managed, somehow enlisting a legendary Godling as my tutor.

It required all of my Court training to keep my voice calm. "Take a boat to the Gate of Moons at sunup tomorrow. Falun will retrieve you and I'll see that you're paid. We'll have our first lesson in the morning."

When I offered my hand to shake, Baccha pressed a chaste kiss to it instead.

⇢ CHAPTER 8 ⇠

EVEN THE NEWS that I'd found a tutor did not soothe Captain Anali's ire on the way back to the Palace. Hers was a quiet anger, but I felt every second of it on the ride back. I didn't blame her. We'd returned to find them searching for me, afraid there had been another attempt on my life.

Nonetheless, once she learned of my forthcoming lessons, she resolved to meet Baccha with Falun in the morning. I knew she and Mirabel would want to take the measure of the Hunter themselves before trusting him alone with me.

Sarou let me borrow a short biography and a book on the Killeen bloodline, with promises to return them in a week. I declined the other two biographies she offered after flipping through the opening chapters. The writers seemed intent on deifying Raina, just as my tutors had done. Besides, why read a secondhand account when Baccha was a primary source?

It was late evening by the time we returned to the Palace. My rooms were dark, the only lamplight spilling beneath the door of Mirabel's bedroom. Surprised to hear the murmur of at least two voices behind it, I knocked.

Mirabel opened the door. "Good, you've returned." She yanked me into the room and shut the door. "The new guard arrived while you were gone. I thought you should meet him before I sent him down to the barracks."

"Mirabel, wait, I have to tell you about the library."

She ignored my words, shoving me deeper into the room.

Mirabel's bedchamber was mostly bare, with just a small sitting area, an armoire painted with lavender songbirds, and a four-poster bed. The round latticework window above it gave a glimpse of the royal courtyard. The room was fairly plain because Mirabel kept most of her possessions at her flat in the city.

A young khimaer man in travel-worn soldier white sat in a chair in the corner of the room; he stood at my approach. He was tall and lean, with russet skin, long dark hair in braids, and the spiraling black horns of an impala. Though not quite as tall as Falun or Baccha, he still towered over me. He looked young, no older than twenty, and had one of those infuriating faces. So ridiculously handsome that I wanted to roll my eyes. The sharp, stubble-shadowed jawline and full, downturned lips alone were worth a lingering glance, but that wasn't the worst of it. Thick, sooty lashes framed eyes of limpid gold.

Gold.

Nothing muddled or common about the color.

He returned my appraising gaze, heat in his eyes sweeping from my face down to my thighs. My cheeks warmed as I smoothed damp palms across my hips.

A smirk curled one corner of his mouth before his

expression smoothed into polite interest. I couldn't believe two men had struck me speechless in one day.

"This is Aketo Jahmar, Eva, of the Sher n'Cai Enclosure." Mirabel's voice came from behind me, making me jump. *Sher n'Cai*, which meant "trap in the sky" in Khimaeran, was the Northern Enclosure. It was buried deep in the mountains far north of Ternain, near the Dracolan border.

Jahmar, I wondered. She couldn't mean . . .

"Do you mean *Prince* Aketo Jahmar?" I asked.

Only two noble khimaer Houses had been allowed to retain their titles after the Enclosures were set up. One had died off and the Jahmars were the only ones left. Descendants of the last khimaer Queen, they were Princes and Princesses whose claim to the land would never again be recognized. So why would one of them want to serve me?

I turned to Mirabel, arms folded. "Does my mother know that the khimaer Prince has enlisted in the Queen's Army?"

Her eyes slid past me toward the Prince. "Your father thinks we should keep that as quiet as we can for now."

Of course he did. Mother would not be pleased if she found out.

I started to inquire exactly how we'd do that, but Aketo lifted his chin. "I enlisted under a different surname, Your Highness. It will not be a problem." His voice was smooth and musical, if a little cold.

"Why did you accept this position? I know my father would've given you some choice."

"We are lucky to have Prince Aketo here after everything that's happened," Mirabel chastened me. "He is known to be a skilled fighter. Ask your Captain."

"It's a fair question, but I didn't accept the position. I requested it. This is the only place where I could have a khimaer Captain, and my father lives in Ternain. He's the bloodkin ambassador to the Queen's Council. As I'm sure you can understand, we've been able to see little of each other." Aketo arched a dark eyebrow, gold eyes flashing. "Your Highness."

Abashed, I bowed my head in apology. "It seems Ternain is the right place for you. Please call me Eva. Welcome to the capital."

He nodded in thanks and left the room to meet the Captain. With the height of his horns, he had to duck to clear the doorway.

I would have to ask her to have a few of the guards keep an eye on him. If his welcome to the Queen's Army was anything like the Captain's, he would need allies nearby. From what I could tell, we wouldn't get along, but I still had to see to his safety.

Even if he was arrogant as a cat.

Citing my hair's current state, Mirabel followed me to my room. Riding always left my hair in a tangle; half of it was matted and the rest defying all sense by springing up in every possible direction. I settled down on the floor at the foot of my bed and Mira sat on the goose-down mattress, my head cradled between her knees. While she worked, detangling and twisting my curls into simple plaits, I told her about Sarou and Brother Jorin, saving Baccha for the end.

"You taught me not to trust anyone until I know their motives. So I need you to dig up every detail of Baccha's more recent past that you can." As much as I was glad to have met Baccha today, simply stumbling upon him at the library felt too . . . convenient. I needed to know why he'd come back to Ternain and soon.

"A man like the Hunter may not like that." Though I couldn't see Mirabel's face, I knew from the cunning lilt in her voice that she was intrigued.

I didn't much care for what Baccha did and didn't like, as long as his lessons proved fruitful. "We'll just have to be discreet."

"The Hound of Death is certainly worthy of study," she mused, working at a particularly tangled knot. "But it won't be easy."

"He said an old woman asked him to return. It might have been a lie, but . . ." The look in Baccha's face when he had said it indicated otherwise.

"I'll start looking tomorrow since I have little else to focus on."

So far she'd turned up nothing on who might've removed the assassin's body. "I've no doubt that you can manage the workload. You'll find something, Mira. You always do."

"I hope so." She wrapped my hair in a scarf and made for the door, dousing the lamps around the bedchamber. I fought a jaw-cracking yawn. "Did you know Papa was sending Prince Aketo to Ternain?"

"No, if I'd known about the Prince, I would have tried to change the King's mind, though the Gods know I've never been able to convince your father of anything he's already set his mind on."

"Why would you have tried to change Papa's mind?"

"If any courtiers actually know something of khimaer, he'll be discovered. Only those born to the noble families have such long, beautiful horns." There was a yearning in her voice. With a sigh, she put out the last lamp. "Have a care with him, Eva. I'm sure Prince Aketo can be a resource to you. That's probably why your father sent him."

After Mirabel left, I didn't fall asleep for hours, my head too full of Hunters and Princes and Kings. Eventually I dreamed that I was back in the Patch, drumming a beat while all three danced at my will, but whenever my song stopped, I found puppet strings tied to my ankles and wrists. No matter how long I searched, I could not find who held them.

→ CHAPTER 9 ←

I HAD MY first lesson with Baccha the next morning in my father's office at the Little Palace. The cornflower-blue home was flanked by rows of orange and lemon trees, with even more fruit trees and date palms in the interior garden. Anywhere else, it would have been a sizable estate, but in the shadow of the Queen's Palace, it looked as small as a cottage.

It was traditionally used as a residence for the King's family, but had sat unused until Papa and Mother became estranged and Papa moved out of the Palace. Though eventually even that distance hadn't been far enough, because he left for Asrodei the following summer and I ran away to join him shortly after that.

An unseasonably cool breeze blew through the window that stretched the length of the office, ruffling the map spread across the oval table in the center. My father's desk was shoved into a corner on the opposite side of the room, a nest of crumpled parchment, myrrh candles stuck in pools of dried wax, overturned inkwells, and porcelain cups with dried kaffe grounds stuck to the bottom.

When Mother called for my return to the capital, Papa had given me free rein to use the Little Palace as I pleased. I hosted dinners for my guard here and walked the citrus grove when the gardens around the Queen's Palace were too crowded with courtiers. Until now I'd barely used this office, and hadn't had the heart to clean off the desk. I wasn't harboring any hopes that he'd return to the capital permanently. After all, if I didn't want to be here, why should he? The desk simply reminded me of him—of long rides over frost-crusted hills, sword-fighting lessons at dawn, and late-night card tournaments over cups of mint tea.

Baccha was bent over the larger table when I arrived. Like yesterday, his hair was unfettered, hanging to mid-thigh. I approached and found him inspecting the tiny jade and onyx paperweights atop the map. He held up one with a tiger's head and the body of a crocodile.

"Do you know what this is, Princess?" I shook my head; the set was my father's. "Dracolans call it a *tirimsho*, a river spirit."

"How do you know that?" I asked, voice deceptively light. Of course Papa would have a set of paperweights from Dracol. He collected all sorts of things in his travels across the realm.

"I spent the better part of the last century in Dracol." He returned his attention to the map of Akhimar, tracing a jagged line from Myre's western coast up through Dracol, the small human Kingdom in the North, beyond the A'Nir Mountains.

Thirty years ago my grandmother Queen Eryna had one of Dracol's Princes assassinated after she learned of his plans to declare war on Myre. Since then, Dracol's current monarch, King Lioniten the Fourth, threatened revenge often. They had not forgotten the assassination, but since war with Myre, a nation more than double the size of Dracol, would likely end in defeat, their hostility came in the form of raiders burning farmland on their way in and out of Myre. The incursions had become increasingly deadly for soldiers stationed in the North. As a result, Mother had closed the border, not allowing any of the Dracolans who lived in Myre to return to their homeland. There were whispers around the Queendom that we were on the cusp of war—the first since the Great War two centuries past—but Papa and Mother wouldn't enter a conflict without true provocation.

The news that Baccha had lived in Dracol sank like a stone in my gut. His loyalties could have changed, which had the potential for danger. I couldn't imagine Baccha working for the King of Dracol, but I also hadn't imagined that he was still alive, so anything was possible. I would need to tell Mirabel about that and every other detail he let slip. "But why? Dracolans fear magick and hate us."

"Of course I wore a human guise," Baccha replied softly. "You would be surprised, though, Princess. Many Dracolans are tolerant to magick."

Having watched my father tally the dead from Dracolan raiders, I ground my teeth. "Whatever they believe, soldiers are dying on the border every day."

"Yes, they are." His expression was troubled, but he smoothed it away and straightened, returning the figurine from Dracol to a map of the Kremir Sands. He gave me a quick once-over, and then frowned. "No escort today? Your Falun seemed rather enthused at the prospect of keeping an eye on me for the duration of my stay."

I failed to hide a grimace. Falun was waiting outside, likely listening in on our conversation. He'd asked to come inside, but I refused to have an audience for my first lesson. Or the second, third, and fourth for that matter.

"A pity," Baccha mused.

"I'll make sure to convey your disappointment, Lord Baccha."

He rolled up the map and we sat across from each other. "Now, in order for our magick to coalesce, I must first know the place where your magick lives."

When I stared blankly at him, he took on a look of long-suffering patience. "Your mindscape, Princess. The place in your mind that offers up the magick."

"Like . . . my lake?" I always saw one when I thought of my magick. And when I'd killed the assassin, it had offered me power.

"Yes, exactly like that. Everyone visualizes differently. When I first became aware of the magick inside me, it took the form of a river running through a vast forest. There I found my wolves and the wind, among other gifts." Baccha rummaged in the pocket of his coat—black leather again— and produced a dagger with a bone hilt carved into the shape of a wolf's head. "For our magick to coalesce, we must merge mindscapes. It shouldn't be too difficult to combine your lake and my river."

He slid the dagger across the table. I studied its wolf hilt.

Its teeth were bared in a snarl, and like his jewelry, it was highlighted with hints of gold. "And why do I need this?"

"Coalescence requires a bit of your blood and a bit of mine." He sat back, waiting for me to begin. "Believe me, Princess, you will be fine."

I pulled his dagger from its sheath, and hesitated. "Baccha, yesterday you said you would have access to my magick."

"I did."

"Will you be able to control it?" I swallowed. "Can your control stop me from hurting someone who doesn't deserve it?"

He bit his lip. "I could do that, but, Princess, I wouldn't worry about such things. All magick is dangerous—"

"I want your promise. That if I do this—develop my ability to use my magick—you'll stop me if I ever lose control of it." If only I could trust this to someone I knew well. All I had to go on of Baccha were the stories about him. In them, he was half rogue, half hero, forced to execute the Queen's will, often mourning even those he was forced to kill. Who knew what secrets lurked in his recent past, but I trusted that he would not revel in the death of an innocent.

The Hunter's eyes met mine. "I swear it."

I drew the blade down my palm in a sinuous line, wincing as blood welled.

Baccha slipped one of the rings, half bone and half gold, off his hand. He took my bleeding hand and slid the ring onto my thumb. It was too large, but Baccha tapped it twice. I gasped as it shrank until it fit snugly around my finger. "This will reinforce our connection, as well as allow me to track you if you're ever in danger."

Baccha didn't flinch as he carved a circle in his hand. He tucked the blade back into his belt after wiping it on his pants. The black hid blood well.

He shuddered once and held out his hand, narrow rivulets running into the creases of his palm. We joined hands. For a moment, I felt nothing but the singular sensation of our skin sliding through a thick coating of blood.

"Now," Baccha murmured. "Picture your mindscape, picture yourself there."

I conjured the lake. It hardly required any concentration to find myself at the lake's edge. Black water lapped at the shore. I imagined my bare feet planted in the damp mud. I could hear the rushing of rapids somewhere beyond this place and I knew it was the Hunter's magick.

I gave a start as Baccha appeared beside me at the lake's edge, our hands still clasped.

Wind slammed into us, making Baccha's hair spin into a tornado of gold. The lake of magick began a slow churn, not the intense boiling of two nights ago in the alley, but a slow building of power. Water lapped at my ankles, threatening to pull me under.

Suddenly my hand burned like I'd pressed it against a hot iron. I clenched my teeth around a scream and tried to pull away, but Baccha held me fast, and only the calm on his face kept my panic at bay. The ground quaked beneath us as my lake and his river became one. Trees surrounded us, growing from saplings to ancient in a blink. Above us, night birds careened through their branches.

As abruptly as the wind had started, it stopped. My lake was still again.

Baccha's voice floated through my mind. *In this place, we can communicate easily, but only when we're here together.*

What's next? I tried thinking it at him.

Baccha cringed, dropping my hand and massaging his temples. *No need to scream, Princess. Next we test the waters.*

I held my foot over the water. As I tried to dip my toes in, there was a moment of resistance. I pressed forward, and the ground dropped off completely. I fell into the lake.

The water was utterly black as it closed over my head. I was a strong swimmer, but that didn't seem to matter here as some unknown force pulled me to the bottom of this underwater chasm. I sank like a stone. Even knowing the illogic of drowning inside my own mind, I panicked. Kicking wildly and choking on that black water, I fell even faster.

I tried to scream Baccha's name, choking on more water, until finally I hit what I thought was the bottom of the lake. Instead I was lying on top of a barrier. It was translucent, flexible, moving with the water in the lake. I tried to push through it, but burning pain spread through my body. It consumed me—there was no thinking around it. I couldn't remember where I was or how I'd gotten there. Finally my hand dropped from the barrier and it all came rushing back. I tried to swim away, but my body was sluggish, still reeling from the pain.

Come back, Eva! This isn't real. Return to your body. Baccha's voice sliced through my terror.

I opened my eyes and found myself back in my father's office. I still held Baccha's hand. I pulled it from him. The wound had healed, leaving a faint scar.

"What was that, Hunter?"

Baccha looked shaken, eyes wide and unfocused. "I told you to *test* the waters, not swim right to the bottom. Human magick can be volatile."

"I would've appreciated that warning beforehand. I didn't swim, Baccha, I fell," I bit out. "And I couldn't even reach the bottom of the lake. There was some sort of boundary."

"I know. And that is only the second thing that went wrong." He squinted at me. "Can't you feel it?"

I closed my eyes and felt around in the back of my head. There was the lake, as always, dark and deep and full of magick, now connected to a pocket of awareness that was Baccha's river of magick. My thoughts stretched toward it; the sensation was like dipping my hand in rushing rapids, like I could be swept up in the current. A sudden, rather sharp annoyance poured through me, but the feeling wasn't mine. It was Baccha's. "What did you do?"

"It's a . . . side effect of coalescence. The emotional exchange is rare, but happens from time to time. I thought your guard mentioned it when he expressed his discontent."

"He said it could create a bond, not whatever this is."

"This is the bond—it's an emotional bond. We will . . . experience each other's emotions."

"You should have told me. You want your secrets, fine, but if it involves me, I want the truth, plainly stated."

"My apologies, Princess," Baccha said. "In my defense, I truly didn't expect it. The bond usually occurs only when two people who know each other well coalesce."

"Then why did this happen?"

"I'm not sure, Princess," he said, the sharp points of his ears going pink.

I groaned, poking at that new awareness. "And you can feel . . . everything?"

"If I concentrate, yes, but usually only the strongest sentiments come through."

"I don't like this, Hunter." I had no desire for anyone to be in my mind but my own self, feeling, reading, *knowing* my emotions. It was a horrible prospect; I would have preferred a stroll through Ternain without a stitch of clothing than be laid so bare.

"If you would like to end your lessons prematurely, I can reverse it. Though I fear that might make the other problem worse." I could feel his confusion coming through the bond. "Did you know that someone put a binding on your magick?"

"That barrier was a binding?" I rose from my seat and began to pace around the table.

Baccha went on. "Yes, unfortunately. A binding indicates—"

"You may have taken me for this empty-headed thing—this silly Princess—but I am not," I snapped. "I know of bindings, Lord Baccha."

A binding was one of the foulest uses of magick. During the Great War, Sorceryn put bindings on khimaer whenever they were taken prisoner, which stopped them from using their magick. They could be broken—magick won out, it always did—but not easily.

I thought of the pain I'd felt when I had pushed the barrier. How could I fight that? It had turned my thoughts to dust. If Baccha hadn't called me back, I would've been lost there, stranded in my mind.

"Then you know a binding can only be removed by the Sorceryn who created it. I can only think of one circumstance where a binding could have been placed on you without your knowledge."

My Harkening, the spell set upon every human babe in the realm to determine our magick. I wrapped my arms around my stomach, trying to hold in the panic.

"What I can't fathom is, why would a Sorceryn put a binding on their Princess?" Baccha continued. "Especially the one favored—because of her magick—to become Queen."

Whenever anyone spoke of my birth, they always recounted the length of time I had spent in the spell—ten days, which was five days longer than the average child. The binding must have been placed then. I knew one person who could've convinced the Sorceryn to do such a thing—my mother. She feared my magick enough to do it, but could she have resigned me to such a fate just after I was born? I couldn't believe that of her, no matter how broken our relationship was.

I pushed those thoughts aside with difficulty. "But, Baccha, I've used magick twice before. I used it the night before we met. Shouldn't the binding have stopped me?"

He asked me to recount the incidents. I explained both—the time I'd hurt Isadore and my killing of the assassin—without going into much detail. Still his pity effused from the bond, flowing into my mind as if it were my own. Baccha didn't express the revulsion or scorn I expected after confessing that I'd taken a life, but then, he had no room to judge.

He shook his head. "Bindings can be created to block a

specific ability, or to fade away over time, though I suspect yours is the former if you used magick when you were just a child. This is good news, though. We can still complete your lessons. We'll simply have to avoid magick that strains the binding until you discover who placed it and get it removed."

"How will we know what can and can't be used?" I couldn't stop the tremor that crept into my voice. Who could have done this? And why?

"Oh, you'll know," he said, scrubbing a hand over his face. "What you felt when you tried to force your way through the binding . . . you'll feel echoes of that pain if you put too much pressure on the binding."

Part of me couldn't help but see the upside to this. If the binding held something back, it must have been more terrible than the power I'd used to kill the assassin. It would be easier to learn the rest knowing there was something holding me back. But Baccha's next words made my heartbeat quicken. "But we'll have to be careful, Princess. If the binding breaks and you aren't ready, your mind could be left tied in knots."

No, I knew where I would end up. Trapped deep within that lake forever.

"How do you know so much about this, Baccha? None of your stories connect you to the Sorceryn."

"It's not a story you would know." Baccha clenched his jaw, the river between us flowing with aching grief. "After the war, I was asked to remove the bindings on a family of khimaer before they were sent to the Enclosure. The Sorceryn who'd bound their magick died at the end of the war, so the task fell to me. The crown wanted the bindings removed because they were driving people to madness—and accidents. When a binding is ripped away by force, the magick that comes rushing out can kill not just you, but anyone close. I was only able to break the bindings in two of them."

"And the rest?" I whispered.

He sighed, forcing a hand through his golden hair. "They died."

We lapsed into silence. Standing by the window, I looked out at the grove below. Baccha had spelled it out quite plainly. If I didn't find the Sorceryn who did this and convince him to reverse it, the same thing would happen to me.

✦

After I left Baccha, I went to see my mother. I had planned to visit her today anyway, so that I could explain why I'd missed Court, but the binding made it all the more important that we speak.

The Queen's Palace was like any other traditional Myrean akelae, but on a much grander scale. Instead of one central courtyard, there were four: the Throne Room, the Sun Gardens, the Silver Pools, and the Royal Courtyard. All of the royal suites overlooked our courtyard, and only the royal family and our guests were allowed in it.

I walked through it on the way to my mother's rooms, hoping the gurgling fountains and flowering trees would calm me. The cobalt and white tiles shined in the high summer sun, and the air was warm and smelled sweet because of the fruit trees. Figs and sour oranges and blue mazi were all in season. Since returning to Ternain, I looked out on the courtyard often, but had never seen Isadore or my mother visit it. Despite the team of servants who must have worked to maintain the courtyard, it was still and deserted.

By the time I reached her rooms, Mother hadn't yet returned from Court, but the soldiers guarding her rooms let me inside to wait. The Queen's suite was much larger than mine, with several bedrooms, two bathing chambers, a formal dining room, and a salon with a wide balcony overlooking the Red River, its waters colored rust by the red-brown clay at the bottom.

I waited there, watching the river ships—swift cutters with colorfully painted hulls, and low-slung passenger boats, prows hung with colorful lanterns—sail past. Upriver, where the water was shallower, there was a floating market of narrow canoes piled with melons, bright citrus fruit, fish, and cut flowers.

There was a soft knock at the door. It was one of Mother's maids, a pale woman in her middle years with bowed shoulders. "Her Majesty will receive you in her bedchamber, Your Highness."

Exactly what I'd hoped she wouldn't do. I hadn't entered my mother's bedchamber since I was still a child. All of my memories of it were bitter.

When I stepped inside, I was surprised to find it was smaller than I remembered. Still larger than mine, but not the palatial cavern my mind had made it into. The room smelled of orange blossoms and instead of light coming from the lamps hanging from the ceiling, tall, pale blue candles burned on every table. They smelled of the sea. The walls were painted a soft gold, with gilded friezes across the ceiling. Mother sat at a teak desk in the corner, reading a stack of reports. In a heavily embroidered silk robe, with her white-blond hair falling softly around her face, she looked much younger than she did sitting upon the throne every morning.

I approached the desk, head bowed. I would have to do this very carefully. Mother liked me contrite, but not weak. "Thank you for seeing me, Mother."

"Well?" She glanced up, bottle-green eyes meeting mine, before turning back to her work.

"I . . . came to ask your permission to miss Court for the next few weeks."

"You come to *ask* after missing two days." Her voice was emotionless. Her eyes continued to scan the page. "When you returned to Ternain, you agreed to obey me. I see, despite your father's assurances, nothing has changed since you left. You are as willful as ever."

"As anyone who hopes to be Queen should be, Mother." At this, she arched an eyebrow, but nodded for me to continue.

"I missed Court yesterday because I met someone who can teach me magick," I said. "Our first lesson was this morning. I thought you would agree that the development of my magick took precedence."

That at least drew her attention. She sat up, pinning me with a sharp gaze. "Who?"

"I fear you won't believe me if I say. He is new to the city. A fey bone-worker from the North." I held my breath, hoping she wouldn't dig further. I had bluffed in my first meeting with Baccha. If my mother became aware of the identity of my teacher, no convincing would keep her from ordering Baccha away.

The Queen wasn't supposed to play favorites, but my mother did. She had put Isadore's needs over mine for as long as I was old enough to remember. If she thought Baccha would jeopardize my sister's chances of becoming True Heir, she would take him from me.

"A fey bone-worker. Only you could find such an improbable thing," she murmured softly. She folded her hands on the table, nails long and lacquered bright blue, with rings on each of her fingers. The smallest was a small gold wedding band. I was surprised to see she still wore it. "Very well. Bring him to Court at the end of the week. You may miss Court until then."

She returned to her work without another word.

"There is one other thing," I said quickly.

"Evalina, you know that I am busy. I have a Council meeting in an hour."

"I wanted to ask about my Harkening," I blurted. "You never told me about it and I am curious."

She sighed, massaging her temples. "Your father could tell you more than I can. I lost a lot of blood during your birth. I was sick for days afterward; even the healers had trouble keeping me alive. I'd barely recovered when your magick was announced to the city."

My heart thumped in my chest. Was that why she seemed so averse to my presence? I'd nearly killed her coming into the world and then I'd been born with magick that threatened the daughter she loved long before I came around. No wonder our relationship always chafed. "I never knew, Mother."

"You never asked, dear," she said coldly.

I blinked away tears before they could fall. "But the Sorceryn, Mother. Did you choose them? Do you know who they were?"

"No, your father handled all of that. He always saw to everything with you." Her stoic mask fell away, but whether her eyes were shining with sadness or fury, I still couldn't tell. "He brought you to the Temple after you were born. He left in the mornings to visit with me, but otherwise he stayed at the Temple all ten days until it was done. Now, if that is all, Eva . . ."

I wasn't sure what words I said as I backed away from her desk. My hands curled into fists to hide their trembling. I shut the door behind me and sank to the floor.

It made no sense. My father couldn't have done this. Why would he make efforts to keep me from my magick and then spend the last three years searching the Queendom for a tutor? I'd gone on many of those journeys. We'd gone to Korsai, the peninsula jutting into the Fair Sea, and Soli Port, and a dozen different villages where elder Sorceryn retired. He could have told me—would have told me—at any time.

No.

There must be another explanation. Something Mother didn't know, or had left out, to torment me.

⤜ CHAPTER 10 ⤛

I WALKED WITH Baccha through the citrus grove outside the Little Palace. The branches were heavy with lemons and bitter oranges. Already sweat clung to my skin. In a few hours the heat would be intolerable. It was the sort of high summer day where everyone retreated from the heat in the afternoon. Even Baccha had exchanged his leather coat for a black silk one embroidered with gold leaves.

I was late in meeting him. I'd barely slept last night. I couldn't think of a single explanation for what Mother had told me. If Papa had stayed at the Temple for my entire Harkening—with Mother sick at the Palace—he must've had a good reason. There had to be some explanation, some justification. I considered sending a raven north, but this wasn't the sort of question I could ask in a letter. He was supposed to return to Ternain for my nameday ball in the coming weeks, but how could I afford to wait that long?

I thought about asking Mirabel, but I hadn't yet told her or anyone else about the binding. I didn't want to worry them yet, especially when there was nothing I could do about it now.

"Tell me, Princess," Baccha began, "what do you know of human magick?"

Unfortunately I knew little. When the Sorceryn finished my tattooing, they sent me away without a single lesson after admitting they had no way to instruct me. "The nature of human magick is to control a substance, physical or metaphysical. Magick of illusion controls the imagination, and magick of water . . . controls water."

"And do you know why tattoos are used in human magick?"

"The ritual brings magick to the surface and the Sorceryn use the tattoos to shape our unformed power into specific abilities. Touching them is supposed to trigger that magick," I said. Though nothing as simple as touch had ever brought any magick out of me. I'd tried with every tattoo, clutching them as I focused on the lake. But always it remained placid.

I shut my eyes and was nine again, in a dusty inking chamber with two robed figures leaning over me, my arms bound to a table heaped with vials of powder and ink. One recited their spell, while the other applied a needle and hammer to my skin. Magick in the air smelled of burning sugar clove and the coppery tang of my blood. I flinched each time the tools met, tiny beads of blood flowing down my arms like a fine lace.

"Princess?" Baccha's low voice drew me from my memory. "Are you well?"

"Fine," I muttered, pushing away the memory. His worry

seeped into me through the bond. "Why must we be inked so young, at nine? Why not once we're older?"

So that we could understand our magick, before we were made to bleed for it.

"Nine years was chosen because eight was thought too young and ten was often too late," Baccha said quietly. "Between nine and ten years is how long it takes magick to . . . ripen, if you will. That's true for everyone, but when humans' magick matures, it comes pouring out unfettered. I was still quite young when the men who would eventually be called the Sorceryn created the tattoos that let humans control their magick. Back then, those who mastered their magick lived . . . but many more died or were killed when they became a threat to others. The greater the magick, the worse the accidents were."

My chest grew tight. If what Baccha said was true, then it hadn't been my fault when I hurt Isadore. It wasn't my wicked nature that caused the accident; it was the inherent volatility of human magick. But it flew in the face of my tutor's insistence that humans had come to Myre with magick of their own. Surely we couldn't have made it across the Fair Sea with constant magickal accidents. "I was told we had magick before we came to Akhimar."

He tilted his head, squinting through the sunlight. "Is that what the Sorceryn say now? Your study of history has been insufficient."

"Then teach me."

"Will you pay me for those lessons as well?" He arched a pale eyebrow. "My rooms could be more spacious."

"No, you'll do this because you should. The next Queen should know Myre's real history. Shouldn't I be armed with more than just magick?"

"A fair argument," Baccha agreed, rubbing the golden stubble on his jaw. "Very well, I will tell you the old stories after our lessons each day."

"I'd rather you told me about Raina now."

"Oh no, Princess. I'll teach you my way, or not at all. Raina is only the middle of the story; what would you learn if I skipped the beginning?" Of course he would be difficult. Baccha only did things his way. He still hadn't explained why our lesson today was outside.

We came to a clearing in the trees. Baccha settled down in the shadow of a heavy bough and patted the crisp grass beside him.

"Tell me of the assassin," he said when I sat. "With detail this time, please. I'm sorry to make you relive it, but I must know everything if I'm to know where to begin your lessons."

I fought to keep my voice steady as I described it—the blood that scalded my skin, my tattoos' sudden luminescence, and the power itself, writhing and ravenous as it sought the assassin's flesh. With every word, my chest tightened.

Memories were fickle things. I could not, for example, recall what tea Mirabel served this morning, but when I thought of the assassin, things I'd missed that night leaped to my attention. The scar on the assassin's chin, tugging at his lips as he snarled at me, and overhead a clump of wilted poppies hanging from a terrace, petals leached of color.

If Baccha felt my growing horror through our bond, he

hid it well. "So you've already learned the secret to blood magick. While touching one's tattoos is sufficient for most human powers, blood magick can only be triggered by the presence of that which it seeks."

"So . . . blood?"

"Yes, preferably from whoever you plan to use it on. Place it on one of the tattoos tied to your blood magick, and it will draw out your power."

"What of using your own blood?" I was sure mine had been the catalyst to using my magick against the assassin.

"Though that might work under less than ideal circumstances, I don't advise it. If your concentration slips, you could accidentally turn the magick on yourself, which could be a fatal mistake. Besides, I find it's a good rule to leave your enemies to the task of hurting you. Best not to give them any advantage." He pulled out the dagger with the wolf handle from our first lesson and rolled up his sleeves. "Cut me. Preferably somewhere on one of my arms, but whatever you can manage is fine."

"Just like that? Is there more to explain?"

"Oh, for the Mother's sake. You will only stop fearing your magick if you understand it." He grabbed my hand and brought the knife down, too sudden and quick for me to resist. Blood dripped from a deep cut in his forearm. "The only way to understand magick is through its use."

Baccha held the arm aloft, blood seeping into the dirt. "One of the benefits of training with me is that I can heal almost anything."

The wound began to knit closed, leaving a coating of

blood but otherwise unharmed skin. "Impressive, Hunter."

"Thank you." He held out the dagger. "Now place my blood on one of the blooms and go to the lake."

I laid the blade, still wet with Baccha's blood, over one of the roses inked high on my forearm, but hesitated, remembering how the lake had sucked me into its depths.

"You won't have to swim into it, I promise."

I pressed the flat side of the blade to my skin and swallowed a pained gasp as the tattoo began to burn. Baccha's blood lit an unseen fire beneath my skin. Its effect was immediate, waves of dizziness striking me as the lake boiled.

I shut my eyes and found myself on the shore next to Baccha. A thick forest surrounded the lake now, a sign of the coalescence. Our mindscapes had combined. The cries of birds and pocket monkeys swinging through the trees overhead filled the air.

Watch. I gave a start as the Hunter's voice whispered through my mind.

A moment later, a red flower burst from the lake. It wasn't a real rose; its petals seemed made from flows of scarlet energy, pulsing with darkness. It hovered over the churning waves, slowly revolving. I could sense its lust for blood and for Baccha's especially. Just like with the assassin, Baccha's pulse sounded in my ears.

I started to back away, but Baccha grabbed my wrist. *Remember our promise, Eva. I am safe and so are you.*

Right. I'd decided to do this. I couldn't quit now. I drew in a deep breath. *What should I do?*

Call it to you.

Come, I thought. The flower drifted closer until it floated just beyond my fingertips. From a distance it had seemed as large as a dinner plate, but when I reached out to cup it, the rose fit in the center of my palm. The flower bobbed, petals flaring, and then sank into my skin.

All the red roses tattooed onto my arms began to glow with the same crimson energy as the flower. The magick of the lake coated my hands like gloves.

The Hunter smiled. *Good, now let's go back.*

I opened my eyes and the sun's heat returned. Magick still covered my palms. From where I was sitting just a few feet away, it leaped toward Baccha, but stopped short of touching him.

"Do you see?" He placed his hand an inch above mine, and the magick licked at his skin. After a moment, he held up his palm, the skin unbroken. "It can't bleed me unless you tell it to. You are in control, not the magick. It only lands where you direct it." He offered his hand. "Now I want you to try."

I touched the center of his palm. *Bleed.*

When I pulled away, my fingers were slick with Baccha's blood.

The Hunter sighed as he inspected a few shallow cuts in his palm, exactly where I had touched him. "You can do better than that, Princess. This is barely worth healing."

I let out a shaky breath and stared down at the magick cloaking my hands. Beneath it, the roses on my arms looked aflame. To Baccha it might have been nothing, but for me, it was stunning. "Do you have more advice to offer, or is your plan just to berate me into getting better?"

"The magick senses your hesitation." He spoke as if it

should have been obvious to me. "You need to want it. Strengthen your resolve."

"Fine," I snapped. I caught his wrist, feeling the steady thump of his pulse. Baccha was not at all afraid I would hurt him. Even as the magick coating my hands flowed over his skin, his expression remained placid. *Open his skin*, I instructed. *Bleed him.*

And it did. Three slashes, as if cut with an invisible and wickedly sharp knife, appeared on his forearm. Blood, smelling of salt, iron, and Baccha's magick, sprayed.

I caught a flash of white bone and covered my mouth as my stomach threatened to empty its contents. In my surprise, the magick left me, the glowing power seeping back into my skin.

It had been so . . .

So easy.

And felt so wrong for that ease. I'd expected my magick to demand great toil and sacrifice. Isa spoke of how her Sorceryn tutors would make her practice the same method repeatedly for hours and test her on the location of every one of her tattoos. I thought my lessons with Baccha would be much the same.

The Hunter barely flinched at the wounds, and I felt no pain from him through the bond. There was only warm satisfaction, like fresh toffees, as he smiled at me. "You will get used to the blood. To get close to the throne, you must."

"I'd rather it shocked me every time." Papa always said that to become numb to violence was to forget to cherish life. Better that my magick disturb me. Like Anali said, it was better that I felt guilt. Or else I might come to see this violence as my only solution to everything.

"Fair, as long as you don't let that shock hinder you." He stanched the blood leaking down his arm with a handkerchief patterned with running wolves. "Now you've used blood magick by touch, but I'm sure you can understand how much of a disadvantage it would be in armed combat."

I'd actually been wondering how Raina had killed thousands with a magick that had such a small range, but I said nothing as he continued. "Another method would be to *direct* the magick using a weapon. That way you can fight at a distance, as well as close range."

"How?" I asked, eager. Wielding magick with a weapon I already knew well had so much more potential than doing it by touch. I never again wanted to feel someone's lifeblood wash over my body as the assassin's had.

"Summon your magick as you did earlier using my blood, but instead apply it here." He helped me to my feet and pointed to a tattoo just below my elbow. Next to a cluster of rosebuds, there was a curved dagger hidden among the leaves. "That ought to serve you well."

I did as he said, using blood from Baccha's handkerchief. My eyes fluttered shut as the tattoo became uncomfortably hot.

Baccha said, "Remember, you'll be using this magick in a fight, Princess. Keep your eyes on your foe."

When I looked into his amber eyes, I could still sense the lake, the waters swelling and rippling until a red knife, shaped just like the tattoo, burst from the depths. It hovered over the surface, pulsing darkly.

"You see it, don't you? You don't always have to travel to the lake. Open yourself to the magick and it will respond." Baccha smiled.

I pictured the lake's red knife covering Baccha's dagger. After a moment, the red tattoos on my arms flared to life. I watched, mouth ajar, as the red energy rushed down my skin to wrap around the dagger.

Baccha let out a low whistle and backed away. "Now, Princess, I'll show you—"

I didn't wait for him to explain. Somehow I *knew* what to do. Baccha had said the weapon would direct the magick, and that this would allow me to fight at a distance. That must have meant that I didn't need to actually strike him with the blade.

I sliced up with the dagger, aiming for where his chest would have been if he was standing closer. As I'd hoped, the magick lashed out in a thin streak of red and struck Baccha. Blood suddenly spurted from his shoulder.

I dropped the knife and ran to Baccha's side.

"Well done." He looked especially wild, blood from his shoulder staining his hair. "Now let's see how many times you can land that when I'm not standing in one place."

He barely waited for the wound to heal before he was calling for my next attack. I chased him back forth through the trees. He dodged and feinted, neatly escaping my attempts until I realized he wanted me to anticipate his next move. Most of my attacks missed, but the few that struck him opened dire wounds. Without his healing ability, practicing this way would have been impossible. As it was, I was glad no one else was there to see his blood-soaked clothing.

And thankful that Baccha hadn't yet sensed the pounding in my head through our bond. The pain must have been from straining the binding, but I decided not to tell him unless it became truly unbearable. Baccha had been quite adamant about the dangers the binding presented, but a headache seemed a small price to pay for the safety the power would grant me.

An hour later, when I was exhausted and dripping with sweat, Baccha told me his first story as we walked back to the Little Palace.

✦

Before there were things such as beginnings and endings, two souls drifted, waiting for the dreamgod, Hesa, to create their home.

Hesa dreamed all things into existence, but she chose their souls first, you see, because souls are easier to dream than worlds. When Hesa fell into her last sleep of creation, seas poured from her eyes, land rolled at her touch, and red sand cascaded down her skin. She dreamed of flowering trees and crocodiles and rivers. And finally she dreamed of power planted deep within the soil.

When she awoke, Hesa named this land Akhimar, which meant "place of magick." For the power she sowed would flow into everyone who lived in this land if they chose to embrace it.

With this in mind, the dreamgod sent the souls, whom she called Godlings, to Akhimar.

They were not born, but awoke full-grown. The first, Khimaerani, gasped her first breath on the banks of the river, which then ran pure and blue. The second, Safiron, woke upon the boughs of a mountain pine, covered in a blanket of snow.

The two Godlings lingered in their corners of the realm, thinking themselves alone. But one day Safiron flew to the top of a mountain. He looked to the south, watching the great river that cut through the land. Though the mountains of his domain were cold, he could see that the sun favored the southern regions.

His eyes were as sharp as a hawk's, and even from that great height, he saw a woman bathing in the river. Her form was different from his, with horns that curved back from her brow and legs that were like an impala's. But even as she waded through the water, she changed. Her body shifted, horns becoming antlers, arms becoming wings. But her face remained the same, high sharp cheekbones, hickory skin, ripe lips, and velvety black eyes.

Safiron flew to her.

Khimaerani saw the man coming. She could not have missed him, flying through the air as he was, without wings, sunlight dancing off his umber skin, white locs kicking in the air behind him. His eyes were the green of new leaves and his ears were pointed.

"How can you fly without wings?" she asked when he landed on the riverbank.

"How do you change without breaking apart?" Safiron asked as she swam to the water's edge.

The wind whispered an answer: magick.

The two became lovers, wandering from the red sands of the south to the mountains of the north. They swam to the isles and back.

Their children were as different from one another as their parents were. The first had Safiron's form and unyielding beauty, and he could make others see whatever he wished. The second grew horns like her mother and wings like those of a golden eagle, and could call forth a storm with a thought. The third child craved fresh blood and could enchant all who looked into her eyes.

From these three became many. The son who took after Safiron called his people the fey and formed a Kingdom in the North. And the daughter who was like her mother, Khimaerani, named her people the khimaer and established a Queendom in the South. The last son, who called his people the bloodkin, roamed both lands, kindred with all.

The two lands lived peacefully, until they didn't.

✦ CHAPTER 11 ✦

THE FOLLOWING AFTERNOON, I walked beside Prince Aketo on the way to the Sandpits. Anali had proposed a trip to the sparring grounds attached to the barracks after I returned from my third lesson with Baccha.

I hadn't seen him since the night we met. It required all my concentration to stand next to him and relax. Each time I glanced over, I wanted to linger on the details of his face. I resented its perfection. I'd always longed for a face like his, or Isadore's. My father used to say Mother's smile, when it was real, felt like sunlight hitting your skin. Isadore had the same smile. I'd spent years chasing it.

Would I swoon if, instead of scowling at the floor, Prince Aketo smiled at me?

We walked in silence until I felt him stiffen at my side.

I followed his gaze. In this part of the Palace, the white sandstone walls were inlaid with detailed mosaics of colored glass, stones, and crystals. Only khimaer artists created mosaics like these.

He was staring at an elaborate scene depicting the Throne Room in great detail. The silver-white pillars were made from crushed crystal and there was a small carving of the Ivory Throne in the center. The woman seated on the throne had a snake's tail curled at the foot of the dais, and massive antlers rose from beyond the red spires of her crown. Just like Khimaerani in Baccha's story. She was beautiful, and utterly foreign; khimaer with such obvious animal attributes weren't allowed outside of the Enclosures.

Aketo's nostrils flared as he took it in. It must have galled him. Khimaer art decorating the Palace walls, while his people weren't allowed to walk through it.

"I'm sorry. Sometimes they hang tapestries over them, but the mosaics are fashionable right now," I said as we turned a corner. His full lips pressed into a flat line. "The most talented artisans in Ternain have been trying to imitate the style for months to no avail. I've heard some try to visit the Southern Enclosure to study with the khimaer, but . . ."

"The soldiers allow few visitors." He offered a wan smile and tugged at his hair. It was tied back, black curls falling well past his shoulders.

The curls shifted and I saw the narrow strip of gold scales down his neck. They were the exact same color as his eyes. I gasped before I could stop myself. He was lami khimaer, part of the tribe whose forms resembled snakes, just like the Queen in the mosaic.

Aketo's expression froze, his eyes flinty, but he kept silent as we continued down the hall.

"I didn't— I wasn't—" I scrambled for words, for an explanation. "Your tribe is lami, correct?"

It took him a moment to answer, and when he did, the words came out through clenched teeth. "Yes, Your Highness."

My face was aflame. "I've heard lami khimaer can read and change the emotions of others."

"If you're wondering whether I'm busy nosing through yours, I learned to tune out most everyone when I was a child." His eyes met mine. "People's minds and hearts should be their own."

"How good of you," I said. Though my voice was sharp, I meant it.

He glanced at me through heavy lashes. "I wonder if you could answer a question for me."

"Of course."

"I assume you learned about our tribes and our magicks through Mirabel or Captain Anali, but what of the rest of the Queendom? How much do they know? It's just . . . curious to me that the signs of our rule are still kept throughout the Palace. Is the history of the Usurpation taught?"

"Here it is called the Great War, and yes, it is taught, though my tutors skimmed over the unsavory details. Mirabel taught me about the khimaer long before they ever did, but no, most Myreans don't know the complete truth about the Great War or the rebellion that followed."

They didn't know humans had relished shedding blood on khimaer holy days. They didn't know that Raina had forced the khimaer to relinquish the throne by slaughtering a nursery full of children, some infants.

They didn't know that to me all that cruelty wasn't shocking. The same depravity had created the Rival Heir system and allowed both to persist.

"Would it change anything if everyone understood?" His eyes were so gold and piercing, so earnest. "Would most Myreans see the Enclosures as unlawful if they knew the truth?"

I wanted to say yes, because it had changed me.

But then I thought of how many Khimaeran folktales were told by our bards and story-weavers. And how during certain festivals, common citizens costumed themselves as khimaer with paper horns and jeweled claws. Khimaer weren't real people to most human Myreans. They were mysterious, fearsome figures in the tale of our rise to power.

"Unless the crown took action, it would change little. They would pity you more, but what good is pity? After all, everyone pities me. None of them would see their children in my place or Isadore's, but they've never demanded a change. And they never will.

"No one relinquishes power easily. If we are to return the khimaer to their rights and station, it isn't knowledge that will do it. It will take force. Or months of political maneuvering. You'd need the entire Council in your pocket."

"The Council?" he echoed.

"The Queen's Council. All thirteen members must agree in order to change the law requiring that khimaer live in the Enclosures. It's feasible now. There are many more khimaer living in Ternain than when I was a child. But it would require much."

"You seem to have given it some thought." Sunlight spilling through the windows made the gold studs in his ears flash.

"Yes."

"Is that what you'd do?"

It was exactly what I planned, when I allowed myself to dream about becoming Queen. To first abolish the laws that said every khimaer child had to be raised in a cage, and then to get rid of the Rival Heir system. "I would have to be crowned first, which, as I'm sure you've learned by now, is unlikely."

"How does it work? With you and . . . the other Princess?"

"At my nameday ball, the Sorceryn will lay a spell upon me and my sister called the Entwining. It binds our lives together so that only we can kill each other. It's done to keep others from interfering." If I made it to my nameday, I would at least be safe from whoever was trying to kill me now . . . unless my instincts were wrong and Isadore really was the one behind the assassin. "Then one of us will challenge the other."

"That night?"

"Tradition calls for a grace period of a single day." Isadore, two years older than me, had had years to grow stronger. The older Rival Heir always had such an advantage. "After that it could be days, weeks, years even."

"I'm sorry." He lifted a hand to my arm.

I stared down at it until he removed it. "You, of all people, do not have to apologize."

We lapsed into an uneasy silence. Hadn't he been listening? Pity was useless.

I only made it three more steps before realizing I'd pitied him first.

✦

Falun shoved a wisp of carmine hair out his eyes and raised his sword. "Ready?"

I nodded and he struck, swinging a practice broadsword in a wide arc. I ducked it and pivoted easily in the sand, deflecting his next swing.

"So how goes keeping an eye on the Hunter?"

Falun blushed, but I couldn't tell whether it was because of the exertion or the mention of Baccha. "Other than your lessons he hasn't left his suite." He crouched and delivered a sharp strike to my calf.

I danced away, my feet sliding in the sand. I let my practice sword fall to the ground, though neither of us had won the bout. "And no one from Court has visited him?"

"I'll tell you if anything changes, Eva, but whatever reason he's come back to the capital after all these years, I don't think we'll find out by watching him."

Mirabel's research into Baccha also had setbacks. She'd tried to find out just when he'd returned to the city. One of her ghosts checked the records of who had come in and out of the city gates going back several months, but so far that had yielded nothing. I had half a mind to visit the Temple again just to ask Sarou, but I probably wouldn't get a straight answer out of her. She'd known Baccha much longer than me and was probably loyal to him.

A shout sounded from somewhere in the pits. I froze, twisting toward the sound. Someone was cheering.

"My Gods." Falun dropped his sword.

Fifty feet away there was a whirling blur as Anali and Prince Aketo fought. Their blades caught the light from the sun filtering through the netted ceiling above the Pits. They looked like flames flaring in a cloud of smoke. My eyes couldn't pull them apart. They moved beyond a pace I could follow, fighting with blades, and with sudden blistering speed limbs were thrown about.

Prince Aketo leaped into the air—I knew it was him, because the curls swinging behind him were dark where Anali's would've been white. With a cry, he came down with his knee in her chest. Their movement had practically kicked up a sandstorm. It took a moment for the sand to settle and when it did, the most perplexing scene lay before me.

Anali was on her back in the sand while he crouched above her with his curved short swords, one in each hand. After a moment he stuck both swords in the ground and held out a hand.

A few of the guards let out whoops of laughter and rushed toward them, stumbling with their boots through ridges of golden sand.

Falun glanced at me. "Looks like the new guard came at the right time."

I muttered a curse. Mirabel had been right. He was a brilliant fighter. Even without a weapon, he could probably put everyone in the guard on their backs.

We walked toward them, and I hoped I was doing a decent job of hiding my annoyance at his apparent perfection.

"I've forgotten how to dance, it seems," Anali said, dusting sand from her pants.

"Your feet are more nimble than most, Captain. Truly."

"So dancing is the key to besting the Shadow?" one of the guards, Malto, asked, clapping Aketo on the back. Malto was bloodkin, short and barrel-chested, with bronze skin, and arms as thickly muscled as a blacksmith's.

Aketo ducked his head, but a satisfied smile curled his lips. He looked up, eyes meeting mine, and the expression wasn't unlike that first pleased smirk.

Though heat simmered beneath my skin, I lifted my chin and ignored the flush of warmth in my cheeks.

He tugged at his hair—I marked this nervous habit and added it to a list of flaws I would compile until I reached at least one thousand—and glanced at Anali. "It is called *kathbaria*."

"*Kathbaria*, 'blood dancing,' or 'death dancing,' depending on who's translating," Anali added. "It's how we train. You learn the dance first, no weapons. If you can't move on your own, how can you move with steel? But kathbaria has no forms; it is only continuous movement, just dance."

"Impossible," a gravelly voice called from beyond our group. "The Shadow, bested by a new recruit? I don't believe my eyes. We can't have left the Princess in such inept hands."

The Shadow was Anali's moniker within the army because she was as hard to catch as a shadow, and because her magick granted her the ability to control shadows and darkness. It was a gift everyone in Anali's tribe, the nozin, possessed.

A grin broke out across my face. I started running before he even finished talking, questions spilling from my lips. "Dagon, what are you doing here? Where's Papa? Is he back in the Palace?"

"Oh, hello, Eva girl." Dagon rubbed a hand through his short, neat hair. I'd known Dagon all my life. He was in my father's personal guard, and was one of his closest friends. Dagon had taught me to ride and to shoot from horseback when I was ten. Much to his chagrin, I was never a good archer. My arms were too short and my aim was better with a throwing knife.

Anali appeared beside me and clasped Dagon's hand. "Welcome back. Has the Lord Commander returned to Ternain? I'd thank you and the King for taking this one from my inept hands."

He chuckled. "I'm sure I didn't say inept. You must have misheard me. But no, the King is still in the North." He carried something behind his back, but his other hand came around to pat my cheek. "I'm sorry, Eva. I came alone."

As the shock wore off, I remembered the binding. I wrapped my arms around the sick feeling in my stomach, wishing I could sink into the sand below. Part of me was glad only Dagon had come. I wasn't ready to confront my father.

Anali filled the silence. "When will he return south? The Princess's nameday is in less than two months."

"I'm not certain when he'll be able to get away. The raids along the border persist and there has been an increase in unrest in the Enclosures. The King travels to and from Asrodei often, as it's much easier to direct military presence and operations from the base, and he's been meeting with the Archdukes in the Sister Citadels as much as possible."

The Citadels were located at the Myre-Dracol border, one on each side of the river. They were Myre's second most important military center, with the vast majority of the army stationed between there and Asrodei. In the North, my uncles, Archdukes Kel and Roshanon, were like kings.

"The King sends his regrets, and I've brought gifts." Dagon pulled a cloth-wrapped sword from behind his back. "There are other things, but I thought you would find this most useful."

I pulled off the cloth and stared.

"It's old," Dagon said while I turned over the sword in my hand. Its guard was dull steel, nicked from use, and the hilt was carved bone that had yellowed with time. "You'll have to wrap the hilt, as the leather rotted off long ago. Anyway, it's best you see it this way. Do you recognize her?"

It was the carving that struck me silent. My thumb roamed over the feathers and the narrow, feminine face. With her curling horns, feathered wings, and one leg that of a leopard and the other a serpent's body, I knew her immediately.

"Daei sher'khimaer." Aketo's words rolled from his tongue like his mouth had been fashioned specifically with them in mind. *"Daei Khimaerani."*

"Khimaerani, the Mother," I echoed. The shape-shifting Godling from Baccha's story, from whom the khimaer race had been born. "Dagon, where did Papa find this?"

"Some merchant in the mountains who didn't realize what a treasure he'd found."

Khimaer didn't hold to the presence of Gods, not like the fey, who had hundreds. Nor were they like bloodkin, who essentially worshipped one God, who represented all things. Instead their ancestors were held sacred, none more than Khimaerani.

During the Great War and the rebellion, all statues of Khimaerani were destroyed. I'd seen drawings, but this was . . .

My hand curled around it protectively.

I pulled the sword from its scabbard. It was similar to my other long sword, double-edged and curved, but in this the strips of silver and gold were etched with peaked and arched symbols. The design was intricate, and though they looked similar to fey runes, I didn't recognize any of the symbols.

"It's beautiful." It was easily the most marvelous thing I'd ever touched.

"May I see the sword?" Anali asked.

I laid it across her hands and Aketo stepped forward to run his finger down the center. "We call these symbols *iktar*. They're an alphabet used specifically for noble surnames." He glanced at Anali, his eyebrows knitted together. "Nbaltir. A royal name and a . . . dead one."

Anali held out the sword. "Well, it's a great find by His Majesty."

I hesitated as I took in the soft awe on their faces. If the name was royal, this should have been Aketo's, but he looked down at it with the sort of distaste reserved for a dead body. Was that because it was in my hand?

Wrinkles framed Anali's smoky eyes as she smiled. "If King Lei wanted you to have this, there is a reason. I trust you'll carry it proudly."

Anali returned the sword to me. I ran my thumb absently over the bone hilt. A pulse went through my hand, making my heart stutter in my chest. It was so soft I thought that I must have imagined it.

"Are you going to stand there staring at it till we all fall over dead, Evalina?" Dagon grinned at me, whistling. "Or shall we see if your Captain has been keeping you sharp?"

I looked down at the sword again. I didn't want to use my

father's gift, not until I could talk with him about the binding. But my father's guards had been challenging me like this since I learned how to fight. There wouldn't be any harm in using it for this one match.

I lifted the blade over my head and leveled it at Dagon's throat. "Shall we?"

The bone was smooth in my hands and unyielding, and yet the edges of Khimaerani's feathers fit comfortably into the grooves of my hand.

I stepped back at the sound of his sword escaping its scabbard. I beckoned him forward, deep into the dunes until the rest were far enough away that any errant blades wouldn't do much damage. Dagon didn't even bother removing his boots.

"Are you still as quick as I remember?" he asked.

"I am!" I called. "And you're still lumbering."

Dagon had always been surprisingly nimble for his size. Now he charged toward me, kicking up sand, with a wide grin to match mine.

"You may be quick, but you're still mad with youth." His sturdy fey-made broadsword swung toward me quick as a viper, a hair away from my stomach.

Dagon's wrist twisted as he tried another open slice across my midsection—my sword arm vibrated with the clash of our weapons as I parried the strike. I dropped to a crouch as Dagon's sword cleaved the air where my head had been.

Dagon charged forward, but I slashed at his arms, forcing him to retreat as I came closer and closer.

I grinned at Dagon and for a suspended moment he smiled back. "Eva girl, you are quicker than I re—"

I struck out at him. Our swords crossed with a resounding strike that vibrated down my arm. Time slowed and the air . . . changed. It became viscous, thicker than water and warm as blood.

I smelled wildflowers and myrrh—magick.

Dagon's face went completely blank. Not only devoid of emotion, but also devoid of self, of *anything*. He blinked slowly and his eyes focused on my face.

"Dagon?" I whispered.

He shoved me away with his cross guard and I went stumbling back into the sand. He stood above me and lifted his sword. I still found nothing in his expression.

I grabbed a handful of sand and threw it at his face. I backed away as he clawed at his eyes.

My attention slid past him, in search of Falun or Anali, but the air was strange past the space between Dagon and me—almost warped.

My gaze swung from the shining blur of the blade to Dagon's face, searching for a sign he'd come back to himself. I barely dodged his strikes. The sword, once unfamiliar, became light in my hand—striking with such uncanny speed and accuracy that I managed to avoid his attacks.

I leaned back as Dagon's sword flew near enough to cut off a lock of my hair. It didn't matter that Dagon wasn't himself, taken over by some strange magick.

Whoever he was, he was trying to kill me.

I couldn't hesitate. Luck and near misses had kept me from death when the assassin attacked; now I would have to depend on skill. I struck out as his guard opened, cutting a line across his chest. Blood welled through his clothing, but Dagon continued forward with no reaction to the wound. I drew my sword back and lifted my right arm to block him. His sword bit deep into my arm.

I cried out, stumbling away from him. For a desperate moment, I considered using blood from the cut to call magick, but Dagon raised his blade again. I knew he was going to put me down. I screamed as I thrust out my sword, stabbing Dagon deep in his stomach. He didn't flinch or make any sound. The ground seemed to melt beneath my feet as his flesh parted around the blade, but I pressed forward, fighting my roiling stomach the whole time. My arm was steady, blood slipping over my fingers, until the sword was buried in his gut to the hilt.

I let out a sob as the blade scraped against his spine. Confusion knit his brow and he fell, taking my sword with him. I collapsed, retching and trying to wipe his blood off my hand. It was the assassin all over again. My skin burned where his blood had touched it. Magick simmered beneath my skin.

There was another burning, though, in the arm Dagon had wounded. It didn't feel magickal, because it was *inside* my arm. I peeled back the fabric of my shirt. Blood leaked steadily from the wound, soaking the sand.

Anali appeared at my side. I could see the shadows of others gathered around. She was speaking quickly, but I didn't hear her. "Check the sword, Anali," I whispered. Fearing I would vomit, I turned over on my side.

Shadows hovered around me; someone touched my shoulder, my hair. "Check Dagon's sword," I repeated. "Poisoned."

My entire arm seemed set upon by scorch ants crawling inside and outside my flesh. I screamed, scratching at it.

Bile filled my stomach, and my words were garbled, incoherent. The others couldn't hear me and I was going to die because of it.

Only one thing cut through the pain: Dagon was dead. Someone, some magick, made him attack me.

A weak groan escaped my lips as I started to cry. The world went sideways as I fell back into the sand.

✦

"Why should it take this long to find a healer?" Anali groaned.

I opened my eyes to find Prince Aketo drifting in and out of focus above me. "Captain, I can help her."

I writhed as the pain in my arm remembered me.

Someone's hands ran over my brow, rough calluses surprisingly gentle. "Explain." This was Anali's voice, sharp as a well-kept blade.

"I can heal her."

"The healers will be here soon," a man's voice protested. Falun?

Prince Aketo's voice hardened. "Captain, forgive me, but there is only a short window to keep this poison from killing the Princess."

It was in my shoulder now and moving toward my heart, like sand boring pathways through my skin. A newer, more primal fear gripped me. A shaky breath rattled in my chest. "Do it now," I breathed. It took all my strength to force out those words.

Aketo's eyes flew to mine and held. The skin was tight on his face, like he was in pain just watching me. He dropped down beside me in the sand.

Aketo's fingers probed the wound. I cried out and jerked away.

"I am sorry, Your Highness," he said as he tilted my head to the side. "I can save you by using my venom to slow the flow of poison in your blood. My other small magick will keep both of us safe."

I shook my head. His words made no sense. *Small magick.*

He opened his mouth so wide, it seemed like a smile. But his lips pulled back farther, revealing fangs.

It wasn't like a bite from the bloodkin boys I knew, whose fangs slid neatly into my neck with their lips there, pressing a soft and careful seal around the wound to catch all the blood and their magick drawing away the pain. When Aketo struck, his fangs drove into my neck with shocking force, the pain enough to surprise a scream to my lips. I clenched my teeth and let only a whimper slip out. A numbing sensation spread from the bite, cooling the burning in my chest until I felt nothing of my body. This venom spread faster than the poison had.

He turned my head back toward him and looked into my eyes. "She shouldn't be feeling any pain now."

I tried to open my mouth, but I could barely lift my eyes to watch him work. He cut open his palm and pressed it to my skin. Seconds later the numbing weighed on my eyes until they fell shut.

→→ CHAPTER 12 ←←

WHEN I WAS seven and Isadore was nine, the royal family left Ternain at the start of Far Winter and traveled with a caravan the size of a small city for three months. We passed through the edge of the Deadened Jungle, our wagons and carriages painted with fresh lamb's blood to sate the wretched—the restless ghosts, furies, and old, long-dead Godlings lurking in the jungle.

Next we journeyed to Adonsai, the Desert Crystal, greatest of the five desert cities. It sat at the edge of the Kremir Sands, part citadel and part temple, marked by seven towers piercing a relentless cerulean sky.

The citadel seemed to be the only thing holding back the Kremir's seething gold dunes. Great masses of them shifted by day, as if hulking beasts lived deep within the sand. The Lady of Adonsai Citadel's bard told stories about the desert creatures—the *hekerrita*, a serpent large enough to swallow villages whole; the *krakai*, who crawled from the bottom of the Silvern Sea, up through the sand; and the *karansa*, wing-ing through the sky, part vulture, part lizard, with acid poison in their throats.

Isadore loved it all—the dry, sweltering heat, the sun turning her skin a rich copper and bleeding every trace of color from her blond hair. She wanted to march into the desert and command the karansa to fly her to the bottom of the world, where even the ocean ran dry and the sand turned black. She wanted to challenge the hekerrita to a duel, where she would climb into its mouth and savage it from the inside.

I hated it all—the grit of sand everywhere you stepped, shaking out my boots for fear of enterprising scorpions and horned vipers, and, most terrifying of all, the dunes. Nightmares of being buried beneath them with the beasts as my only company woke me every night.

Waking now was like those nightmares.

A cruel slumber of memories turned nightmares wore down my strength the way desert storms ate away villages.

In them I stabbed Dagon over and over. Sometimes I wasn't wounded and after I gutted him I bent over his dead body, weeping. Other times it wasn't Dagon I cut down at all, but the assassin. In the next, I turned away from the corpse without a second glance. Details changed, but every time I still cut him down and left him bleeding in the sand.

Then the dreams changed. I was in the Patch: kissing a faceless boy beneath the half-collapsed eaves of a building; sleeping curled up on a threadbare pallet; lining my eyes with kohl before I went out at night. In these dreams I wasn't a Princess—my wish finally fulfilled—but they were somehow still equally terrifying.

Wading through my nightmares was like clawing my

way up the dunes as sand sucked at my feet, teeth and claws scratching at my ankles. There were moments of clarity. I heard snatches of conversation, felt rough hands on my face, and smelled sandalwood candles and incense. But every time I began to rouse, fine sand seemed to draw me under.

Finally I woke with a gasp that dissolved into a coughing fit. I opened my eyes to find Mirabel peering at me from a chair next to my bed.

"How long?" I asked. A rough whisper was all I could manage.

"I've been bending over backward to keep your mother from moving you to the Palace infirmary. She said she wanted to keep an eye on your progress, but I told her, why should the Princess move if the same healers in the infirmary have already seen you? It's my care she objects to," she said, rising from her chair. No question of how I was, no such warmth from her. "It's been three days. Took you long enough."

I tried to speak, but coughed instead, my throat dry and itching.

She lifted a cup of water to my mouth. As I sipped, she continued. "Rumors of your death reached the city soon after the attack, but the Queen came to visit and, after several of her favored healers inspected you, it was announced that you were in good health. Still, there is unease in the city. You'll have to issue a statement of your own and be seen in public. I believe a short ride around the city will do."

"And what of Dagon?"

Mira shook her head. "I'm so sorry."

Why feel sorry for me? What about Dagon's family?

Guilt cut through me cleanly, so sharp and keen that I

couldn't speak. I swallowed thickly, closing my eyes against tears. "Do we . . . do we know why Dagon attacked me?"

I couldn't yet force myself to ask about his body or whether news had been sent to his family. I wanted to write those missives myself and personally sign off on his pension. I wanted to pack up his medals, folding them carefully around Myre's flag, and tuck a cobalt-handled dagger into a rolled-up Killeen banner.

Mira's lips thinned. "There was some sort of compulsion laid on him and a spell that repelled anyone who came near you two. Lord Baccha arrived soon after you'd passed out. He could detect it in the air, said it was Sorceryn work. Thank the Mother Prince Aketo was there to heal you."

"How did he heal me?" I remembered the bite. I pulled my hand from the blankets and found a bandage on the side of my neck.

"He used his own venom to slow the progression of the poison in your veins, then used his own blood and its immunity to poison to heal you—no poison can kill lami khimaer." That had been the cut on his palm, then. "He said it would take your body some time to heal, though we did not expect it to take this long. He didn't either, it seems. Everyone has been quite beside themselves. Falun most of all."

I bit my lip hard enough to draw blood. "Have you found out who might've set the spell? Or who might have *ordered* it set?"

"No. Anali thought to connect Dagon to your sister or her allies, but it seems no one spoke to Dagon in Ternain before you saw him. Even the gatemen hadn't registered his arrival in Ternain. But we will keep searching for a way to connect him to the Sorceryn who set the spell." She paused. "I did find something, though."

She held up a gold coin with a square cut out of the middle. I'd never seen any like it before. The gold coins minted in Ternain were thicker, with my mother's profile on one side. "Falun brought Lord Baccha along when he came to visit you yesterday, per my instructions. I slipped into the Hunter's rooms while they were here. The easiest way to know where travelers have been is to check their coin."

I inspected it. The square seemed to have been cut out after the coin was minted, because it was engraved with a castle, those massive dwellings of the North. I couldn't read the words etched onto its other side, but I recognized the letters, small and sharp and artless. "This is from Dracol."

But this wasn't news. It only confirmed Baccha's story.

"It *was* minted in Dracol, but I've only heard of coins with this square cutout coming from one place—the Roune Lands. Every coin in his possession is like this."

I stared at her, mouth ajar. The lawless land in the northeast corner of the realm was populated with roving bands of thieves and criminals exiled from Dracol and Myre. The country was barely livable; the soil was rocky and little grew there. Only one city, Yrsai, held to a set of laws. In truth, it seemed the sort of place where Baccha could've whiled away the decades. Except if he had been in the Roune Lands, why lie about Dracol?

"There's only one way to enter Myre from the North," I said.

The A'Nir Mountains between the Roune Lands and Myre weren't navigable. The only way to reach Myre was to travel downriver through Ydara's Pass. Every ship that came from the North was stopped at the Sister Citadel.

Mirabel smiled broadly. "I sent a raven north early this morning. I know a few of your father's contacts there. But at least now we know where Baccha truly came from."

At the mention of my father, I sank back into the pillows with a heavy sigh. It was time I told Mirabel about Papa. If anyone could have guessed his motivations back then, it was Mira. "I have news too. Really it's more of a puzzle I can't work out. There's a binding on my magick. I found it during my first lesson with Baccha."

I explained what I'd learned from Mother. When I finished, Mirabel's face was ashen. "I can't think that your father has betrayed you, but what the Queen said is true. Lei brought you to me the day after your magick was named."

"What other explanation is there?"

"I'm not certain. Your father is a man full of secrets. Like you, he tends to keep his plans to himself, but he couldn't have done this," Mirabel said. "Have I told you the story of how we met?"

I shook my head and she continued. "I stopped keeping track at some point, but I marked my hundredth nameday decades before you were born. Fey long-livedness is a fickle thing, passed down from our Godling ancestors, but even with the little fey blood and magick that I have, I inherited it. I outlived my mother and all but one of my seven siblings. Once I realized my aging had slowed, I left my birthplace and came to Ternain. It was not an easy time for me. I couldn't find a job because of my horns, and I'd taken to cutting purses to survive."

I knew some of this—that Mirabel had grown up in the desert, and her mother, a human with distant fey relatives, had been the steward of a minor Fort near the Southern Enclosure. Her father had been khimaer, and he lived in the Enclosure. But she'd never told me why she left or what came after.

"I'm not proud of it, but it kept food in my stomach. I survived. One morning, I saw a young lord with a heavy purse. He was without guards, so I tried to steal it, but he stopped me and asked if I wanted a job. When your parents first married, your father used to walk the streets alone just like you. He said he was in need of a secretary, but what he really wanted was a spy. No one would've suspected that the King had an old khimaer woman to do his bidding."

She laughed, and there were tears in her eyes. "I worked for Lei for two years until the Queen became pregnant with you. It took Lei months of convincing, of begging, but eventually I agreed to care for you. He knew your life would be . . . difficult. He wanted someone who could protect you, and see to your interests, just like I'd seen to his. I'd cared for younger siblings and watched them age and die. Outliving you or your father would be one thing—I've lived that and I will live it again—but having you ripped from me? I couldn't—I still don't know how to accept that.

"I only decided after I saw the way your father held you, like you were blown from glass, draped in gold, and would break if he just breathed the wrong way. I knew he would spoil you within an inch of your life, most everyone here would, and I knew a girl, a Queen especially, would need more than that. So I coaxed you from his arms and held you tight, just long enough for you to get the measure of me, and then pressed you into the wet nurse's hands. I loved you instantly, before I saw that your eyes were like petals of a flower on fire, before you gasped out my name like a growl, and spat up in my hair. I knew I would do anything to protect you, long before I accepted that your safety wouldn't always be up to me."

Hot tears slid down my cheeks. I knew Mirabel loved me, but she rarely said so. Hearing it just now released something in me.

"If your father asked the Sorceryn to do this, it could only have been to protect you."

I wiped my face. I wished I had her faith, but I'd been disappointed too many times by my mother and sister. Even when you loved them, people were unknowable. "Then I need to see him."

"Your mother left two of her guards outside your rooms to keep an eye on you, I suspect. If she believes you're attempting to leave this close to your nameday . . ."

She would keep me under guard, probably locked in my rooms, until I turned seventeen. "I'm not going to run away again, Mira. I'll tell her I'm leaving."

"Are you sure you want to go now? It's been days since Dagon attacked you. Whoever's trying to kill you, they will probably try again soon."

My heart gave a stutter. "You're right, but Ternain isn't exactly safe. I'll be better protected on the road with the guard to watch anyone following, and at Asrodei, Papa will be there." I asked Mirabel to have the guard start preparing for the journey. After Court tomorrow, it would be time to ride back to Asrodei. Somehow I would get my mother to agree.

Finally Mirabel left. Alone, the weight of Dagon's death struck me again, memories pouring over me until I could barely breathe. I retreated into my dressing room because I didn't want anyone hearing the broken sounds coming from me. What would Papa say when he learned I'd killed one of his oldest friends?

As I wept, I prayed he would forgive me, because I knew I would never forgive myself.

→ CHAPTER 13 ←

I RESTED MY hand on Baccha's forearm as the doors before us swung open. The crier's magicked voice echoed through the Throne Room. "Her Highness Princess Evalina Grace Killeen, Rival Heir to the Throne of Myre." There was a pause, just long enough for me to draw breath. "Attended by Lord Baccha, Lord of the Wild Hunt, Lord of the Hounds."

Word of my appearance needed to spread through every inch of Myre, rooting out rumors of my death. As the Court turned to stare at our entrance, I knew bringing Baccha had been the right decision. News of his presence in Ternain for the first time in two hundred years would soon be on every lip in the capital.

I was sore and stiff from so many days in bed, but I kept my back straight as we glided forward. Though healed, the wound I'd taken when fighting Dagon throbbed steadily. I liked that it served as a reminder, never letting me forget.

Dagon is dead and you killed him.

Mirabel had dressed me in a cobalt gown, the copper coins sewn onto the hem making music of my every movement. The tight bodice narrowed my waist, and the fitted skirt made much of my hips. It was beautiful and bright and not at all me. The cobalt dagger was House Killeen's sigil. I hoped Mother would at least notice my efforts.

The weight of the Court's attention pressed against my skin, but I focused instead on the one member of my family in my sight.

Mother's face was its usual emotionless mask, unlike all the courtiers floating around her, who craned their necks in order to catch a glimpse of me. She positioned a silvery fan near her mouth, but held my gaze as Baccha guided us forward. Her bottle-green eyes flickered over him and she inclined her head, the barest smile passing her lips.

The crowd parted around us, all either too low in standing to approach or too surprised. A servant, a brown-skinned bloodkin girl with blank round eyes—she must have worked hard to perfect that look—greeted us with wine. I accepted a glass and thanked her.

Baccha looked down at me with a stiff, though still adequately dazzling, smile. It took me a moment to return it. I'd tried to bury my mistrust of Baccha when Falun brought the Hunter to my rooms, hoping he wouldn't sense it through the bond. But I wasn't sure my efforts had been successful. I had to stop myself several times on the walk down from asking him about the coins. He'd been uncharacteristically quiet all morning. Though perhaps that could be attributed to the twenty-five soldiers who escorted us here.

Getting the truth out of Baccha would have to wait until I'd found my way out of Ternain.

He glanced toward the dais. "Her Majesty the Queen, I presume?"

I nodded. "Thoughts?"

"I see her in you," he murmured quietly, for my ears only. "Although I hope you won't petrify with age as she has."

"You might amend your opinion. She may seem icy now, but she can be charming, especially to handsome fey men."

"I shall not," he announced. "Any woman who would greet her daughter with such a cold expression will have trouble charming me. Besides, my fearsome reputation always trumps my stunning visage—unfortunate as that may be."

"We'll see."

"And what of your sister? The overwhelmingly pretty?"

I arched an eyebrow. "How do you know she's overwhelmingly pretty?"

Baccha just smiled, all slow and filled with wicked mirth. "I gather, from the tone of your voice, I'm *not* allowed to bed her."

His efforts to distract me made it difficult to maintain my Court expression—pleasant, vacant, and aloof—because I wanted to both laugh and step on his foot.

I dug my nails into his arm. "No, Baccha. You're not allowed to bed any Killeen Princesses or Queens."

"Oh, but what about Princes? You're sure you don't have an older secret brother hiding among these lovely creatures?" He cast an admiring look around the room. "I could do well with a Prince, especially—"

I pinched him and he let out an undignified yelp.

"Baccha." I sighed. "Please, let's just . . . see my mother."

I tugged him forward. I hoped I wouldn't encounter Isadore today—at least not until after I'd dealt with Mother.

I hauled him through throngs of gaping courtiers—the smiles Baccha threw their way ranging from rakish to blood-thirsty—until we reached the dais.

I let go of Baccha, threw my shoulders back, lifted my chin, and mounted the stairs of the dais.

I curled a finger and Baccha followed.

Mother's eyebrows lifted slightly as she took us in. I stepped close to the throne, my eyes falling on my favorite carving, a woman like a lioness with flowers trailing down her body instead of clothes. I was surprised to see concern in Mother's eyes when I reached out my hand to brush her cheek.

We put on quite a show.

A hush had fallen over the Throne Room. Now every-one watched as I looked at Baccha and nodded in Mother's direction.

He fell to one knee. Any other Lord would have dropped to both knees before the Queen; even the Archdukes in the North did. One knee was the proper bow for a foreign digni-tary—meaning he respected Mother's authority but consid-ered himself not bound by her rule.

And our earlier maneuvering had made it perfectly clear that Baccha fell well within mine. We had planned this, but it was no less satisfying to see Mother smother her annoyance beneath a smile.

But that was no surprise; she allowed nothing to show on her face unless it served her. At least not for long.

She gestured for Baccha to rise, while I grabbed a new glass of wine from the tray. Mother favored wines from the northern vineyards. This one was dry and bitter, a perfect pairing with trays of jellied guava, little gilt cups of pomegranate seeds, and painted paper sheaths of candied nuts.

It was a perfect representation of this place: bitterness among sweet luxury.

Mother made no effort to lower her voice when she spoke. Almost as if choreographed, the courtiers surged forward, straining their ears. "You might've mentioned that your fey bone-worker was the Lord of the Hunt, Eva."

"My apologies, Mother," I said. "As I said when we last spoke, I didn't think you would believe me about his identity."

"Well, I am glad to see you've recovered from the attack. I hope you didn't mind the guards I left by your rooms. It . . . troubles me that you were attacked right in front of your guard," she said, voice thick with worry. "Perhaps a change in leadership is necessary?"

"There was a spell keeping them from helping me."

"Nevertheless, please keep my guards near you. We don't want any more incidents." She paused, glancing out at the Court. "Some courtiers were suggesting naming Isadore True Heir. If I hadn't assured them you were well and safe, I might've had trouble putting them off."

As if anyone could make my mother do anything. Only the Queen's Council could force her hand and she had them all under her thumb.

"I was under the impression that a body was required to initiate the naming of the True Heir," I said slowly. Anger hummed beneath my skin. An *incident*. That was what she called an attempt on my life. Like it was a mere inconvenience.

"Eh." Mother shrugged, a minute lift of her shoulders that somehow exuded queenliness. "That is the usual custom, but these are pressing times. Your father writes often of new boldness in Dracol's attacks on the border, and all of our eyes and ears at their King's Court speak of new machines they believe will rival our magick. Impossible of course, but their wishful thinking nonetheless will result in death. Besides, after your . . . long absence, many in the Court still harbor concerns about your commitment to the crown."

"The Court should be pleased, then, that my nameday approaches," I answered, careful to smother the frustration in my voice. "We can only move ahead when I am of an age to ascend to the throne. I doubt we would become more stable if Myreans doubted the veracity of a Rival Heir's claim to the throne."

She blinked at me. "Yes . . . that is true. Speaking of your nameday—it troubles me that your father seems to have pushed back his return from the North. I pray his work doesn't keep him from your celebration, but who can know what these savage Dracolans will do?"

It took an effort not to roll my eyes at her hollow words. *Savage* was the insult leveled at all our enemies, even those within our own borders. Was she operating under the illusion that Myreans were tame?

Still, her mentioning my father before I could threw me. "Have his plans changed?"

"No, but they may," Mother murmured. A smile flowed across her face, cold as Far Winter wind. "You never know what will happen in the North, sweet. Circumstances, matters of war, change not just by the day, but the hour. I would be surprised if he makes it before your nameday. At this point, even making it the day of seems a stretch."

"That is why I'd like to visit him in Asrodei." My face burned, but I fought to keep my expression smooth. "With your consent, of course."

"So close to your nameday? There are less than two months left, darling."

I mimicked her overly sweet tone. "Asrodei is only a week's ride away, Mother. I will be gone for three or four weeks, at most. I'll be back with time to spare."

Mother's eyebrows lifted mechanically, but her hands clenched the arms of the throne, blue lacquered nails like claws. To allow a glimpse of truth beneath her facade, she must have been truly surprised. "And what of your safety? If your guard can't protect you in Ternain, how can I trust you'll return to me unscathed?"

"That is why I planned to ask if you could spare five soldiers from your guard. Captain Anali will be glad to have the help." I hated every cursed word. Any soldiers of hers would likely spy on me for her, but I could live with that.

"And will your guest be traveling with you?" Mother asked, in a voice like spreading frost. "What are your plans, Lord Hunter?"

Baccha, who had watched our exchange from beside me with growing discomfort, met my eyes before answering. "I plan to accompany Her Highness wherever she goes until her instruction is complete."

I'd asked if he was willing to travel to Asrodei, or if he

preferred to wait to resume our lessons when I returned. He'd agreed to join us and spoke of training on the ride there.

Mother turned her attention back to me. "Wonderful, especially that you feel so comfortable leaving Ternain at such an . . . overwhelming time. I know Isadore oversaw every detail of her coming-of-age ball."

I took a steadying breath. "I trust Mirabel to see to all of the details that we haven't already ironed out."

Mother's mouth puckered. She made no secret of her prejudice against Mirabel. For a long moment, silence lingered around us. "Very well, but you'll bring fifteen additional soldiers."

Relief coursed through me, though it was stymied by her demand. Fifteen soldiers, in addition to my twenty, would slow our progress. "Thank you, Mother."

Before I could ask her to excuse us, she turned her attention to Baccha's slender form. Baccha stood close, tension vibrating down his body.

"Lord Hunter," Mother said, her voice adopting a husky quality. "I must admit some amazement to see you standing here, especially next to my dear Eva."

How lovely to know I'd suddenly become her *dear* Eva.

"Your Majesty, I am honored that you even recognized my name. Few have seen me for who I am on this recent visit to Ternain," Baccha answered in a broad, courtly voice. "In fact, that is why Princess Eva earned my respect and affection so quickly."

Mother's eyes brightened. "Eva loves her stories. I remember we once got into a heated discussion of one of the less famous tales surrounding your name. 'The Robber Girl.'

Evalina believed you should have disobeyed the Queen and spared the girl. Where she got such a silly, romantic notion is beyond me."

At the mention of the tale, Baccha's face closed off, eyebrows flattening into pale, neat lines, and his lips pursed.

Although "The Robber Girl" was one of his lesser-known tales, mostly because there was no way to spin it in his favor, I had been fascinated. *A girl with black hair and silver eyes had been seen stealing jewels all over Myre. She'd even snuck into the Palace and stolen from the crown. The Queen bade the Hunter to find her and demanded her punishment be worse than death. So the Hunter stole her away and kept her as a bride, just until she fell in love with him. The night she confessed her love, the Hunter returned her kiss, and then slit her throat.*

Still coated in her blood, he carried the Robber Girl to Ternain and dropped her body at the base of the throne.

Or so the tale went.

I pinched the inside of my elbow, willing myself not to snap at her. "I was a child, Mother," I said. "How heated can a discussion become at nine years old?"

"I remember you older, darling. And I remember you being quite adamant about it."

Baccha lifted a hand to the small of my back and shook his head. "In those days, Princess," he said, voice gone cold, "an oath taken to the Queen was set in one's blood. It was virtually impossible to disobey."

I looked up at Baccha, surprised to find he was smiling at me. But it wasn't one of his usual ones, full of flirtation and guile. This was soft and terrible—and it cost him.

The river flowing between us bled wracking grief and rage. It was thick and thorny, even centuries later.

Baccha's eyes widened as mine filled with tears.

Mother stared at us as if we'd both just sprouted an additional set of limbs. I straightened, smoothing damp palms on my dress.

I was busy thinking of some way to end this conversation, or at least steer it toward another subject, when my mother said, "If you'll excuse me, Lady Shirea's just come in and I must speak with her about news from the border."

Lady Shirea was on the Queen's Council. I opened my mouth—if she had news of the border, I wanted to hear it—but Baccha took my arm. He swept us away, dodging every courtier who drifted close enough to speak.

We ducked around a wide pillar in one of the private alcoves of the Throne Room. "Why did you do that?" I asked.

"What do you think your mother saw between us?"

"I don't know. She saw that you were upset and that I became upset as well."

"Think, Princess. You became . . . agitated because of me. What do you think will happen if your mother decides you're in the thrall of a powerful fey? One as powerful as I am? If she should share that suspicion with other nobles?"

I would never see the throne. Every human noble would rebel to keep me from it. I sank back against the pillar. I started to rub my eyes, but remembered the layers of powder, kohl, and paint I'd applied this morning, and tugged at my hair instead. "I'm sorry."

"No, I am. I shouldn't have . . . I should have known she

would find some way to manipulate me. After all, I'd just watched her do the same to you." He massaged his temples. "Now, shall we see your sister or have you had enough of this place?"

I'd had more than enough, and as much as Baccha had returned to his usual self, I knew from the aching silence of the bond that Mother's words had cracked open something in him.

"Let's get out of here," I said, but as soon as we returned to the wider room, I heard familiar laughter and groaned.

"I assume that your sister is in the group of courtiers walking toward us. Shall we make a mad dash for the doors, then?"

An emotion suffused from the bond. Calm.

I wouldn't run from Isadore again. Baccha pulled me forward and into the den we went.

She stood in the center of a large group of courtiers, each one carefully ignoring my presence until I stood before them.

She looked lovely, in a simple gown the color of the sky, with a square neckline and long sheer sleeves. Her fingernails were lacquered white and her hair hung down to her waist in elaborate golden spirals. She, like Mother, carried a fan. Although it hid half her face, her eyes were tight with an emotion I found impossible to read.

She stood between two young fey men, Lord Katro and Lord Patric, both sons of Lady Shirea. They stared openly at Baccha, an edge of hostility puckering their lips.

I stepped forward as Isadore lowered the fan. My thumb traced the line of her jaw, while she cupped my cheek.

Isadore smiled. One of her dangerous ones—light as a petal, sharp as a knife.

Like a rabbit catching sight of a looming hawk, I went still.

Baccha cleared his throat and I remembered myself. "Lord Baccha, may I introduce my sister, Princess Isadore."

My eyes fell to Isadore's hands, moving beneath those long sheer sleeves. I'd been expecting it, given the show she put on last time I was at Court, so I felt the exact moment magick blew from her skin.

She cast it in a wide net; it fell over my mind like a light shroud, making the air around me shimmer and twitch.

Isadore's hair became shot through with silver and gold, her eyes a more intense green. Her skin was flushed and luminous—near metallic, as if she were fey.

I swayed, drawn to the sweet smile on her face, the wondrous color of her hair, but I pinched my arm, the pain sharpening me until her magickally enhanced beauty faded.

Katro and Patric stared at Isadore openmouthed, eyes dull.

"A pleasure to meet you, Lord Baccha," Isadore said. My skin crawled when Baccha bowed and pressed a soft kiss to her palm. My sister watched me, making plain the admiration in her eyes, hoping, probably, that she would see jealousy in mine.

"The pleasure is mine, Your Highness," Baccha said. Her magick didn't seem to affect him.

With a irritated frown, she drew back from Baccha, her magick melting away.

"Just how did you meet the Princess?" Katro leaned forward, sweeping back his hair. Its pale green color had always fascinated me. With his tawny brown skin, he was lovely, like a dream. It was a shame the sneer on his lips marred his beauty.

Baccha answered in a voice smooth as fresh cream turned to butter. "Ours is a recent but inextricable partnership," he whispered conspiratorially. "We share an . . . affinity for each other's magick. Marrow, blood, and the like."

Isa's eyes narrowed, but she said nothing.

"Lord Hunter, if I may ask, why are you here today? Most fey believe you shunned the Court and refused to return to it after the"—Katro's lips thinned—"Great War. Why return now?"

"Well. Some time ago I heard word of a Rival Heir born with marrow and blood magick, born under a Blood Moon no less." Every courtier around us fell into rapt silence. "I had the privilege of being alive during the time of another with such powerful magick. I felt it then, and I feel it now. There is nothing quite like the lure of a strong Queen."

A pretty speech, but certainly not the truth. It shouldn't have had the power to fill me with such bitterness.

"Well, there are two Rival Heirs, you know," Patric said, puffing his chest out like a buffoon. "I myself prefer the winning side in such disputes."

I gave him a look that should have, if there was any justice in the world, sheared the flesh from his bones.

Baccha chuckled dismissively. "Power is power. There's no mistaking it."

"I would hate to think you had made a miscalculation, Lord Baccha, but there is raw strength and then there is influence," Isadore countered, an undercurrent of anger in her voice. The silence around us broke and whispering voices rose, like silk gliding over tulle.

"Yes, and political influence can shift like the changing tide, Your Highness. It is important to remember that power can't be swayed. Power simply is." Baccha's eyes flicked in my direction, smile strained.

My body felt coiled tight as I laughed breathlessly. "Such a serious turn our conversation has taken! If you'll excuse us, we really must go. We've business to attend in—"

"I'm glad you're well, Eva." Isa's cool facade faltered, her brows drawn tight, her bottom lip trembling. "With the rumors, I thought . . ."

She stepped toward me, reaching out a hand. Only Baccha's iron grip on my arm kept me from jerking away from her, from all of them.

"What? Weren't you relieved that someone else might've done your job for you?"

Everything fell away but Isadore's frozen expression. "Of course not. I was sorry to hear you were hurt," she answered, but she sounded anything but apologetic. She sounded agitated and confused.

"Why, Isa? We'll be attempting to kill each other in a few months. Why should you care that I was injured? You do plenty to hurt me at Court. In fact, I would think you'd be quite pleased, unless you're sorry to have missed the pleasure of doing so yourself."

Her eyes went wide at the use of her childhood name. Isa to my Eva. I never said it aloud anymore. We weren't

Isa and Eva to each other now, just Rival Heirs set on a murderous path. It would be best if we could both forget everything but that.

"Are you implying that I had something to do with it?"

"Did you, Isa?" I whispered.

"Of course not," she snapped. "The law is clear."

An acerbic laugh fell from my lips. I should have been relieved, thankful that Isadore had no hand in these attacks, but what was the difference? Even if she wasn't behind them, she would still try to kill me when the law said she could.

"Excuse us," Baccha said. He smiled something bright and beautiful, and tugged at my arm. Isadore and I were inches apart, glaring right at each other.

"Yes," I muttered, leaning back. "If you'll excuse us . . . we have a trip to plan."

"Oh?" Isadore arched an eyebrow. "Where are you traveling?"

"To Asrodei."

She smiled. My mouth went dry—that smile was all Mother. "Running away again, Eva?"

"No, Isa. I'll be back."

And when I returned, I would have the magick she'd once begged me to use. I would make her fear it as she should have then.

I let Baccha say our goodbyes.

The next time I saw Isadore would be in the days before my nameday. I wished this last glimpse of her was less painful—so I replaced it. As Baccha and I walked away, I drew a simple memory: Isadore's fey nursemaid, Kitsina, using glamour to conjure a ballroom within my bedchamber full of swishing skirts of heavy brocade, crystal and pearl, glittering stones, and kohl-sharp eyes. Isadore and I danced wildly through it, creating a revelry all our own.

But even in the memory, her eyes looked as cruel as they were now.

→ CHAPTER 14 ←

I DIDN'T LEARN the truth about the Rival Heir law until I turned thirteen.

It started with Isadore's anger.

We were in my bedchamber. She sat beside me with her legs folded underneath her, while I assembled my toy soldiers around a model of the Queen's Palace. The miniature Palace was about three feet tall. It was all dazzling white, with a flat roof and intricately tiled courtyards, and a parapet lined with arrow slots. It was a nameday gift from my father, who had left Ternain two days before on a trip north.

I still hadn't received a nameday gift from Mama and didn't expect that to change.

Isadore had been put out all afternoon and had sneered at the Palace. Fifteen now, she'd decided she was too old for such things, but her eyes ran over the glittery mosaics inside. Isadore reached into the toy Palace and pulled out one of the portraits from outside the Throne Room. It was no bigger than her thumb.

She inspected it for a moment before returning it to the model. "Have I shown you the bracelet Mama gave me? She said it was too mature for you or . . . she would have given you one too. I'm sure of it."

Isa couldn't help gloating over all the gifts Mama had given her, and loved finding excuses for why I hadn't received the same. It was her misguided way of trying to make me feel better when Mother favored her. Even in her selfishness, she had room to feel my hurt—at least that was how I imagined it. Maybe Mama had said such a thing, though try as I might, I couldn't hear those words in any voice but Isa's.

I didn't blame my sister much. I shared my gifts with Isa, because the only things Mother bought were trinkets and jewels. Every gift Papa gave her, which were usually ones worth sharing, Mama sent back and replaced with something of her choosing. And since Isa's gifts weren't usually sharable, she told me about them instead.

Still, it wasn't an even arrangement. At least Papa tried with Isa. I hadn't even seen Mama on my nameday, or in the days before it—she'd been off celebrating the arrival of an important outlying fey Lord and had little time for me.

"I prefer this." I gestured at the model. "You can't *do* anything with a bracelet except wear it. Besides," I added, knowing the real reason Isa wasn't wearing it, "doesn't Mama know that you don't like bracelets anymore?"

Didn't Mama know that Isadore hated anything that got in the way of her magick?

Isa's eyes narrowed, focusing on the bracelets hanging around my wrist, but she didn't dispute what I said. Instead, she called for her nursemaid, Kitsina, who'd been given charge of us this afternoon. When the nursemaid, a lithe fey woman with tawny skin, hazel eyes, and a narrow chin, entered the room, Isadore spoke without even glancing her way. "The bracelet from Mama, Eva wants to see it. Go get it."

"Isadore," Kitsina said slowly, "it grows late, and we are going back to your room soon anyway. We will show your sister tomorrow."

Isadore stood up and smirked cruelly. "I'd like to see it now. You can go on your own, or I can make you do it. It's your decision, Kitsina."

Silence stretched out between them, fiery gazes warring. Dread pooled in my stomach. I hated watching Isadore use her magick. In the throes of it, she became a different person. Finally Kitsina bowed her head and swept out of the room.

"You shouldn't do that," I blurted.

Isadore said slowly, "Do . . . what?"

"If Kitsina doesn't listen to you, ask Mama for a new maid. There's no need to force her with magick."

"You only say that because you don't have magick, Eva. If you did, you wouldn't fear it so much."

"I'm not afraid," I protested.

Isadore waved away my words and proposed a game of story while we waited for Kitsina to return. She grinned, tucking the long blond wisps of her hair behind her ears. "Let's play Enchantress."

I pouted, knowing what was coming. One of Mama's favored bards at Court always told the story "The Enchantress and Her Princess" when Isadore and I were present. In the story, the Enchantress stole the beloved Princess away from her Palace. The Enchantress then put the Princess into an enchanted slumber so she could steal the Princess's beauty every night.

The Enchantress was some old khimaer woman cursed with hideous features. She had horns, bloody claws, and fangs as long as a child's hand. Her eyes were bright like fire, the bard said, and he always looked at me when he said it, for my eyes were similarly unfashionable. Isadore made me play the Enchantress for that reason. Also because she'd never consent to playing a khimaer and I did anything Isadore asked me to do, no matter how unhappy it made me, just to keep her from using her magick. Since learning how to wield it with the Sorceryn, she was constantly looking for a reason to summon it.

"Kitsina will be back soon," I hedged. Isa's room was just a short walk away. "I thought you wanted to see the bracelet."

"I'll let you play the Princess," Isadore said, and then she took off her necklace, a long emerald pendant, and hung it around my hair, like a diadem. I watched her eyes. They had calmed some, but there was still a dangerous stillness in her expression, though none of the magickal light. I kept quiet so I wouldn't do something to make her change her mind.

I sat back, closing my eyes while Isadore rambled a long spell. Playing the Princess was easier, but it wasn't as fun as Isa made it out to be—all you did was lie there. I tried to think of what Isadore did when I was the one to cast the spell. Her lips were always smiling slightly, the long feathers of her eyelashes fluttering as she snuck glances at me. Isadore leaned against me on the couch. I didn't peek, though; I concentrated on the cool weight of the jewel on my forehead, another one of Isadore's gifts from Mama. My fingers longed to touch it and have it glitter in my hands the way it did when it hung around Isa's neck.

Finally my eyes flickered open to look at Isadore. By now I should have been the Princess without her beauty, the jewel hanging from Isadore's head instead of mine.

"Isa?" I whispered. She leaned over me, staring down at my face.

Her eyes were storm clouds again, containing the same quiet anger as when Kitsina challenged her orders. I glanced around, thinking her nursemaid had returned, but when I tried to sit up, Isadore put her hands around my throat. I didn't struggle at first, because I didn't understand. But it was painful; I couldn't breathe as her nails gouged my neck.

I tried to pry her fingers off, but panic made me slow and confused.

I struggled and tears flooded my eyes. I bucked off the settee as Isadore pushed me down.

"Eva," Isa said. "Try to use magick. The Princess uses a spell to break free from the Enchantress!"

She let up a bit. I gasped in air and shoved her off. "Why would you want me to do that?"

Isa grunted as she slid across the floor, but when she looked up, she was grinning. "Because. You need your magick, don't you? I learned some of mine on my own, maybe you can too."

"You know my magick is dangerous." I'd told her a hundred times before. She knew firsthand the damage it had wrought.

"All magick is dangerous," she scoffed, crawling back over. "You are such a child. You're afraid of everything."

I tried to withdraw, but she grabbed my ankle. Magick rolled off her skin and anger ripped through me.

I should use my magick. Isadore used hers. It was what she deserved. I should show her—no, I *would* show her.

But no magick rose up in response to the anger she was making me feel. I kicked wildly and my slippered foot connected with Isadore's chin. Blood dripped down her dress.

The door banged open, the swish of skirts telling me Kitsina had returned.

"What have you done?" She gasped. I thought she was talking to Isadore at first, but then she strode up to me and yanked me to my feet.

She dragged me to my mother's bedchamber, where I was left to wait for hours. When Mother came into the room, well after nightfall, I lay curled up at the foot of her bed, all my tears dried in messy streaks.

We sat on a cushioned bench in front of her bed. "What a mess you've made," she crooned at the sight of me. I tried to speak, but she hushed me. "I already know what you did. Your sister told me about your magick. How you've been asking her to practice. You should have told me you had learned to use it, Eva."

"But I didn't, Mama. Isadore is the one who—"

"That's enough, dear. I should have done this years ago. From now on, you and your sister will only see each other at Court events."

"Mama, please," I whispered, tears clogging my throat. "Isadore asked me to use magick but I didn't. I swear."

"I'm sorry, dove. We were fools to have waited this long. It's inevitable."

"Waited . . . for what?"

My mother canted her head, pity softening her expression. "Waited to separate you. There always comes a time when Princesses can no longer be sisters in the true sense." She frowned, tapping her chin as if suddenly reminded of something. "Oh, I'd forgotten you didn't know. Your father wanted to tell you himself but . . . only one of you can survive. That's what it means to be a Rival Heir. One of you must kill the other."

I trembled as I tried to make sense of her words, but they were incomprehensible. "Me and Isa? What?"

"You and your sister. The law demands this sacrifice. I would save you two from this if I could, but I can't." She patted my cheek with a cool hand. "You understand, don't you, Eva? The older you get, the more you'll want to use magick. You know it isn't safe."

I *knew* that, but it was Isadore who'd hurt me this time. It was Mother who would believe whatever lie Isadore told her, without attempting to hear my side. They were the true danger, not me.

My mother told me to wash my face and called for a servant to take me back to my rooms, where I was to stay from then on, unless I had Court or lessons with my tutors.

The next night I left a note on my bed for Mirabel, and walked through the passages alone, carrying a small pack with the meager scraps from my dinner and a few precious items, hoping to never return.

- II -
MARROW MAGICK

Bone bright, clean and white—
Teeth to shred your flesh—
Horns used to bore you through—
Power true as true.

—Child's rhyme, of khimaer origin

⤜ CHAPTER 15 ⤛

WE LEFT TERNAIN two days later, exactly six weeks before my nameday. The moon sat low on the horizon, and the distant glow of a coming sunrise diffused waves of amber and lilac across the sky.

Captain Anali, Prince Aketo, and the three other soldiers beside me in the boat were all obscure smudges watching the river for crocodiles. The rest of the guard, and my mother's soldiers, had gone ahead last night, bringing horses and the rest of our supplies on the ferry. We would go straight north once we crossed the river, first passing through the Slender Forest and then riding along the edge of the Arym Plain, until we reached the highlands where Asrodei was located.

From our flat-hulled boat, the Palace rose like a pale mountain, casting the rest of the city in shadow. Without the sun lighting its mosaic facade, it seemed more fortress than Palace—its crenellated walls standing stark against gilt domes and crystal towers. At this distance the seams of Ternain were laid plain, whitewashed stone resting against colorful clay flats and the Palaces of noble houses made from carved marble and glass. Ternain was both ancient and ever new, a garden yearly growing more vibrant, more true.

By the time we crossed—gifting the riverman with a heavy bag of gold, and gratitude for his discretion—the sun had risen higher, filling the world with hazy pink-gold light. The only signs of life were water birds: scarlet ibis to match the river, and blue herons, their feathers unfurled like crepe skirts upon the water.

Already, there was peace here, before the city churned into motion.

The riverman docked at a wharf dipping precariously into the water and we walked through the Slender Forest, named so for its thin blue-green trees and the forest's shape, only forty miles deep as it stretched along the river. We met in a clearing just a mile or so beyond the river.

Already there was an obvious divide in the camp. My mother's fifteen guards stood together by the horse lines, packing their saddlebags. They were older than my guard, near middle age, and mostly men. My guards were still breaking down their tents from the previous night.

While Captain Anali set off to double-check supplies, I was left standing with Prince Aketo.

His dark curls hung loose about his shoulders, and his horns shined like obsidian beneath the sun. He'd dressed simply, in cotton breeches, a dark green tunic, and supple, well-worn boots. The trees around us suited him more than the Palace, and his presence held a weight I hadn't seen when we first met. He seemed to carry who he was on his shoulders—a khimaer Prince in a world that didn't want him—but instead of bending his spine, it bolstered him. I couldn't help but envy his comfort, especially as buzzy sparks of anxiety stirred beneath my skin.

It would take a week to ride to Fort Asrodei, but my stomach fluttered as if my father waited among the trees. My insides had begun aching when we left the Queen's Palace. Knowing I would see and confront my father in a week made my chest tight.

My mother's soldiers had noticed our appearance and watched Aketo with cool expressions. He stared back at them with utter calm. The soldiers looked away first.

"If they cause you any trouble, tell me or the Captain."

Aketo's nostrils flared, a sign of annoyance I recognized from our last conversation. "If they trouble me, I will handle it on my own."

"That seems wise," I muttered. I drew in a calming breath. "I haven't thanked you yet, for saving my life."

"Such a thing does not require thanks, Eva," he murmured, eyes fastening onto mine.

I smothered annoyance. He wouldn't even let me apologize properly. "Nevertheless, I am thankful, Prince Aketo, and if there is anything you should ever need—"

"Call me Aketo," he corrected, smirking.

And just that quickly, I wanted to knock his gorgeous teeth in. "Do you really think you can take on those veteran soldiers so easily?"

He arched an eyebrow. "I've been dealing with veteran soldiers all my life."

And again I had put my foot in my mouth. Soldiers were the law in the Enclosures. "Is that how you became so skilled?"

He grinned. "So you've been convinced of my skill already? After watching one sparring match?"

I gritted my teeth for a moment before returning his smile. "I would say yes, but I'm afraid if your ego grows any larger, it may impede on your faculties. Like, for example, your ability to hold a civil conversation."

I started walking across the clearing.

"Wait, Eva," Aketo said, following. "My apologies, that was childish of me. I watched your fight. You are very good, quick and ferocious with your blade . . ."

"But?" I looked around, trying to spot Falun's crimson mane among the tents.

" . . . But what you lack in hand-to-hand training makes you easy to read."

He could not be serious. I'd thanked him for saving my life, and now he was critiquing my sword fighting.

"If you're so sure of that, we'll spar after we make camp tonight." Once the words were out of my mouth, an image of Anali on her back in the Sandpits flashed in my mind. And I'd never once beaten Anali.

"Are you quite sure?"

I wasn't. Not even remotely. But Gods, if I could beat him, just his surprise might be worth risking embarrassment. I gave him a smile sharp as any dagger, and said, "I look forward to it."

We took an overgrown road about a mile off the main road north. It was only a road in a loose sense, packed red dirt about the width of four riders. Azure and lilac-breasted birds careened from the branches overhead, their percussive cries echoing around us. We rode for most of the day and made camp just as the sun was beginning to set.

Baccha saved me from my match with Aketo. In an effort to extend my limits with blood magick—I could use it only three times before the magick melted away—he'd proposed a combat lesson. We fought at the edge of a field of yellow wildflowers where we'd made camp.

So far it had amounted to me being battered with Baccha's blunt practice sword. He wanted me to learn to summon my magick while under attack. Unlike our last lesson, I'd first have to draw his blood through combat to use my power.

I cursed as I blocked the Hunter's next thrust. I surged forward, but he deflected my next attack with ease. I'd expected it and dropped to a crouch. The tip of my sword opened a wound on his thigh.

I scrambled back and wiped the flat of the blade on my forearm. Beneath Baccha's blood, the tattoo of a sword there became hot and the magick reared up in my mind. I wrapped the blood magick around the sword just in time to block Baccha's overhead swing.

I only had to twist the sword to direct the magick. Aiming for Baccha's center, I struck. Dark red energy shot off the blade; where it touched Baccha, blood sprayed from his chest.

"Good," Baccha said through his teeth.

I barely had time to deflect his next assault as my vision blurred. The light-headedness from my first lesson hadn't lessened with experience, as I'd hoped. Now pain radiated from the center of my head, an effect of the binding. I hadn't told Baccha yet, just in case he thought about slowing down my lessons.

I managed one last slash across Baccha's stomach with the magick before dropping my sword. I collapsed to the ground beside it. "No more, Baccha."

He grunted as he settled down next to me. "That is just as well. This"—he looked down at the wound low on his torso—"needs healing."

We watched the sun disappear below the horizon as Baccha's wounds knit themselves back together. "How did you learn that?"

His hair was braided back away from his face, the style and complexity rivaling Mirabel's finest work. Even braided, ribbons of his hair shone like platinum and spun gold. "I learned it from a retired Sorceryn that lived in the Deadened Jungle."

"Be serious."

"I was born with the ability to heal and glamour, but that is all," Baccha said, cutting through my thoughts.

"And what about the rest?" I thought of his mindscape, that vast forest and river that now were enmeshed with my lake. Many of the noble fey, who were descendants of Godlings like Baccha, inherited other magickal powers from their bloodline. Though his father's line, Falun had a gift of tracking. But if Baccha hadn't been born with all his strange magick, how had he gained such power?

Through the bond I felt his contentment as well as his disinterest in my question. Since Mira found those coins from the Roune Lands in Baccha's rooms, I'd been trying to find a way to tell when he was lying by using the bond. That way I could confront him about it and possibly get some clue on why he had returned to Myre. The duality of knowing Baccha had, if not lied, skirted neatly around the truth while being intimately aware of his emotions made it impossible for me to judge him accurately.

"It is a long story, Princess. And besides, I've already decided what story to tell you today."

"Which is?" I prompted.

He smiled. "I told you of Akhimar; now I will tell you the story of Myre."

Many years passed in peace since the age of the Godlings, but peace, by its fragile nature, always ends.

The fey Kingdom and the khimaer Queendom thrived, growing in strength and eminence. But war broke out, as wars do, because the King coveted the lands below the river, because the fields there bore more grain and its trees more fruit.

But he made one mistake. He'd chosen to declare war during a succession. Khimaer Queens were not chosen by birth or power, but by skill. In every generation there were ten Princesses—one from each of the noble tribes—and when the old Queen died, the succession began. The Princesses were always given a task, one fundamental to the fate of the country. Whoever completed it most skillfully would be chosen as Queen.

When the Elder council learned that the fey King planned an assault on the capital, they asked the Princesses to find a way to end the war before it began.

Many Princesses amassed soldiers on the border between their lands—the Great River—and others made plans to assassinate the King. But one Princess, named Aaliya, simply gathered information on the fey monarch, including every rumor that had ever plagued his House.

On the eve of the King's planned assault on the khimaer Queendom, Aaliya crossed the river and snuck into the fey army camp. She passed a large tent with the King's sigil on the front and continued until she came to another.

It was smaller than the King's tent, with a sigil of a leopard's paw on the front. She slipped inside and waited. Finally a young man entered the tent. His hair was the color of the sky in high summer, a pale, perfect blue. His skin was tawny brown and freckled.

Aaliya knew of the strange beauty of their neighbors to the north. Even so, Prince Rhymer startled her.

She put her knife to his neck and bade him to sit. Besieged in his own tent, he listened carefully to her proposition.

"If we marry and join our nations," she told him, "we can save our people from war."

"And you will be Queen?" he questioned. "What shall I be?"

"As my husband, you will lead my armies. You will protect the realm."

"And what of my sons and daughters?" the Prince wondered. "Are they to lose the honors of their station, the chance to rule?"

"One daughter of the fey, I will take as my handmaiden, to one day be married into my line," Aaliya promised, binding the oath with her blood. "One son, I shall have as my most trusted adviser."

It didn't take long for Prince Rhymer to decide. Aaliya was lovely and her deal was more than fair, but her research had served her more than her beauty. The King had killed his wife in a rage just a year ago and the Prince still hated him for it.

The next morning they crossed the river together, with the King's head on a pike. Weeks later, the fey army traversed the river, not for war, but for a coronation.

They called their new Queendom Myre. In the Godling tongue it meant "no creation without sacrifice."

✦

I was still thinking about Baccha's story by the time I crawled into my tent. The image of the Prince and Princess wading the river with the King's head in tow wouldn't leave me. I'd never once heard any tales about Queen Aaliya, who had established Myre, which didn't surprise me. Why would our bards tell stories where the khimaer were the heroes of this country, when humans had done all they could to paint them as villains? I wondered how much House Killeen had done to cover up the past.

I thought back to my conversation with Aketo in the Palace before Dagon attacked. Then I'd said the truth wouldn't change Myre, but I'd been wrong. The erasure of the truth already had.

From the outside, my tent looked the same as the rest in the clearing, but on the inside the canvas was lined with strips of pale blue and soft orange cotton, and three rugs were laid on the ground. It was large enough to sleep three, but only Falun shared my tent. He was already inside unbraiding his hair.

Aching from the ride and from my lesson with Baccha, I sighed as I sank into the cushions on the tent's floor.

"Difficult lesson?" Falun asked. The oil lamp in the center of the tent offered dim light, but Falun's pale skin was still radiant.

It had been exhausting, but worthwhile. "It was many things. If I said them all, I would contradict myself."

He snorted. "Just like him, then."

I rummaged through my saddlebags until I found the coin from the Roune Lands. I hadn't yet gotten a chance to tell Falun about what Mirabel had discovered while searching Baccha's rooms in the Little Palace. Why had Baccha said he'd come from Dracol, instead of the Roune Lands? People did not go to the Roune Lands unless they had business there. Perhaps he was trying to keep me from finding out why he'd truly returned to Myre.

Falun's face was unreadable while I explained where it came from. He'd finished undoing his hair and stared down at the coin. "What are you going to do?"

"Keep having our lessons and wait for him to lie again or betray me, I suppose." I paused, contemplating the wisdom of my next statement. "I saw you two riding together today."

Falun blushed. "I recall you telling me to keep an eye on him."

"I know. I want you to keep doing it. Just . . . be careful."

"I will, Eva." Falun put out the lamp. "Make sure you do the same."

→→ CHAPTER 16 →→

I LAY ON my back in the dirt, trying to catch my breath.

Aketo peered down at me. He seemed to be holding in laughter.

I stood, brushing dirt from my calfskin leggings. "Again."

I heard snickering behind me and gestured rudely at Baccha and Falun. They were sitting on an overturned tree with the other spectator to my humiliation, Anali. Every so often she called out advice. "Eva, don't try to follow his movements. Look toward the next!"

It was the third day on the road to Asrodei and my proposition to spar with Aketo had finally come to fruition. Yesterday I'd only escaped it by hiding in my tent until supper. I'd been too sore from my lesson with Baccha to contemplate getting trounced again.

We faced each other again. Aketo licked his lips and smirked. His brown skin was slick with sweat, his horns fading into the dark trees behind him. "Captain, she can't yet hear, so how do you expect her to sense my next move?"

"What are you talking about? My hearing is fine," I muttered.

"Exactly my point. *Fine* is not *good*." He beckoned me forward. In our first two matches, he'd let me come to him. Perhaps that was my mistake.

I blew out a breath. "What exactly is it that can't I hear?"

"Everything," he said. "It's a part of kathbaria."

Kathbaria, the khimaer death dancing. That unbelievable fighting I'd seen between him and Anali in the Sandpits before everything went to ruin.

"Kathbaria is a dance," he continued, absently rubbing his jaw. "A communion with the world around us. A world with an undeniable pulse, a rhythm and song."

He couldn't be serious. My reaction must've been plain on my face, because Aketo sighed. "Don't take my word for it. Listen to your body, listen to the wind. Can you hear the movement from the camp behind us?"

Yes, I could hear the creak of horse lines and the crackle of the fire, but the wind? "I don't think—"

"If you don't want to try, then why did you ask?" he said. Fair point.

I watched as he began to sway, just slightly, to music I supposed he'd conjured in his head. I tried to match his posture—balancing lightly on the balls of my feet, right foot in front of the left, hands at my sides, relaxed but ready.

Every so often curls fell into his eyes and the gold of them was made brighter by the darkness.

I tried focusing on the sounds of guards just a few feet from us—Kelis's throaty chuckle, Malto murmuring what was surely a dirty joke, and someone being punched quite soundly in the chest—but it wouldn't come together. All the other notes were discordant: wind twisting through the clearing, whipping at the tents, the natural stirrings of the trees.

After a minute, I gave up. I matched his gentle sway and hoped we would move past this soon.

Aketo's eyes narrowed. "This will be tedious if you only try for a moment."

Not so patient after all.

I straightened and rested my hands on my hips. "How do you know I'm not trying?"

"Please," he muttered.

I threw up my hands. "Well, I'm not sure what you expect. Random noise cannot just become music."

"Provided you listen closely for more than a moment, you will find it." Aketo moved less than an arm's length away from me. Too close; I took a step back. He followed, pinning me in place with a glare. "Close your eyes."

I folded my arms across my chest, but did as he said. His voice floated between us, low and rich. Sharp. "Now empty your mind and listen. Start with the trees."

"What—"

"The wind through the trees. Focus on one sound, find the music in it, and let your consciousness expand beyond it." He paused, hand touching my arm briefly. I jumped. "You can't dance without music and you won't always have some-one around to play it. You must find it."

I tried to relax. The wind in the trees made a sound like

muted chimes. I could find no music in it, though, and soon latched on to another sound—the steady rhythm of Aketo's breathing.

The high, clear notes of thrushes in the trees, all while the soft exhalations of his breath kept time.

I heard feet stepping through the brush and distant movement from the camp. Still, there was no percussion, no bass. And then I felt it—the steady drum of my heartbeat.

The rhythm of Aketo's breathing changed, stuttered and sped. I opened my eyes and dodged on instinct. His hand sliced the air where my neck had been.

I could still hear his breathing, and my pulse raced along with it. The thrushes shrieked as I twisted away from him, their calls shifting to a staccato beat. Under this new rhythm, I ducked and kicked, trying to sweep his legs out from underneath him. Aketo leaped over my leg easily. As I straightened, he caught my arm. With a flex of his, he flung me out and spun me around, until my back was pressed against his chest, one of his arms loose around my neck. Had he been holding a knife, I would've been dead.

Even with my heartbeat thundering loudly in my ears, I could still hear the wind, the birds, and damp wood popping in the fire. The music.

"I'm surprised you can actually listen," Aketo said, warm breath tickling my neck.

I elbowed him in the side, and he laughed against my skin before stepping away.

Even apart, it seemed I could feel his pulse against my back. My breathing that was matched to his. But if Aketo felt anything, it didn't show on his face. "Next time, move from one attack to the next without waiting for your opponent to move. It is a dance, after all. You don't forget the music as soon as you've done one step. You're quick, like a bird. Use that—never hesitate, never slow."

His voice cut across the space between us. "Again."

We were too far apart for me to hear his breathing, but the wind worked just as well. I swayed, letting my body move to the sound of branches creaking, leaves slapping each other as they rustled, time still kept by my heartbeat.

In all that sound, his movements were misplaced notes. I heard them and knew when to evade, dodge, attack.

I swung away from him, ducking blows, dipping into a crouch, and rising as soon as his arm whistled through the air above me. This time, when he made the grab to spin me into his chest, I pulled him to me instead. I jabbed him in the gut, pleased at his noise of pain. This victory was short-lived, as his leg swept me to the ground.

The next time, he set me whirling to avoid his blows. It felt so much like a dance—the sweat beading his brow, cheeks flush with color, and our feet pounding the dirt—that I forgot myself. We could have been in the Patch, but this dance was far more intimate.

The heat from his body warmed my skin and his eyes never left mine. My heart raced as I fought to match his grace, and I could barely breathe when he touched me.

The illusion faltered when his elbow caught my chin and a kick sent me down into the dirt. Still, my pulse thundered in my ears and my skin felt hot, tight. I closed my eyes and imagined the world was a wholly different place, one where I met him in the Patch.

"That's enough for tonight," Anali yelled, chasing away my foolish imaginings and calling us back to our tents.

Cheeks burning, I ignored Aketo's outstretched hand and climbed to my feet on my own.

He stared at me like I was a problem he couldn't solve, brow knitted, bottom lip sliding between his teeth. I fidgeted, avoiding his eyes. After what felt like a long time, he smirked. Half in shadows, I couldn't read him as he murmured, "Until tomorrow, Eva."

Falun woke me early the next morning with news: last night he'd seen Baccha leaving camp between a change in the watch. Falun had tried to follow, but without Baccha's blood, he could only track the Hunter for a few miles before the fey's trail disappeared. And when Falun awoke the next morning, he saw the Hunter emerge from his tent as if he had never left at all.

⇥ CHAPTER 17 ⇤

THE NEXT DAY, the road took us along the edge of the Arym Plain. The grasslands were like a massive bowl; the forest dropped off and below swept a flat sea of golden grass, dotted with islands of jutting rock where golden lions lounged. In the distance there were streaky dark lines of swampland and shallow lakes. If we rode any farther, we would find herds of wildebeest, packs of hyenas and jackals. My father's family home was located deep in the Plain, but he'd never taken me to visit them. It was a hard and dangerous ride through that wild expanse of golden earth.

We made camp in a sparse stretch of trees between the plain and the distant hills where Asrodei was located. In just three more days I would see my father. I'd done perhaps too well at keeping him out of my thoughts for the first part of the trip, but now I couldn't stop thinking about the binding. I dreamed of swimming to the bottom of my lake. I always woke just as the pain lanced through my body.

This wasn't the first time my father had failed to share the truth with me. Instead of telling me what it meant to be Rival Heirs, he'd left that to Mother, who delivered the news in the cruelest way possible.

Had the binding also been to protect me, as Mira thought? I wanted to believe that, but hope made the wisest of women into fools. It didn't escape me that I was looking for an excuse, wanting a reason to forgive him before he'd even confessed. Was it wrong to want someone to trust?

We'd camped near an offshoot of the Red River and I decided to take my horse down to the stream for a wash—for me and for her. Four days on the road and washing with a bucket of water warmed over the fire had begun to get old.

I led Bird through the trees to the stream downwind of camp. I let out a groan when I found Aketo, waded in up to his thighs, washing his great buckskin horse. He didn't see me approach, so I stopped to admire him.

He was shirtless, naked but for low slung breeches and a leather band around his left arm, and he'd somehow knotted his hair into a bun atop his head. Even from far away, I could see those gold hoops lining his ears.

He was beautiful, of course. Long and lean and hard in all the right places, curving sinew and gold shining through his brown skin. Shadows traced his jaw—he still hadn't shaved—and scales flowed down his back and stopped just short of his hips, in a knot-work pattern of gold and copper and black.

I let myself imagine touching him. I wanted to trace the curve of his bottom lip, half captured between his teeth, half poked out in a ridiculous pout. I wanted to stare at every curve and hollow of his chest and flat stomach until I'd memorized him. Then I wanted to do the same with my hands.

Aketo turned and looked right at me, that familiar smirk now tugging at his mouth. "I should warn you, Eva. I can feel you."

My mouth fell open.

He coughed, flushing as I stared. "I mean, I can sense you. I can sense anyone's feelings when they're near me. It's more intense, more exact, the closer they are. I thought I should tell you. Didn't want to interrupt your admiration, but you might've stood up there feeling all manner of things . . ."

He bit his lip again and I wondered if he'd somehow perfected that look by sensing its effect on the people around him. There was a distinct connection between the sight of it and me wanting to throttle him or kiss it away—an utterly infuriating and useless reaction.

It took a long moment for me speak, as my tongue was stuck fast to the roof of my mouth. He looked pleased and I could feel his eyes on me, heavy and warm and impossibly diverting. "Ad . . . mir . . . ation?"

"Yes." He shrugged, a sly set to his lips.

I counted to five in my head and swallowed the slick reply desperate to leap from my tongue, and then walked with Bird toward the stream. I stopped at the edge of the water and pulled off my tunic, leaving a light chemise behind. Aketo hadn't moved. I could feel him watching me, though I couldn't have said what he felt.

I dove into the water, because it was hot and I hadn't been clean in days. And because I needed to escape the pressure of his gaze.

I washed Bird, moving as quickly as possible without appearing rushed. When I finished, I turned to find Aketo at the banks of the stream, still staring. I stared back, wringing water from my hair. "Aketo?"

"Hmm?" He licked his lips, eyes flashing and matching the gold rings in his ears.

"It isn't very fair. You get to know what I feel, but how am I to read you?"

"I've heard the same all my life and I never have an adequate reply," he said, eyes never leaving mine. "If it helps, I rarely talk about others' feelings aloud, but sometimes these things are necessary. In this case, so you would know I admire you, too."

"It does help," I said, and slipped beneath the water to cool the burning in my cheeks. When I emerged, he was gone.

Blessedly clean, I dressed in calfskin leggings and a soft blue tunic and headed back to camp. Once I saw to Bird, I walked back to my tent, fighting against a smile, but Baccha stepped in front of me before I could go inside.

An atypical frown tugged at his lips.

I jumped—I hadn't even seen him since we first arrived in camp. Falun had ridden with him during the morning ride. I'd watched them from the back of the procession, wondering if Falun would confront him about last night, but they barely spoke.

I crossed my arms. "Hello, Baccha."

"Let's go," Baccha said. Today his hair was loose again, blond strands dancing when the wind caught them.

"Where exactly?"

"Get your things—a sturdy blade, but not a sword, throwing knives, something serrated." He tapped a foot impatiently. "We're going on a hunt. It's time we moved on to marrow magick, Princess."

Before I lost my nerve, I asked him, "Where did you go last night?"

He sighed heavily. "I went in search of our quarry for tonight. Are there any more questions, Your Highness? We need to go straightaway. It's already late. I spoke to the Captain and she wants us back before the second watch."

I couldn't hide my shock as I crawled inside my tent. I picked out a set of throwing knives on a belt made to hang around my hips, and two large hunting knives.

Baccha helped me to my feet and we walked away from camp after I confirmed his words with Anali. I couldn't afford to be careless, not with the coin from the Roune Lands eating a hole in my pocket. Though after his direct answer, a coin felt like flimsy evidence of treachery. I decided I would ask him when we reached Asrodei, where he couldn't stalk into the forest and disappear.

I let Baccha walk ahead of me once we reached the trees. They were different here; though this area wasn't near dense enough to be called a forest, the low leafless branches reached out and twined around one another, like dancers in an embrace. It didn't take long walking through these trees to feel like the camp didn't exist at all.

I fought to keep Baccha's pace. Though grace always marked his movements, here he became something more. He looked taller, grander, and when my thoughts brushed the bond, he felt vaster—like the river between us was where the Red River met the Silvern Sea—and even less knowable than I'd always thought.

He flowed through the trees. Their twined branches bent to his will, easing apart with his touch, never once catching that great swath of hair flowing behind him, whereas when I wasn't within a few inches of him, they snatched at me.

I should have expected his ease in the forest—he was Lord of the Hunt, after all, who once led a host of wolves, night stags, wraiths, and magick-workers hoping to be absolved of their own crimes through Myre at the behest of the Queen. Of course these trees welcomed him. Might the great sands of the South open a path for him? Would the northern snows that piled higher than villages melt at his touch?

My usual fear of Baccha washed over me. How much of the real Baccha hadn't I seen? How much had he hidden away? And could I trust him, well away from the camp?

"What are we hunting?" I asked after we'd been walking for nearly an hour. The sky was darkening and so far Baccha had said nothing.

He ducked under a particularly twisted web of branches and held them apart for me. I touched the trees, wondering if I might feel the soft buzz of glamour, but I didn't even smell his magick. As soon as Baccha moved away, the branches slid back into place.

"Antelope, hopefully. They stray from the grasslands sometimes."

We continued forward, though sweeping the ground for double-teardrop-shaped tracks proved impossible when I could barely see in the dark.

"Baccha. The sun is going down. I have to *see* the beast in order to kill it," I said.

Any eagerness I felt had worn down to anxiety, and the bit of flatbread I'd stuffed down my throat when we first set off wasn't doing much to curb the gnawing in my gut.

Baccha stopped so abruptly that I ran right into him. I swore as I fell onto my backside. "What's wrong? What is it?"

"I forgot that . . . you can't see at night." He slapped a hand to his forehead. "I actually *forgot*."

"So we're heading back to camp?" I climbed to my feet with the help of his outstretched hand.

"I don't think so, Princess," Baccha answered with a laugh. "For someone so eager to use their magick, you sure are quick to try to get out of it."

"My apologies for not realizing stumbling around in the dark was an integral aspect of your teachings."

He held up his hands. "What did you expect?"

"I don't know, Baccha," I mumbled. "I *expected* something like the tutoring of my childhood—tidy, stuffy rooms, musty Sorceryn scrolls, and towering piles of books. Hunting *during the day*."

Baccha laughed, holding a hand to his stomach. "It was your idea to leave Ternain. Come on," he said, waving me forward. "I'll give you a bit of me to get you through the night."

I folded my arms across my chest and Baccha grinned. Before I could blink, he held his palms over my eyes, pressing down slightly. "Like that," he murmured, and then he stepped away.

I blinked a few times, feeling like I had gotten a bit of dust in my eyes. I looked up at him and leaned away. Moments before, shadows had hugged his sharp features. But now, as I stared, his face had cleared. I spun around, my eyes devouring the vivid colors around me. It wasn't just that the darkness had limited my field of vision; all the colors were richer now, with greater contrast. I could differentiate the shades of green of the vines, the leaves on the trees, and the wilted ones half buried beneath dirt.

I turned back to Baccha, wanting to devour him with this sight. His hair was even more beautiful. I stepped forward to catch a handful of it, my eyes picking out individual strands of white, yellow gold, rose gold, and even silver. Even the color of his skin was richer, warmed with more honey and gilt than my eyes would normally pick up.

"Don't let this add to your ego, but you're wondrous, Baccha. I wish I could see myself like this, or . . ." I swallowed the rest of my words, but held them close inside. Aketo. My mother. Or even Isadore. Perhaps that was why the fey loved her so, if they could see her like this.

"You'll have to take my word for it, Eva." He reached out to pull one of my braids. "You're wondrous too. And you'll be even more wondrous with a pair of horns around your neck."

We started through the trees again and I moved with more energy, lighter on my feet than I had felt in days. I followed Baccha easily, and as I did, our speed increased. As we traveled farther east, the trees grew together, their branches woven even tighter, but that wasn't a problem for Baccha.

He began to run. The wind that gathered in his wake was the same one I had smelled the first day we met. It whistled through the trees, stirring my hair, moving through my shirt and pulling me along. I stayed as close to Baccha as I could, stepping only where he stepped, sure that the wind would drive me to terror if I strayed from him.

By the time Baccha slowed, I was breathing heavily, but not as tired as I should've been. I should have been clutching my sides, cursing the soreness in my thighs, bent over trying to pull air into my lungs. I could tell we'd traveled a long distance, longer than seemed possible. I whispered, "How did you . . . How did I do that?"

Baccha looked over at me. "We traveled on the wind. And before you ask, no, it is not a gift you could borrow. It took me the better half of my first two centuries to learn it."

"Which was . . . when?"

"Hush, now." He pointed at a set of tracks in the underbrush. "We'll walk from here."

I tried to be as quiet as Baccha—his steps made no sound—but mostly I failed. Even with my new keen sight, I stumbled over roots and slippery lichen. But I kept my eyes open and listened.

We walked for about five minutes until I heard it—the soft crunch of leaves crushed underfoot, the wind whistling in a different way, moving around something new. I stopped Baccha with a hand on his back. I pushed urgency through the bond, willing him to stay still.

I lifted my shirt, easing a knife from the band around my stomach, and stepped around a tree. My vision narrowed until it was all I could see.

The antelope was lovely, a soft and buttery brown, with stripes of white around its narrow neck. It stood less than fifteen feet away, bending over to gnaw at a tuft of grass. Its horns curled back and then forward again, ridged and sharp.

Beautiful. My eyes ran down its thin but powerful legs, the wide white stripes on its back.

I shifted and the antelope lifted its head. Those eyes met mine just as the knife left my hand. A second later I heard the sound of a bowstring being pulled taut, released, and then the impact of three arrows into its body. One in its chest and two in its midsection. The antelope fell on its side, one of the arrows snapping beneath it.

"I had it well in hand, Baccha."

"You dealt the killing blow, which is really all that counts. I just didn't want it stumbling around spilling blood all over."

I showed him the other two knives in my hands.

"Well, I apologize for underestimating you, but you don't exactly exude skilled huntress," he huffed, while wrestling his hair into a knot at the back of his neck, then stuffing it into the collar of his shirt.

"What about you, *Hunter?* I spotted the antelope before you even noticed," I said, jabbing one of my knives in his direction.

He smiled with enough viciousness to make me step back. "Watch where you point that. This is your hunt, Princess. If you'd like to see how I . . . hunt, I can arrange a demonstration. I should warn you, I am better at hunting people than beasts."

"I'll pass," I said, shaking off a chill.

"Then we might as well begin." Baccha pointed to the antelope.

I walked to where it had fallen and removed my knife from its throat, grimacing at the smell of blood and death.

I cleaned the knife on a patch of moss at a nearby tree. Heat still rolled off the beast as its blood leaked onto the forest floor. Even with a thick mess of blood at its throat, it was beautiful. Liquid black eyes stared up at the stars, and those horns were half the length of its body.

"Well?" I asked, once Baccha had removed his arrows.

He blinked at me, and then laughed. "Retrieve the horns, Eva. That is the only part of marrow magick we will do tonight. You only need to claim them."

"How . . . ?" I paused, trying to find the right question. "There isn't a more delicate, magickal way of doing this? Where the horns just fall off?"

"I suggest a serrated knife." Baccha tried to shrug as if he wasn't enjoying this, but his smirk was telling. "Get as close to the head as you can get."

Insufferable immortal bastard.

"Your amusement is leaking into the bond, Baccha," I muttered as I bent to pull the long-handled knife from my boot. It gleamed in the moonlight, as wide and as long as my forearm. Made to butcher and pull through layers of fat, muscle, and bone. *Not* meant to saw off horns.

I rolled the antelope's head so its eyes faced away from me. My hands brushed down the length of both horns and a pulse of energy went through me. I took a deep breath before laying the knife along its left horn; then I clenched my teeth and set to sawing. I didn't realize I'd closed my eyes until Baccha called out, "Princess, *look*."

The white tattoos on my arms—bone tattoos, animal silhouettes winding in a chain from the tips of my middle fingers up past my elbows—glowed brighter than the moonlight. I gasped, jarring the knife away from the notch I'd created on the horn. I began again, watching the light intensify with every stroke of the knife. The glow the tattoos emitted twisted around the horns, outlining them in a misty white effulgence.

With one hand at the base of the horn and the other sawing back and forth below it, it didn't take me long. Still, the muscles in my arm burned even as I reached halfway and sweat stung my eyes. I stopped and started a few times, worried I would lose my balance and bury one of the horns in my stomach.

As I sawed through the last edge of it, the light flared and pain exploded in my mind. It was so sharp that I bit my tongue. The light was gone. Baccha moved close to me and lifted the horn from my hands.

"Thank you," I whispered as he gave me a waterskin. My headache started again and I clenched my teeth against the pain.

Baccha bowed and gave me a cloth to wipe my face. "Do you want to take a break?"

I peered at him. Something like respect rested there, in the straight line of his eyebrows and the flat set of his mouth. It was always worth noticing when Baccha wasn't smiling. "I can finish."

He bowed his head again and backed away when I returned the water. As soon as I wrapped my hands around the horns, the headache started again. Sharper this time, pressing at my thoughts like needles boring into skin.

But I had to endure this. Baccha was expecting me to claim both of these horns, and I refused to give him another reason to question my commitment to magick. As long as I told myself I could live with the pain, I would be fine. There was the binding to consider, but if I'd claimed one already, that meant this was one of the magicks the binding allowed.

Instead of that burning starburst of pain in my head, I focused on the pinching ache between my shoulders. The smell of blood and rotting leaves clogged my nose, and the only thing I could see was the mingling of the light my arms emitted and the silver moonlight reflecting off the blade. Once I was halfway through the next horn, I sucked in a breath and stood up, shaking my head. Baccha called my name and I waved him away. As soon as I wasn't touching the horn, my mind cleared.

I would be fine—I could finish—I just needed a moment of not breathing such death.

I closed my eyes and counted until I stopped feeling faint. I fell to my knees, too tired to crouch. The still-warm blood from the antelope's neck soaked into my pants. I didn't even feel the pain of the headache anymore, I just knew I needed to be done.

When the knife bit through the last inch of the horn, I sagged with relief. Baccha was there before I had to ask, lifting it from my hands.

"Some bones are harder than others to claim," he murmured as he took the horn. "Horns are the most difficult."

"And we had to start with the most difficult?" I crawled away from the dead antelope, in the opposite direction of where he placed the horns, and collapsed at the base of a nearby tree.

"Your nameday is soon, too soon for me to regret pushing you."

I glared at him, hoping it might relieve some of the pressure behind my eyes.

"I know it was difficult, but I couldn't help you. You can only create a lasting bond with a bone you claim, a bone you remove yourself." I watched as Baccha wrapped the bones in coarse brown cloth. A sense of relief eased through me. Half of me never wanted to be near them again. "If you don't properly claim the bones, their usefulness runs out in less than a year. I have bones that I've been wearing for well over a century. That ring you wear is one hundred ninety years old."

"So I won't have to claim another pair of horns for the rest of my life?"

"That's right, unless you live as long as I have, and at that point, you'll have greater things to worry about than a new pair of horns." Sorrow flowed through the bond. "Come on. Let's get you back."

"What about the antelope?"

"It's too far for us to carry. Jackals roam these woods. They'll make better use of it than we can." Baccha stuck out his hand.

I ignored it, pushing up to my knees first, and then used a low branch on the tree to pull myself up.

On the walk back, he told me the next story.

✦

Once more, the realm was irrevocably changed—when twenty ships arrived on the shores of the Fair Sea.

The voyagers had left their homeland, a vast Empire across the Fair Sea, and become lost on the vast ocean. They called themselves human, and in form they were plain, shaded only with the colors of the earth. But strangest of all was that they had no magick.

Myreans had long known of lands beyond the realm, where there was no magick, but these were the first people from there to arrive on their shores.

The humans approached the current Queen and requested refuge. She told them they could stay in Myre for five years, to recover from their long journey, and in exchange, the humans would build ships so that her people could explore the realm by sea.

When their work was complete, the humans sought the Queen again. They had forgotten their home, they said, in the decade sailing across the sea, and Myre had taken its place. They wanted to stay but knew that without magick, neither the land nor its people would accept them.

"What would you have of me?" the Queen asked.

"We ask that you make us Myrean in blood, in exchange for our loyalty and craft," a Lord among the humans said.

The Queen was shocked by the boldness of their request, though the trade on the sea with the help of the human-made boats had already yielded much wealth. But a gift of magick, on such a scale, had never been done before. She considered her decision for exactly one year and then called the humans back to her Court. She offered them an elixir made from the blood of khimaer, fey, and bloodkin. It would not give them all magick, but it would make magick grow in the blood of their children.

When the humans learned of the elixir's contents, half fled north to the mountains and eschewed magick. The rest drank it and pledged fealty to the Queen, swearing upon her Ivory Throne.

A generation passed and the first humans with magick were born. Their powers were as vast and varied as the sea, most given multiple gifts. There was magick of water, magick of fire, magick of speed, and magick of foretelling. There were magicks of the mind and of healing and of blood.

But their magick was cursed and impossible to control. When human magick was loosed, it killed.

The Queen of the next generation—who believed her predecessor had been a fool to give the humans this gift—declared that they would have to leave the realm if they could not restrain their abilities. However, she was not cruel. It was not the humans' fault that the previous Queen had been foolhardy.

She assigned the task of conquering this magick to a group of human men who'd learned to use their magick through sorcery and ritual. To aid in their task, she created a council of the most powerful magick-workers in Myre.

This was a mistake.

Together the council and the human men, who by now called themselves the Sorceryn, found a way to link magick to symbols emblazoned upon their skin. Human magick became the most potent and feared across the realm.

It was this power that convinced the humans that they should rule.

⤞ CHAPTER 18 ⤝

WHEN WE RETURNED to camp, Aketo was waiting outside my tent, smelling of mint soap.

"Do you . . . Can I have a word?"

I stared at him. I'd never heard Aketo stumble over his words. He rocked back on his heels and smiled. "If you aren't busy, that is."

"Just, ah, a moment." I pulled up the flap and ducked into my tent. Blessedly Falun wasn't inside. I washed my face with a towel and the last of the waterskin Baccha had given me and invited Aketo in.

Once Aketo crawled into the tent and sat across from me, the space seemed to shrink. His horns brushed the top of the canvas and his legs were so long. I flushed when his knee touched mine. My eyes traced the straight line of his broad shoulders, winding up his throat until I noticed the slight depressions in his bottom lip, from his fangs.

Staring, again.

Someone, one of the guards, had set out tea. I busied myself with pouring us a cup. "Honey?"

"Yes." I glanced up and found him watching me. Even when I noticed him staring, he didn't seem to care.

He was far too confident, far too beautiful to be anything but horrible.

And that smirk.

I pressed the tea into his hands and gulped down half of mine. A bit of honey slid down the side of his cup. He caught it with his thumb and then tasted it.

Gods damn it. What was I thinking, inviting him in here? "What did you want?"

In the same moment, he asked, "How was your lesson?"

"Fine—"

"I—" He chuckled softly. "You first."

"It went well. We hunted an antelope. I brought it down." I glanced up to find Aketo leaning forward. He nodded for me to continue. "I . . . it was strange. Every part of it, my magick, I mean."

I hadn't talked much about my lessons with anyone other than Falun, and then only briefly. No one else had asked. Aketo wasn't whom I would have chosen.

Khimaer magick was used from a young age. Every tribe had a different power. All khimaer from the lami tribe, like Aketo, could read and control emotions. And all the khimaer from Anali's tribe could manipulate shadows and darkness. Skill grew as they aged, of course, but there were no tattoos. No Sorceryn delving needed to find the power within. Magick, Anali had told me, was as easy as breathing for her.

Aketo nodded slowly. "Do you like it?"

"No, I don't. Maybe if I could learn slowly, maybe if I'd started when I was a child, but now? No."

He sat back, tucking his curls behind his ears. "I used to hate my magick. For a long time, I couldn't understand where my feelings ended and everyone else's began. It was overwhelming. I spent most of my time alone until I was ten."

"What changed?"

"My mam decided it was time to start taking me on her visits around the Enclosure so I could watch her work."

"What does she do?"

"She's the head Steward of the Enclosure, which just means that all the Governor's orders are filtered through her to the rest of us. But her most important work is in helping the heartsick. She visits with people, sometimes she uses her magick to soothe them if they ask, and other times we bring food and see that their homes are cared for. At first I would do anything to get out of the visits. I'd just started controlling how much I felt other people's emotions, but it was so much harder around people who were in pain. We can't just soothe them for the sake of our own comfort. We only do what they want. Besides all that, I always knew things I wasn't supposed to and . . . I was put out to learn we were lucky. I had Mam and my brother, Dthazi, and my granna. A lot of the people we help have had their families split between the Enclosures, not to mention the ones the soldiers kill. They kill anyone who makes trouble. That trouble could be as little as being drunk or out past curfew. Or talking back."

I swallowed. "How did you stop hating it? The visits and your magick?"

"I saw the good we did. That and my mother made it clear hating my magick was the same as hating myself. She'd say, 'You can't cleave you and your magick in two. Doing that will kill both.'"

"Oh. That's why I . . . struggle with my magick. If me and my magick are one and the same, I am nothing but a murderer. The most well-known person with this magick was Queen Raina."

"I know."

Did it disgust him? Did it gall him, defending me when I'd inherited magick that killed his ancestors? It would have burned me up inside.

Aketo shifted. We'd been drifting closer all this time. My legs were folded beneath me, my knees pressed against his shins, and one of his hands was half resting on my thigh. I shivered. I wore thick calfskin leggings, but I felt his touch as if against bare skin.

I inched back, putting some distance between us. "What was it you wanted to discuss?"

"Since we're just a few days' ride from Asrodei, I wanted to tell you that I've met your father."

Of course he had. My father knew every member of my guard. Other than Anali and Falun, who'd both been my choice, he'd chosen them all. "I knew that when you came to Ternain."

"What I mean to say is that I know him well. He visited the Enclosures and—" He broke off and canted his head like he was hearing something from afar. The color drained from his face, and his eyes went round.

"Aketo?"

He shook his head, and then covered my mouth. Half a second later, I went cold.

How long had our voices drowned out the screaming?

CHAPTER 19

I DUG THROUGH the weapons in my bags and pressed a sword into Aketo's hand.

His eyes flashed to mine. "Stay here. I'll guard your tent. If anything happens to me, you'll have to run."

I let him go, my heart pounding like a drum in my chest. The only other sword I'd brought with me was the blade with the carving of Khimaerani on the hilt. I unsheathed it, the bone handle fitting perfectly into the contours of my palm.

I waited, peeking through the tent flaps. Someone, a man from the look of his boots, appeared. He and Aketo moved away from the tent and began to exchange blows.

His sword whistled through the air, and then two more attackers stepped from between the shadows. I crawled out of the tent and ducked just before a sword could take my head off.

I jumped to my feet and swung without hesitation. My

blade connected with the forearm of a veiled fighter, jarring against his bone.

He hissed and uttered a curse. I didn't understand his words, but I felt the venom of them.

The slight curve and single edge of his sword marked him as a northerner, from Dracol. I had only a moment to consider this as he attacked. I blocked him twice, and then froze at Aketo's grunt of pain.

I glanced to my left.

Twenty feet away, three men circled Aketo, blades whirling. Blood spread from a cut on his upper thigh, soaking the leg of his pants. The sound of steel slicing the air caught my attention just in time to duck another blow aiming for my head.

I backed away and the Dracolan's sword caught me across my stomach. I was barely aware of the pain, but I could feel blood soaking into the waistband of my pants.

I tried to find the music, but it was all chaos and discord in a storm around me. All I heard was the clang of steel as swords met. I jerked up my sleeve and found the tattoo of a sword on my arm.

I swiped the veiled man's blood across it. My magick reared up within me, and I wrapped the power around my blade and swung, aiming for the man's heart. A wound spurted blood in his chest, seeping through his clothes. It wasn't a killing blow, though it worked well as distraction. As his eyes jerked from my sword—still cloaked in crimson magick that moved like flames in the dark—to his blood drying on my arm, I swept my sword in a long arc, cutting his neck.

When he fell, I'd already turned toward Aketo. He was fighting two men now, as one had fallen. I watched as his blade lashed the air, swift and dangerous as a snake. Even while beating back their strikes, Aketo's eyes met mine. His were telling me to run.

I lifted my sword above my head, waiting for the right moment. Then finally one of them stepped back, dodging Aketo's blade, and I struck. My sword bit into his shoulder and he turned toward me, growling in pain.

I scrambled backward and wiped his blood from the blade and rubbed it on my arm. I lashed out at him with the magick, this time cutting his neck so that blood gushed from the wound, splattering me. He staggered for a moment and then dropped.

I retched at the feel of his hot blood on my face, reminded of the assassin's blood and Dagon's. Pain stabbed at the back of my head, worse than it had ever been for blood magick.

When I looked back toward Aketo, the last man had fallen. Aketo limped toward me. I ran and caught him just before he fell. The wound in my stomach tugged painfully as I lowered him to the ground.

"You said . . . you would . . . stay in . . . tent," Aketo wheezed. His head rolled back with the weight of his horns, and his skin was ashen and cool to the touch.

"Hush now. I had to leave it, you were being overrun." I needed to stop the bleeding. Then I could find Baccha. I tried cutting a strip of fabric off the bottom of my tunic, but my hands were trembling too hard. I poured all my fear into the bond, praying Baccha would come.

"I had things," Aketo whispered, eyes fluttering shut, "well in hand."

I froze at the flash of movement behind the nearest tent and then sagged as Baccha stepped into view; one of his wolves walked beside him, its muzzle red with blood. In one sharp glance he took in Aketo, the bodies of fallen men around us.

Baccha dropped to the ground next to me. "Guard us," he said to the wolf as it prowled behind him, growling with pink-tinged spittle hanging from its lips.

He cut open Aketo's pants to access the deep gash across his upper thigh. I caught a flash of blood still spurting steadily down his leg and looked away. Baccha held the edges of the wound together. As Baccha healed him, Aketo groaned, his back arching off the ground.

Aketo opened his golden eyes and I let out a breath, pushing away fear's tight grip on my heart.

"You're bleeding too, Princess," Baccha said.

His hands were gentle as he pulled my shirt up to look at the wide gash across my stomach. I flinched as the fabric stuck to the wound, tugging painfully. He pressed the ends of the wound together and a shrill scream escaped my mouth. Icy threads pricked my skin, knitting the flesh back together.

When I caught my breath, I asked, "How many?"

"Twenty at the start. We ran them off pretty easily. They must have misjudged the size of our camp," Baccha answered. "I can smell your magick, Princess. Well done. Though I'd like it if next time you could avoid getting gutted. And," he added, looking at Aketo, "that goes for you too."

Baccha stood and walked to one of the fallen men. He removed the dead man's veil. He was surprisingly handsome, with prominent cheekbones and a lush mouth, made macabre in death. Round brown eyes open and unseeing; warm ocher skin the usual northern shade. The veil wasn't just a ruse, then; they truly were from Dracol.

"A raid?" Aketo asked.

"But this far south? We're days from the capital. That makes no sense." I sat up, clenching my teeth as I swallowed a moan. My wound was still tender. "Unless, of course, this wasn't a raid and they're working for whoever is trying to kill me."

"What interest would a man from Dracol have in the contest of Rival Heirs?" Aketo asked.

"What do we know of the interests of men from Dracol?" I asked, glaring at Baccha, daring him to say he did know.

The Hunter wouldn't meet my eyes. "I'm sure your Captain will have more insight. Let's go assure everyone that you two are still alive."

I helped Aketo to his feet and barely looked at Baccha as we walked to the edge of camp. My hands still shook for fear of what would have happened without Baccha, but I shoved those feelings aside. It was neither the time nor the place to investigate whatever I felt for this Prince. Besides, my rule for the Patch still stood—romance was a luxury fit for those with years ahead of them, not weeks.

Thirteen bodies were lined up in a row, dragged there by the guards. All Dracolan, their veils trimmed in gleaming black and red beads—the black for prayer and the red for the lives they'd taken, if I remembered correctly. If there had been, as Baccha said, twenty men, then with thirteen dead here and four dead near my tent, at least three had gotten away.

Other than Aketo, only two of my guards and one of Mother's soldiers had suffered injuries. Everyone else milled around the vestiges of tonight's fire, cleaning weapons and packing. When Anali saw me, she didn't waste any time.

"We're leaving," she said, voice grim, "once everyone is healed and the bodies are burned. Pack quickly. We'll ride through the night and the next day until we reach Asrodei."

Which meant in a couple days I would see my father. I would finally have the truth.

➤➤ CHAPTER 20 ◄◄

WE RODE LIKE demons, beneath a thick cloak of Falun and Baccha's glamour. Anali's shadow magick spread around us when we rode into the night, and Baccha's wolves scouted ahead. Aketo rode beside me, though we didn't speak. I suspected that Anali had chosen him to see to my safety if we were attacked again. That, or he felt as protective of me as I had begun to feel of him after last night. I couldn't shake the image of him bleeding out in the dirt.

And yet, I resented his presence at my side, reminding me of everything I would never have. Aketo was khimaer. Of course there was no future for us. It would be better for the both of us if I remembered that.

The land changed drastically between the sparsely wooded grasslands we'd been riding through and the hill lands where the Fort sat. The road sloped downward gently, green and purple hills steadily growing in size until one understood why they were called the Little A'Nir; their size rivaled the jagged northern mountains.

We cut back and forth around and through the hills until we reached the limestone fortress.

Asrodei was erected atop one of the hills. It was difficult to tell where the fortress began and the hill ended because of the grass and wildflowers that clung to Asrodei's walls. At the top, the Myrean flag kicked in the wind, the silhouette of the blue dagger on it flowing like an undulating snake.

Without the mosaics that decorated most ancient structures in Myre, Asrodei had always felt incomplete to me until I lived here. Now I saw the dignity of its unadorned walls, the beauty in its simplicity.

I heard all of the guards except Aketo sigh when we came within sight, like they were coming home. Without acknowledging it, everyone rode faster. I leaned over Bird's pommel, heart in my throat.

Once we came within a hundred feet of the base of hill, five guards approached. Anali started to guide her horse forward, but I spurred Bird ahead, wanting to dispel with any formalities that could delay our entrance.

I pulled off the scarf protecting my head from the sun and thrust my hand forward. The Killeen ring was simply a silver band fashioned into eagle wings holding a bright blue stone with a black crack down the middle. My signet was a heavy gold ring inlaid with orange moonstones and my profile, underneath which was my name in tiny lettering.

I needn't have bothered. One of the soldiers—fair-skinned and thick-necked, with a long scar down his cheek—took one look at my face and dismounted. He knelt beside his horse and bowed, forehead to the ground. After a moment the others followed suit. They all murmured, "Your Highness."

The first soldier climbed to his feet, and then made us jump by yelling, "She is here, Lord Commander!"

I went still. Anali had sent guards ahead yesterday to alert my father to our arrival, but I hadn't expected him to meet me down here. I'd thought I would have more time to prepare myself. I had no notion of what I would say to my father.

The rest of the guards parted and suddenly there was my father, walking through them, looking almost serious in the gold-and-white jacket of the Lord Commander. It hung unbuttoned, its ribbons and medals splayed carelessly and gleaming in the sunlight. My father always joked that next to his daughters and wife, he looked plain. He was of average height, his skin a rich chestnut, and his face was broad and ruggedly handsome, with heavy brows and a nose at least thrice broken. Though his eyes, a different color than mine, were familiar, their soft brown was still a shock in his dark face. I took in his overlong beard, more peppered with gray than I remembered, and his neatly trimmed hair as black as mine and showing its curl in the tight waves pressed to his scalp.

I dismounted, smoothing my hands down the panels of my riding skirt.

He wrapped me in a hug and kissed the top of my head. He smelled as he always did—of ink smudges, bitter soldier's draught to keep him alert, mint leaves, sword oil, and fresh sheaves of paper. Up close, I could see he was thinner than usual and there were lines around his mouth that hadn't been there when I left nearly a year ago.

Sensing my discomfort, Papa pulled away. "You look almost surprised to see me, *parder*."

Leopard, in Khimaeran. He'd given me the name when, at eleven, I leaped onto his back from the top of an orange tree in the grove around the Little Palace.

"I thought you would be inside." Unable to hold his gaze, I turned toward the guard. They all dismounted and knelt in the dirt. "We've been riding night and day for five days. I'm sure everyone would like to rest."

Papa's eyes narrowed at my mother's soldiers as he gestured for them to rise. "Right. You must be exhausted. Shall we take the steps or . . ."

He glanced toward the base of the hill, where two large wooden platforms were attached to cords of woven leather. The lifts were used to raise supplies and people into Asrodei, because the steps built into the side of Asrodei's hill were narrow, old, and could be treacherous if you didn't watch your footing. I hated taking any of the lifts—often wind would roll through and set the entire thing swinging through the air— and I'd only gotten somewhat used to taking them during my years here.

"The lifts are fine," I said. They were more convenient for everyone. It would be selfish to demand that my guard and everyone else walk all the way up. It was an irrational fear anyway. When the winds became too strong, no one used the platforms.

Anali and my father chatted until we reached the loading area and I didn't hear a word of it, my thoughts too full of what I would say to my father once we were alone. We stepped onto the lifts. Papa, Aketo, and half of the guards formed a tight ring around me; Falun went with Baccha and more of the guards in the second lift.

When the first gust of wind caught the bottom of the platform, my knees buckled. How I hated being at the mercy of this little scrap of wood.

Everyone on the lift was facing away from me, except for Aketo, who held out a hand. I took it, and our fingers interlaced. The lift swayed again; I held on to him so tightly I thought my fingers would cramp. His thumb stroked the back of my hand until my pulse slowed and I could breathe around the fear.

For a horrible moment, I wondered if this was his magick. But no, I decided. Magick was rarely this subtle. And in my tent Aketo had said that he and his mother never changed anyone's emotions without their consent. If he did, he was no better than Isadore.

Seconds later the sounds of twisting leather stopped. The lift had been pulled up to one of the open ledges at the base of the Fort. I let go of Aketo's hand and hurried off behind my father, glad to find my feet on stable ground.

I didn't get the chance to thank Aketo. Anali ushered him off with the rest of the soldiers. Only my father and a few of his Kingsguard stayed. Papa turned to me, brown eyes tight with worry. "Now it seems there is much we have to discuss. Things in Ternain must be truly dire if your mother let you out of her sight this close to your nameday."

"They are, but that isn't why I'm here. I came to ask you about my Harkening."

Papa's eyes widened, but the shock was quickly replaced by resolve. "Very well. I'll tell you whatever you want to know."

We walked through the familiar gray halls of Asrodei in strained silence, a few members of his Kingsguard trailing behind so they wouldn't hear our conversation.

The Fort was a hive of activity. Groups of soldiers saluted Papa as we passed and clerks in ink-stained tabards trotted along carrying maps and long sheets of parchment. The Queen's Army employed hundreds of craftspeople— blacksmiths, fletchers, seamstresses, and more—and many worked in Asrodei, bowing low as we walked by. Papa was well acquainted with most everyone we passed, and I recognized the head blacksmith's son, broad-shouldered with a dimpled smile that had once made me blush, but we didn't speak to anyone as we moved through the Fort.

Hands clasped behind his back, frown etching lines around his mouth, Papa finally spoke. "Mira wrote me. She told me about the assassin and Dagon."

"I'm so sorry, Papa," I whispered, blinking away sudden tears. As with every time I thought of Dagon, I felt the warmth of his blood on my hand. "I didn't want to hurt him, but there was nothing I could do."

My words sounded hollow. Dagon would never draw breath, never laugh or cry again. And it was all because someone so wanted me dead they had used him as a pawn.

"You were defending yourself. You have nothing to apologize for, Eva," my father said.

"He's still dead, Papa. By my hand."

"The cursed Sorceryn who set that spell on Dagon is to

blame. And even more to blame is whoever set the Sorceryn on the task of killing you. I should have never let you go back to the Palace without me. I've been away from the capital too long. I will make certain you're safe here. I confess I am glad your mother saw fit to give you additional guards." He paused as a towering red-haired man approached us in the hallway, seemingly to try to speak to Papa. Even though the cobalt dagger pin on his chest marked him as a General, Papa waved him away. "Mira also told me that you've been learning magick with the Lord Hunter. I think I know why you've come."

I clenched my fists, trying to remain calm. "Why, Papa? Why bind my magick?"

"Because"—he sighed heavily—"of the omens."

"Omens?" I echoed, stopping in the middle of hall. A tapestry hung from the wall near me, depicting some ancient, blood-drenched battlefield. The sight of it turned my stomach. "But what does the Blood Moon have to do with my magick?"

"It was more than that, Eva. Four months before you were born, there was an eclipse, what the Auguries call 'the Black Sun.' It was the day after your mother announced her pregnancy to the Court. Weeks after that, there was a shower of stars in the sky above Ternain. The Auguries had predicted the Blood Moon's rising well before your nameday, and the falling stars, but the eclipse . . . surprised them. It's a rare omen and troubling enough that one of the Auguries went behind your mother's back and came to me. They believed the Queen wasn't taking the threat to you seriously."

I knew the Blood Moon was a harbinger of change, and

all omens of falling stars relate to magick, but the eclipse . . .
"What does the Black Sun mean?"

"It's an omen of great danger. The Sisters believed your magick would threaten you, perhaps even bring about your death. Sister Amya was fearful enough that she suggested sealing away your magick until you came of age, and then you would be allowed to decide to embrace your magick . . . or not."

"And you agreed? How did you expect me to survive against Isadore without my magick?" I growled, rounding on him. A bitter taste coated my tongue.

His hand trembled as he rubbed his forehead. "I spent months researching the effects of bindings and knew I couldn't allow you to be severed from your magick completely. With the help of a Sorceryn I'd known for years, I came up with another solution. A binding that would allow the use of some magick, but would limit the use of your greatest powers. It seemed like the best option at the time."

"Even when I can use my magick," I said, voice cold, "the binding still pains me. It grows worse every time."

"I'm sorry." His eyes, shining with unshed tears, met mine. "I was trying to protect you, parder."

"There can be no more lies between us, Father," I said, voice as cold and remote as I could make it. It was my best approximation of Mother's voice when she was giving edicts to the Court.

He nodded. "I promise you, Eva. I'll tell you everything."

"Why didn't you tell me before? You may have protected me from one danger, but by never telling me and never giving me an opportunity to fix it, you've left me weak," I said.

"I know," he answered, head bowed. "I've wanted to tell you all this time. I tried, but I didn't think you would forgive me. Not after what happened."

All my anger and confusion were like a hard pit in my stomach. "What are you talking about, Papa?"

What more could there be?

My father looked me in the eye as he answered: "Brother Kaar, the Sorceryn who placed the binding, is dead. He was killed eight years ago, just before you turned nine."

Papa continued to explain how Brother Kaar had been found with his throat slit and how when my father went to the Temple to collect the Sorceryn's research on bindings, he found that they were all destroyed. And that Brother Kaar had been attempting to learn the secrets of marrow and blood magick so that he could help me navigate the binding. After Kaar's death, Papa had searched the Queendom for someone else to teach me magick, planning to confess as soon as he found someone. But he hadn't. I'd found Baccha on my own.

I was only half listening; I walked with my arms wrapped around my stomach as my pulse drummed in my ears.

My father had always been infallible to me. Even his mistakes—like waiting to tell me about the Rival Heirs—were made because he wanted to keep me from being hurt. He had protected me from Mother when I asked to leave Ternain. He'd taught me most everything I knew that was worth knowing—how to hold a sword and ride a horse and that Myre was made up of more than the nobles who held power.

But he'd lied. I thought of all the times we'd spent together in these same walkways, every lesson he'd taught me on military theory, the meals shared, each visit to the library when he could have taken me to this Sister Amya. He could have told me anytime, but instead he'd let me believe he was perfect.

He was right. I couldn't forgive him. Rage had coiled around my heart, and my father's apologies only made feel colder.

Unless I wanted to risk my life, I was stuck with this binding. Only Brother Kaar could have removed it safely. And if the omens were true, maybe that was for the best.

⇥ CHAPTER 21 ⇤

I slept long and hard after retiring to my rooms. By the time I woke the following day, it was already well into the afternoon. I declined an invitation to have lunch with my father.

Anger had worn me down till not just my heart but my skin felt raw.

I would have stayed in my rooms for the rest of day, but Falun brought a note from Baccha. It was time for our next lesson.

I sat across from the Hunter at a round table in his room. It was nicer than I expected, large for a bedroom, with a green patterned rug spread across the tiled floor, a spacious sitting area, and a circular window looking out on the green hills around the Fort. There was a long, flat white box on the table between us; Baccha's pale fingers held its edges, flexing ever so slightly.

Through our bond, I could feel his avidity, tart as mazi fruit in the spring.

I dropped the coin on the table. "Before we begin, tell me how you came to have this."

Baccha tensed. "I thought you'd agreed to let me keep my secrets, Princess."

"I did, and that agreement might've held if you hadn't lied."

"Oh?" Baccha murmured. "And when was this?"

"You said you spent the last hundred years in Dracol. Mira said every coin in your possession was stamped like this. Why didn't you mention traveling through the Roune Lands?"

"The next time," he said tightly, "one of your people invades my privacy, these lessons are done."

"They won't need to after you tell me the truth. Why are you here, Baccha?"

"There are things in my past that I am not . . . allowed to speak of. You'll have to be satisfied with not knowing. Remember at Court I told you of oaths made in blood. I was bound three times over: in my own blood, in that of my kin, and in the blood of the Queen who first held my leash. The oath cannot be broken. This, speaking of it plainly, is as much as I can reveal without—" He broke off with a twitch. "Please, Princess."

His pain was like acid, reverberating through the bond. I watched that fine-boned face, those ancient honey-brown eyes that never seemed ancient, the gold color of his skin, and the utterly inexplicable nature of him. He was paler now, his face thinned out with pain, but he was still Baccha. And with him, I'd come farther, come closer to survival than I ever could have alone.

"Isn't there some way we can break it?"

"Short of killing me, no. You'll recall that I am immortal," he said with a sardonic smirk.

"How can I trust you, then?" *You can't,* my thoughts whispered. *You can only trust yourself.*

"You have my oath that I will never hurt you. That is all I can offer." He hung his head. "I'm sorry."

"Is any of this connected to Raina?"

"Only tangentially. I can speak of her freely."

"Good, I want to hear her story now. I know she must be next."

"She is, though I won't tell her story as I've told the others, since in this case I was actually there myself. In those days, the Queen chose three handmaidens—fey, human, and bloodkin—after the tradition started when the fey and khimaer nation became one. They were chosen from among the finest Houses in the Queendom. Often, if the Queen favored one of her maidens, she would arrange her marriage to one of the khimaer nobles at Court. It was considered a great honor, marrying into a noble khimaer tribe. It was Raina's dream to be chosen as handmaiden. Her family was one of great wealth, but of only middling stature at Court. And as humans, they held little power. The Queen wouldn't have considered them at all, but Raina and her sister, Amara, were prodigies.

"Amara could use her magick of wind and flame to take flight. Raina's gifts, though, were less palatable to the Court. She knew the magick of strangers whenever she met them, and she could close wounds just as easily as open them. She treated magick as a Sorceryn would, tattooing her skin every time she discovered a new ability. But in the end, the Queen chose Amara. I met Raina two years after that; she was nineteen, teaching magick at a small school on the outskirts of Ternain.

"When I wasn't working for the crown, I tracked any intriguing magicks so that I might eventually learn them. Raina was a stubborn thing, and troubled. Sometimes she was aloof as a house cat. Other times she wanted to know every detail of the goings-on at Court and if it included news of Amara, even better. I didn't think she would agree to instruct me, but one day she sought me out and agreed. All she asked was that I bring her to the Queen's Palace as a guest. I should have considered the night she chose, but I underestimated her, thought her small. She was scheming from the first time we spoke.

"It was a festival night, and the Queen was hosting the nobles. At the end of the gathering, the Queen toasted Amara and announced her betrothal to the Queen's brother. Raina didn't flinch. The Court dispersed; I lost sight of her and knew then that I'd made a terrible mistake. By the time I found Raina, she'd already killed the Queen and her sister.

"That was the night," Baccha finished, "the Great War began."

"So we'd come to this land, sworn fealty to its rulers, and then betrayed them with the very gift they gave us at every turn."

I didn't realize I'd spoken aloud till Baccha answered, "Yes, you've summed it up quite succinctly."

He pushed the box to the center of the table. "Now shall we begin your lesson?"

"Wait, I want to know more about Raina. Why did she do it? Were you in Ternain during the war?"

"Because she didn't like being denied power. And no."

"Then where were you?"

"In the mountains, helping people fleeing the country because of the war." He tapped the box. "Open it."

"What is it?"

"The horns. I thought we would have to wait until we returned to Ternain to make something of these, but I found a serviceable jeweler among the artisans here who had what I needed. I had a couple coins melted down, and, well . . ."

I lifted the top. The thick bottom parts of the horns were attached by a gold chain and the tips were coated in gold.

"Hold your hand above the box." I did as he asked. "Close your eyes."

This sounded like some grand setup for a joke at my expense, but I closed my eyes without complaint.

"What do you feel?"

Gentle warmth spread out from my palm, tingling in my fingertips. My pulse sped and the pounding at the base of my neck—a symptom of the lingering headache I'd had since the raid—lessened.

The warmth suffused through my limbs until I felt lighter, relaxed, and well rested.

"What *is* that?" I said with a gasp.

"The bone claiming." Baccha hooked a finger around the edge of the box and pulled it from under my hand. The warmth lessened gradually until I felt cold, weak without it. "These horns hold both the energy you expended claiming them and the antelope's energy. It's a heady mix."

"But it didn't make me intoxicated, Baccha. I felt . . ."

"Energized? Better than you've felt in weeks?" I nodded. "That's marrow magick. While blood magick is used on your foe, marrow magick affects *your* body. That energy is what will give you an edge over your opponent."

Baccha pulled another box from his jacket pocket. It was much smaller than the first. "I had the jeweler make another trinket."

Inside sat two round gold bracelets. They were too small to fit around my wrist and much too wide to be rings. Baccha curled two fingers around the bracelets and lifted them from the box. The bond began to hum. "He shaved off a bit from the bottom of each horn and I used a bit of my blood and yours—"

The skin on the back of my neck prickled. "And where did he get my blood?"

"I wouldn't worry about that, Princess. Anyway, he made these—"

"*Baccha!*" I shook my head. "Actually, never mind. I'd rather not know."

"When you were ill in Ternain, I retrieved a sample. Blood is always useful." He smiled, the very picture of innocence. He handed me one of the bracelets and slipped the other onto his hand. I watched as it stretched around his knuckles, and then shrank back down to fit around his wrist. "Go on, put it on."

I slid the bracelet over my fingers; it ran like liquid metal over the back of my hand. A cord of light appeared, wrapped around my wrist, connecting Baccha and me. I tried to grasp it, but it dissolved when I touched it. Even so, I still felt the cord, a gentle tugging, pulling me toward Baccha. "If I left the room, would I still feel it?"

"With concentration, yes. You could go anywhere and find me, just as long as we were both wearing them."

"But why, when I have this?" I held up my thumb with the ring Baccha had giving me during our coalescence on it.

"Because with this, we can communicate both ways. If you should need me, just give it a tug." Baccha ran a finger over the edge of the bangle and I felt a lurch in my stomach. "I will know. It is simpler."

"Thank you, Baccha," I said.

Baccha leaned back and rubbed the golden stubble along his jaw. "Well, I thought they would be useful. After the raid, I thought you should have a proper way to summon me. Now onto using the horns. What do you and the antelope have in common?"

"Speed?"

He tilted his head to the side and thought for a moment. "Hmm, no. The antelope is swift, but its speed is purpose-ful—a different purpose than, say, a cheetah's. Consider the antelope's life. It is prey; it spends most of its life running from cats in the grasslands, dodging death at every turn. The weakest antelopes are killed early in life, but the strongest— one strong enough to live so long that it grew such horns— what do they have?"

"Survival?" I murmured, almost to myself. I didn't love

this idea of me as an antelope being chased by a host of she-lions. "They're survivors."

"Yes, exactly. This is why I chose the antelope for your first claiming. This part of yourself—your ability to escape death—is of great value. Victory is about survival—knowing when to cut and run, knowing what wounds you can take and which you cannot. Leaving Ternain after that last attack was smart—it was survival." Baccha paused, fingers tracing the edge of the box again. "You will take well to these bones, Eva."

I didn't think it was so much my ability to survive, but a strange combination of luck and other people's abilities. While I had survived on my own the night in the Patch, only Aketo's skill kept me from death just a few days later. But why argue this? Perhaps I *would* take to the bones. I hoped so; they were lovely and I wanted to lose myself in that hum—that current of magick looping from me, to the horns and the creature I slew to claim them, and back again.

"Can I use them now?" I asked.

"They are meant to be worn hung around your neck."

I reached into the box and lifted the chain, feeling that warmth flow back into my hand.

I waited for any pain to build in my head, but there was nothing. I grinned and twined them around my neck. The points swung down to my stomach, and considering how heavy they were in my hands, I couldn't help but wonder how much these would impede my movement.

"How can I fight wearing these?"

"I wouldn't worry. Claimed bones have a way of moving out of the way when you need them to."

"If you say so. What's next?"

"Marrow magick is best in hand-to-hand fighting because it doesn't require the constant use of your tattoos."

"So, what, we go down to the Fort's Sandpits and fight?" He wasn't carrying a sword today—he rarely did—just lots of small knives.

I rather liked knife fighting. When I came to Asrodei, it had been a part of Anali's training. But Baccha was so long and quick and full of casual grace . . . I did not look forward to trying to best him.

"No, in here will do. I plan to mostly chase you." A knife appeared in his palm. "Aren't you going to run?"

"You can't expect me to run around this room," I said. The broad chamber was split into three sections, with a large four-poster bed on one side, low sofas for hosting guests in the middle, and the table where we sat now on the other end. There was more than enough room for him chase me, but the sharp edges on some of the furniture worried me just as much as Baccha's knife. "I could slip and break my neck."

"The antelope has amazing footing—hopefully so does the Princess." He leaned forward and the knife slid along the table, brushing the edge of the box. "And you did call yourself quick earlier."

"Please be serious," I said, though I was inching my chair back, preparing to jump out of it at any time. It wasn't as though I feared the knife. It was just that, well, every other time I had thought Baccha was joking about an element of our training—my hurting him repeatedly, the horns sawed off with only the moon to guide me—he'd been completely serious.

I surveyed the room behind him—noting the low settee in the back corner, the narrow table in front of it, and the surprisingly delicate chairs on either side—and then a gust of wind came from under the door.

Baccha vaulted onto the table in front of me. "Come now, Evalina. *Run.*"

One of Baccha's pale eyebrows arched, matching the mischievous twist of his lips, and that was all the provocation I needed. I kicked back the chair and stepped away from him. His eyes followed me, teeth sharp and shining between his lips. "Good girl."

It occurred to me that spending so much time with Baccha was like walking a lion on a leash and forgetting that the lion had teeth and sometimes liked to swallow men whole.

Still: I thought, I hoped, I could take him. "*Good girl?*" I said.

He inclined his head. "*Very* good, Lady Princess. You're finally understanding the hands-on nature of our lessons."

"What am I supposed to do?"

"Tap into the magick in the horns—they're meant for more than that warm energy buzzing through you now." Another knife slid neatly into the palm of his hand. He tested the edge on his thumb. A fat bead of blood welled from the cut and he stuck his thumb in his mouth. "See what they offer."

"That's all the instruction you're going to give me?"

Baccha leaned forward so quickly that I took a step back, even though I was well outside the range of his knives— unless he threw them. "If you manage to draw my blood, the exercise will have ended, but . . . until then."

Wind stirred my hair, sending a spike of fear into my chest.

I concentrated on the horns, my fingers resting slightly on the golden tips, but was only greeted with the same current of energy as earlier. I darted into the corner, wanting to put more space between us as a wild laugh sprang from his throat.

My knee banged against the smaller table on my way across the chamber. I squeezed the horns and a surge of energy pulsed through my limbs, chasing away the pain.

I turned and nearly yelped as Baccha's knife flashed like silver flame barely an inch from my face. I fell backward, the bones in my wrists grinding as I caught myself, scrambling away from Baccha.

I climbed to my feet. "Damn you, Baccha."

I looked around the room, trying to spot him. Shadows appeared at the corner of my vision, but as soon as I turned to face them—nothing. I called out his name, embarrassed to hear tremors in my voice. "Baccha, this isn't chasing. This is just you trying to scare me."

"Is it working?" he whispered in my ear.

The thing was, Baccha made more music than he realized. Each time he came near, I could hear his jewelry spinning through the air and the soft rustle of his hair. He moved dramatically, wildly, but even so, he was too quick for me to catch.

Wild laughter rang out, racing around the room on the wind. *At least he hasn't summoned the wolves,* I thought. Then I realized he might if I didn't figure out something soon.

What did he expect from me? I hooked my fingers around

the horns again, trying to pull some power from inside them. Energy came easily; stumbling around the room hadn't tired me, neither did there seem to be any lasting tenderness from my many falls. But there was nothing that made me a match for a half-visible Baccha. I squeezed them tighter, the twisted edges digging into my palms.

"Run," Baccha barked into my ear, startling me from clear across the room. "Run, run, *run*."

Pain stabbed at the center of my head as I ran. The horns must have only been able to chase away my headaches from the binding for a short time. I found myself leaning against the larger table.

How had I gotten across the room so quickly?

Baccha was sitting on top of the overturned settee, legs splayed lazily as he nodded with satisfaction. "See, I said antelopes have good footing. Well done, Eva. Now, again."

It was the horns, I realized, making me so much faster that it was dizzying.

Baccha blurred before my eyes, disappearing, then re-appearing inches away. Time slowed as the silver flash of his blade swung toward my neck. I ducked under the knife, punching him as I ran back toward the jumble of furniture on the other side of the room.

Suddenly Baccha was behind me. "Better, even better, and you weren't holding them that time."

I didn't think about the speed, the careful footing of an antelope—just felt the force of my annoyance at him. And bloody, *bloody* magick, the pain in my head was causing spots to swirl across my vision.

I drove my fist up under his ribs and plucked one of the

knives from behind his back. I slashed it across his face. Blood leaked down the edge of his slackened jaw.

Baccha wiped it away with a casual swipe of his hand. "Again?"

Instead of answering, I attacked again. We danced through the room, twisting and jabbing, flowing around each other, time slowing and stopping until I could hardly breathe. When we stopped, my hands were shaking.

"Enough," I gasped. I removed the horns and then sat down upon the floor. I was at my limit.

"I told you," he murmured, "it's a heady thing, marrow magick."

Yes, and it wasn't at all like blood magick, which pleased me. If I could use these two powers in tandem, I would be more than a formidable opponent for my sister.

I would be a threat.

⤙ Chapter 22 ⤚

I FOUND A note left on the small desk in my bedchamber when I woke two days later. Just one line. *Care to dance in the Pits?*

Aketo's writing was precise, though a smudge of ink at the bottom obscured half of his name.

Nearly an hour later I found myself in Asrodei's Sandpits, straddling Aketo's waist, sending up sprays of black dust as we grappled in the sand. Breathless at every look we shared, I fought like a demon.

"I think you've won this bout," he said through clenched teeth.

I punched him once more in the side and pressed my forearm against his neck. One of his arms was pinned beneath my knee, the other fisted in the hem of my tunic. His knuckles rubbed against my bare hip. If I'd had a blade, his throat would be slit by now.

I rolled off him and climbed to my feet. The sand was noisier—and more musical—than the dirt we'd fought on during the trip. I could always hear his attacks before they came, but it was difficult to move at his speed in the sand, so the difference was hardly felt.

Aketo, of course, moved with his same careless grace. This was the first bout where I had bested him.

I glanced at the swords cast aside a few feet away, trying not to think about it. "Shall we start with blades, Aketo?"

"Evalina, please. We should talk—"

"Another go, then?" I shook the sand from my hair and widened my stance.

It took only a breath to find the music and then I was twisting as I kicked, aiming for his chest.

Aketo ducked, his leg shooting out so quick, I had no time to deflect it. The breath went out of me and I landed on my bottom in the sand. Before I could jump to my feet, Aketo was standing over me. "Now, please—"

I kicked his feet out from under him. Aketo fell half on top of me, cursing when I punched him in the side. He rolled off me and just lay in the sand with his eyes shut. He might've been sleeping if not for the quick rise and fall of his chest and the sweat beading his brow.

We lay on our backs in the sand. Though we weren't touching, I could feel the heat from his body. I watched Aketo while I could. The black-and-gold line of scales down the back of his neck met black sands, and the rings in his ears glinted in the dull light of the Pits. He rolled onto his side and looked at me. The gold of his eyes was the same as the gold of his scales.

Gods, he was beautiful.

He rubbed at a purplish bruise on his jaw. "Are you done now?"

I sat up, hands fisting in the sand. "You said you wanted to dance. So let's dance."

"I'd rather talk," Aketo suggested.

"If this is about my father, I do not want to know." I did not want any more bad news just yet. I'd begun to feel guilty for ignoring Papa's invitations and had agreed to meet him for dinner tonight. If there was something else my father needed to tell me, I wanted to hear it from him.

"You can ask me whatever you wish, as long as you will agree to stop pummeling me."

I decided not to point out that he'd happily trounced me just days ago. "How does your magick work?"

"I sense the emotions of those around me and with touch I can change those feelings."

"My sister's magick is a bit like that. Her magick is named persuasion, but it is so much more insidious than that. She pushes her will into you. I've seen her magick make a courtier say and do things they wouldn't have said or done without it."

"To me that doesn't seem like my magick at all." His fingers laced through mine. "Can I show you?"

I looked at Aketo; his eyes were shut, his horns long and proud. "Yes."

I smelled cinnamon and orange blossoms as warmth spread from his hand into mine. It eased over my skin, coaxing a sigh from my lips. This feeling he'd given me was peace.

"I should tell you, the more time I spend with a person, the more aware of their emotions I become. Usually it takes years, but with you it started when I saved you from the poison. And grew deeper when you saved me during the raid."

"Well," I sputtered, "in truth, we saved each other. You've saved me twice now, so it is still uneven."

"I hope we can maintain the current ratio," Aketo said, a slow, sly smile spreading across his face. "I wouldn't want to get used to you saving me."

I was afraid that I wasn't ever going to stop wanting to look at him, afraid of how his hand felt in mine.

Aketo leaned over, and the hand that had been in mine moments ago slid up my arm to rest against my neck. "Would you mind terribly if I kissed you?"

I closed the distance between us, the only way I could think to wipe the smirk from his face.

"Oh." He murmured a soft sigh of surprise against my lips, bracing one hand on my hip, drawing us tightly together. Something unspooled in me when I realized just how neatly we fit.

Our heartbeats twined together until we were of one sound. His thumb moved in minute circles on the wing of my hip, his lips hot and instant against my mouth, stoking flames beneath my skin. My tongue slid along Aketo's bottom lip, and a growl vibrated through his chest into mine.

This, I thought. *Why did I wait for this?*

He jerked his head away. "I can feel their attention," he whispered right into the crook of my neck. "I only want to feel you."

We broke apart and I clenched my fists to keep from reaching for him again. I looked around to find my guards had mostly blocked us from view, but they were all looking over their shoulders, glancing furtively at the narrow space between us.

I found that I hardly cared.

✦

As we walked back to my chambers, I was pleased to observe how undone Aketo had become.

When I tried to lace our fingers together once we left the Sandpits, he looked at me like I'd lost all control of my senses. I laughed before taking his hand. It wasn't as if anyone who would have objected could have seen. The rest of the guard, including Falun, stood in a ring around us.

I glanced at Aketo, trying to find some way to break the charged silence between us. He was smiling too, smiling like he had a secret trapped behind his lips. But as we rounded the corner to the royal quarters, a choked gasp came from his mouth. "Where are your father's rooms?"

"What?"

"Eva." His voice was guttural, pained. "Where are your father's rooms?"

"Not far from here. Why?"

He spoke quickly, each word scrambling over the previous one. "I've spent enough time with King Lei that I can sense his feelings from here. He is in a great deal of pain." He grabbed my arm. "We must go to him now."

I rocked back as if he'd struck me. I choked out curt

241

instructions for the guard to fall away from me and pulled Aketo and Falun, the only guard I knew in my escort, aside. "We have to get to my father's rooms."

Falun gave me a blank look. "What's wrong?"

"Something is wrong with my father," I whispered, thankful I still had the presence of mind to whisper. I didn't want the entire Fort to erupt into panic. That would only slow us.

"How do you—"

I pulled Aketo into a sprint. My heart threatened to burst from my chest with each step. I ran faster than I ever had in my life. Aketo suddenly faltered, eyes wide and confused, rolling like a startled horse.

"Hurry," he said, voice gone rough. *"Hurry."*

I threw everything into the next step, and the next step, and more into the ones after that. A strange numbness came over me when we reached the double doors leading to my father's chambers. Aketo pulled the doors apart and then Falun appeared, shoving me behind him. There were weapons in all of our hands and I couldn't remember retrieving them. I couldn't even remember what turns and stairways had gotten us here.

There were no soldiers outside his rooms, as horrible a sign as anything.

I spotted three drops of blood on the woven rug carpeting the foyer. A whimper or a scream tore from my mouth and I pushed past them, so that I was the first one to see the blood covering every inch of the bedchamber and my father's broken body—his cut throat spilling blood as precious as rubies across the floor, and the jagged wound stretching from chest to navel.

242

At first, I was sure it wasn't real. All the blood and the magick and pain of the last days had gone to my head. But I blinked and blinked and everything was still shiny with freshly spilled blood.

And I could smell it, the reek of death and fresh meat and filth. My stomach rolled as I stumbled forward.

My heart gave one last shuttering beat and exploded in my chest.

↠ CHAPTER 23 ↞

A SCREAM POURED from my mouth like a column of fire meant to burn the earth to ash. Aketo and Falun stood near me. I saw them, saw the guards rushing into the room, but couldn't hear them.

There was only one sound: blood in the carpet, squelching and sucking at my boots as I stumbled forward. There were only two feelings: warm blood soaking into my pants as I fell to my knees and the bristle of my father's beard as I placed my hand on his cheek.

"Papa?" I gasped. He was still warm, broadsword clutched in his right hand, and his eyes, blessedly, were closed. His skin free from the creases of worry he'd always worn. If I hadn't had to move so carefully, trying not to touch any of the viscera spilling from his stomach, I could have believed he'd simply fallen asleep. "Papa, Papa, Papa."

My vision narrowed, blackness crowding out vivid color, but a sound drew my attention. My eyes zeroed in on the right side of the room. The edge of one of the tapestries hanging down to the floor fluttered.

The one knife I had left flew toward it. I ran, leaping over a chest, upturning a table, dragging Papa's sword, and screaming as I swung it in a great arc.

The bottom half of the tapestry fell to the floor, finely woven and moving like water. The body behind it was that of a woman with ocher skin and a tangle of raven hair, her face veiled, gurgling, spurting blood from the chest I'd just cleaved in two.

The sword clattered to the floor. I screamed and screamed until the black came again to crowd out all the red.

My eyes opened to Anali's face, her eyes swollen and red-rimmed. I flipped over to the edge of the bed as spasms racked my empty stomach.

The look on her face set me to chewing the insides of my cheeks. Her grief was an open wound, impossible to avoid. Her eyes were wide and shiny.

Her hands moved without ceasing, adjusting her jacket, inching toward her sword. I had left her to deal with everything. I should have been able to handle it, I should have—

"What do we know?"

Anali blinked down at me. "There were six, including the one you killed. All Dracolan."

"The one I killed?"

"The woman you killed was the sixth—"

"What woman?" I remembered only seeing my father, kneeling next to him, and then—nothing.

"One of the assassins, the only one your father and his guards hadn't killed, had hidden behind a tapestry. Falun told me you saw her before the guard did and killed her."

I closed my eyes, trying to remember. There was a face, high yellow skin, and black hair, and the feeling of warm blood splattering across my chest.

I forced myself to keep speaking. "Has anyone been in his rooms yet? Anyone besides you and the guard?"

"I've kept everyone out so far, but I've told the Generals. I told them we wouldn't move forward until you woke."

"What time is it?" Was it the same afternoon, evening?

"You slept all night." She hesitated. "It's early afternoon."

My father had been dead nearly an entire day and I had slept through it. *My father was dead, my father had been killed, my father, my father—*

No. I clenched my fists until my nails drew blood. "Give the Generals my order to keep my father's room sealed until I can sort through his things. We'll have to send people in to clean and attend to the—the bodies." I closed my eyes. There was no part of me that wanted this, but delaying would be impossible. "Assemble the entire Fort in a few hours. I'll have to announce what's happened and choose an interim Lord Commander. I'm sure Papa had someone in mind. Then I suppose we'll have to leave."

Anali bowed her head and helped me out of bed. Someone must have bathed me, because I wore fresh underclothes beneath the blankets.

"Your Highness, I am so—" Anali began as soon as I'd stepped away from the bed.

"Anali, I think for now we should skip all of that." I only had to get through this. Just today, I reminded myself. Then I could dissolve.

"Eva, your father—" Her voice cut off in a ragged sob. I noticed things in small degrees. Her white hair was undone, stuffed into a knot at the back of her head, matted and frizzy. Her jacket was rumpled, the buttons closed incorrectly. "Your father is gone and I—"

"See, Anali, talking about it will only make things worse." I would isolate the pain somehow. Until then, I would ignore it.

I could not come apart until I had cared for my father. "Anali, I'm going to find out who did this."

"Your Highness, they were Dracolan. Everyone is already calling it an act of war."

"Do you think a team of Dracolan assassins could get into this Fort unaided? No, someone powerful is a part of this and they will see justice."

Mirabel always talked about how everyone had an inner core of strength, but didn't realize it until they needed it. I would just have to find mine.

And there was a thing I needed in order to do so. I couldn't ignore my feelings when people around me had access to them. "Anali, I need you to keep Aketo and Baccha away in the next days."

She only stared at me, but finally nodded. "As you wish, Your Highness."

- III -
KHIMAER MAGICK

Of all the wonders in Myre, they kept this from us for nearly a century. The strange, illusive magick of their foremother—the most ancient of them all. The khimaer say they cannot teach us this power, but one wonders if this is the truth. Is it simply another matter of them hoarding power?

—Journals of Kenyon Neion, Sorceryn among the first human settlers in Myre, from *Old Lore and Magickes in the Age of the Godlings*

━ CHAPTER 24 ━

ROBES OF QUILTED cotton and cobalt organza hung heavy on my shoulders.

The humming of the Sorceryn and a sea of courtiers and Myreans buzzed around me, sounding more like a hive of angry bees than was comforting. I should have hummed along with them, but my lips were shut tight. We stood on the banks of the Red River, gathered to mourn my father's death. The sun was high, and the grand city wall of Ternain rose behind us, but the noise and energy of the city seemed far away.

It had been two weeks since I returned to the Palace. I'd stayed at Asrodei for half a week to make arrangements before traveling to the capital, though I had not wanted to return.

In those two weeks, I hadn't spoken one word beyond what was required of me—pretending it was grief that kept my lips sealed and not fear of letting the unending anger spill out. Even as I tried, even as I knew my father *deserved* this tribute, this small thing I could give him, seeing him smoothly into death, no sound escaped me.

I was playing the grieving Princess, empty but for my sorrow over my father's death. Inside I was all rage—and I was helpless. But the show must continue.

Isadore, Mother, and I were all painted accordingly—streaks of gold and white across our cheeks and under our eyes—as if we were all the same in our mourning. A bead of sweat rolled from my temple down to my chin and I almost hoped the dripping paint would stain the robes. The paint was chalky and oppressive and the combined heat of the robes and the sun made me light-headed and dizzy. I wanted to throw off the garments, wipe my face clean, and run back into the Palace before the Sorceryn lit the pyre.

But I couldn't.

My fingers laced through my mother's and my expression held only a pale imitation of the real pain I felt. That pain was a scream that lived deep within my chest. It never left me.

I was dimly aware that I shook, muscles locked tight enough to cramp. My hands were like claws scrabbling at my mother. I wondered if I could squeeze her hand tightly enough for her to show a reaction in front of all these people. The King was so well loved; thousands had journeyed to Ternain once the news of his death spread. It felt like I was standing before everyone in Myre.

And it all felt so wrong.

Mother's gaze didn't waver from the Sorceryn, but I felt her attention shift to me. "Behave," she breathed, in the same cadence and tone as the Sorceryn's mourning chant.

Thoughtless, I glared at her. She squeezed my hand so

tight her nails cut into my flesh. Wasn't she worried about the blood, ruining the perfect sight of us? Blood had no place among all this royal blue and white.

Wasn't she worried?

"Behave," she repeated. I glanced beyond her and watched a sneer flash across Isadore's face. I would burn alive keeping this boiling rage inside.

I looked back toward the pyre, but not before Isa's eyes caught mine. They were swollen and rimmed in red, but when she looked at me, they grew cold.

I shut my eyes and I could still see my sister, the one I knew well. Isadore and I were young, perhaps six and eight years old. We'd joined Mother before some ball we were both too young to attend. We knotted towels around our waists like gowns, relaxing with Mother in her luxurious dressing room, nearly the size of my entire suite. Five or six women floated around her, each applying a different cosmetic. Isa and I got into every pot of cream, every vial of pigment, and all her sticks of kohl.

We'd hung necklaces around our heads like crowns and practiced our dancing.

Mother had laughed at the mess we made and sent us back to our rooms painted, perfumed, and pampered from head to toe, chubby hands full of the fruit tarts she favored.

My eyes filled with tears at my mind's betrayal. It had not always been like this. Mother's hand tightened like a vise around mine, drawing me back to reality. I blinked the tears away, refusing to let them fall.

The pyre lay on a flat-hulled boat, piled with timber at the bottom and a profusion of blossoms on top. They were the plants of our sigils, blue lilies for Mother, orange poppies for me, and Isadore's verdant ivy woven throughout. The pyre was crowned with a deceptively small body wrapped in a white shroud. How many layers had they wrapped him in, to keep all the blood from dampening the shroud?

Beside me, Mother called out: "Now."

I jerked as a stream of fire exploded from the hands of the Sorceryn near the river's edge. Flames caught on the bottom layer of timber. My knees buckled and my chest felt crowded—my heart containing too many things, eating me up inside. Only Mother's iron grip kept me on my feet.

Fit for a King, the magickal fire would take hours to burn, creating a steady flow of ashes down the river. At the banks of the Red River, west beyond Ternain, Myreans would gather to watch the ashes of their King flow downriver. Here we were to stand waiting until the flames ate up his shrouded body. Many would leave to escape the heat, but we couldn't. Hours with my hand in Mother's, with my sister just a few feet away, threatened my sanity.

I didn't know who had ordered the assassination of my father, though I was sure now that it was the same person trying to kill me.

There was one week left until my nameday. How was I to kill Isadore when I was too weak to stand? When the thought of shedding more blood made me want to forfeit everything? If only my anger at Isadore and Mother would focus me, sharpen me like a blade, instead of turning me into this cowering thing. I had little strength, but I did have rage to bolster me.

It whispered a truth I didn't want to face. My family had

done all they could to undermine me. They'd kept secrets, withheld their affection, lied, and manipulated me. I loved my mother and Isadore, but I could not trust them with my heart or the Queendom that I loved despite its flaws. Since they fought to keep me from the throne, I would find a way to take it.

I imagined a narrow box and inside it I locked away everything my mother was but for *Queen* and *obstacle*. And then I made more space, putting away everything Isadore was to me except *enemy*.

I stared into the churning depths of the river, my father's ashes fading into dark red-brown. A river of royal blood, Papa's now, and soon it would also be full of either mine or Isadore's.

It took some time, but I stood taller. I breathed deeply; though the air burned in my throat, I welcomed it. I allowed the smoke to cloud my mind and bade my thoughts to silence, except for one refrain: *enemy, obstacle, Queen.*

⇥ CHAPTER 25 ⇤

HOT WIND CARESSED my back as I climbed over my balcony railing. My fingers, gloved and steady, curled around the wrought-iron ledge. I closed my eyes as my foot sought the edge of a nearby brick.

I braced myself for a moment, feeling just how easily I could fall. It was only a fifteen-foot climb down to the suite below mine, but it was a sheer drop straight to the gardens of the royal courtyard below.

The metal bit into my fingers as my breath eased out of me. I was no closer to death than I'd been in recent months, but this did away with the illusion. And for the first time, I was the one in control of my own mortality.

I began the downward climb. After ten breathless maneuvers over terrifyingly narrow edges of sandstone, I pulled my trembling body over a balcony similar to mine. The door was locked, but after three well-placed kicks, it swung open.

Mirabel had boarded up the hatch beneath my bed while I was away, so I'd had to be more creative in my escapes.

I found a hidden door inside the dressing room of the unused suite below mine and was out of the Palace so quickly I surprised even myself.

I'd braided my hair back earlier and tucked it beneath a cap. In plain brown trousers with a jacket that somewhat minimized my chest, it was the best I could do for a disguise. The particular blood-orange color of my eyes was a problem, after such a recent public appearance, but I would keep them shaded under the bill of the cap. If I saw recognition in anyone's face, I would be gone before they could tell a soul.

There were two slums in Ternain: the Patch and, even worse, the Tiger's Den, where the small Dracolan population lived. Since Papa's death four weeks ago, piles of garbage had been left to fester in the streets. The steward assigned to these streets was clearly ignoring his duty, but few Myreans would notice or care. The crown had announced that Papa's murder and the attack on my camp during the ride to Asrodei were plots orchestrated by the Dracolan King.

I was convinced that if Dracol's King Lioniten was truly involved, he must have had help from someone with power in Myre. How else would six Dracolans have infiltrated Fort Asrodei? But despite the many arguments I'd made to my mother, she would not change her mind.

I had never hated her more.

I supposed it was more convenient for her. She didn't have to pretend she actually cared about Papa's death, and she could turn her eyes toward Dracol. The drums of war were on the cusp of being sounded. My nameday, just three days from now, was the reason for the hesitation. The Court wanted the succession decided before they made any decisions. Dracolans had been aggressive for decades, but this was the first significant attack that Myreans could truly blame on them. War was being discussed, as well as the pressing need to name a True Heir.

I walked until I reached the farthest edge of Ternain.

People were dying in the Tiger's Den, attacked to avenge Papa's death. With the Dracolans possessing none of our magick, they were easy targets, and Mother wasn't doing a thing to protect them. The guards assigned to patrol those streets, soldiers all of them, had abandoned their posts. So I was expecting danger.

When I realized someone was following me, I slid a knife into my palm.

I felt no fear. Death had been perched on my shoulder for months. This was hardly an adjustment.

When the hand landed on my shoulder, I whipped around, my knife sliding across the man's face.

The blood was on my arm and magick coiled around the knife in two blinks. This, at least, I could manage despite the binding. Any leftover bitterness I felt at not having full access to my magick was lost momentarily in the wonder of protecting myself.

Pain stabbed at my mind, raking it with claws, but I gritted my teeth and—

"Princess, it's me," Baccha growled. "*Bloody magick*, couldn't you tell?"

My concentration slipped and the loss of the magick left me reeling.

"What are you doing here?" I shoved him away. "Why are you following me?"

He grabbed my hands when I made a second attempt. "Princess, I happen to think the most important question is, *What are you doing in the Tiger's Den?*"

"None of your concern," I grunted, snatching my hands away.

"Oh, Princess," he said. "Just because you don't want someone to care doesn't mean they can just stop."

My eyes slid to Baccha's right, where Aketo stood. My thoughts stalled and I forgot the next thing I was going to say. I shut my eyes tight, teeth sawing at my bottom lip as I took a deep breath.

The concerned expression on Aketo's face was exactly what I expected. If he could feel the rage that rattled around in my chest like a wild animal, the dread at my quickly approaching nameday, the panic that made it hard to breathe in the small hours of the night. I couldn't handle suddenly being in front of both of them after these weeks alone. Alone like I needed to be to get through this and find out who killed my father.

I tried not to look at Aketo head-on. On my worst nights, I dreamed of how I'd been kissing him before finding Papa dead. And I woke up longing for his touch, because at least I could get lost in it.

I couldn't see Aketo, because he could fix it. If he was with me all day, he could push away the pain so it didn't make me forget where—and who—I was. He could make it so I could sleep at night. So that I wouldn't wake up choking on the smell of my father's blood and having to crawl into my dressing room so the guards outside wouldn't hear me screaming.

But he would tire of me. How long would it take until I snapped at him the way I snapped at Mirabel? How long before he was avoiding me?

When his eyes flicked to me, my entire body clenched.

"Eva, how are you?"

"I'm sure you can already tell." My body shifted toward him, but I kept my eyes to the ground. "Why are you here?"

"We're following you, Princess. So unless you want us to continue and ruin whatever likely ill-conceived plans you have, tell me. What are you doing out tonight?"

I pulled my hat down and strode forward.

They both matched my stride. "Princess?"

"There is a tavern here. A rough place." For the first time in weeks, I let my consciousness slide toward the bond. Worry. Of course. The same feeling colored every word Mira and Anali said to me. I didn't need the bond to know Baccha would feel the same.

"And why are we going to this tavern, darling?" Baccha asked. "You might as well tell me."

"You're a pushy bastard, you know that, right?" I shook my head. Oh, he knew. "I'm going there to see if anyone knows who might have hired the Dracolans who killed my father."

Baccha stopped me with a hand on my shoulder. "What makes you think that's what you'll find?"

"Because King Lioniten did not orchestrate the plan to kill my father on his own. I'm sure of it."

Baccha gave me a long slow blink. "Go on."

"It isn't right," I whispered. "I'm sure there is someone noble involved. I just need proof. Killing the King is a death sentence. And I will deliver the execution myself."

The only person exempt from that sentence was the Queen. But if my mother was knowingly keeping the Queendom focused on Dracol instead of investigating who was really to blame, it might be enough to force her from the throne within the next year.

It wouldn't stop Isadore from challenging me, but without Mother's support, she would have less power over the Court.

"Eva," Baccha said softly, in the kind of voice I'd use to calm someone threatening to step off a ledge. "Are you sure this is wise?"

I ignored him, striding forward purposefully even though I had completely lost my bearings. I clenched my trembling fingers into fists.

For a moment I felt this warmth curling around my thoughts and I drew in a deep breath—because I suddenly *could*. I twisted around to glare at Aketo. "Stay out of my head. If you can't control your magick, maybe it would be better if you stayed away from me."

"That isn't me," he said softly, though he couldn't hide his frustration completely.

"It's me, Eva," Baccha said. "You're feeling my emotion from the bond for the first time in weeks. You can't shut me out when I'm right in front of you."

"Stay out of my—"

"Sweetheart," he murmured. "We're in the middle of an alley in the Tiger's Den. If you want to have it out, we can return to the Palace."

"My nameday is in a few days." I stared both of them

down. "And you are delaying me. You may go back, but I'm doing this."

Baccha and Aketo exchanged a look, but made no move to leave.

"Follow without questioning me or get lost. Got it?"

A few minutes later, we ducked into a dim little room. It was a bleak place, no name, just a sign posted up that said ALE. Seven mismatched tables were spread across the room. The smell of browning pork hung in the air and every table had a greasy sheen. Sawdust covered the floor. There was one barmaid moving through the room and maybe twelve men scattered around.

Once we sat, the barmaid slung three glasses of cloudy wine onto the table. Like most Dracolans, her skin was pale golden brown. She wore a long skirt, stained along the hem, and her hair was in a haphazard knot of silky black tangles at the back of her head.

She gave Aketo a long look, but I was fairly certain it was because he was lovely and not because he was khimaer. He'd worn a scarf around his neck to hide his scales and the lamp-light made something of his eyes, seeming to light them from within.

I pulled off my gloves and reached for the wine, but before I could snag it, Baccha dumped half of mine into his cup.

"I think you'd do better without this, Princess," he said.

I bared my teeth. "I don't care what you—"

He rolled his eyes. "So what is the plan?"

I had a coin purse stuffed deep in one of my pockets. I'd planned to find a way into a game of cards, or dice, or tiles, and then just ask around. I hadn't done all that much planning once I read of the place in Mirabel's notes.

When the barmaid came nearby again, I reached out and caught her hand. "Have you seen anyone strange sniffing around here?"

"You mean besides you?" she asked, voice thick with a drawling accent.

She glanced down at my hand around her arm, her eyes widening at the red lacquer coating my fingernails. I pulled away.

Stupid mistake. Most common folk would not have their nails manicured.

Baccha rattled off a stream of syllables I couldn't understand, but recognized as Dracolan. Of course he spoke Dracolan with the fluency of a native. Hadn't he been hiding out there for centuries?

Baccha and the barmaid exchanged a few words, and then he pointed his chin in my direction and nodded at her. She turned to me, but hesitated.

"Go on, tell her," he murmured in Common. Khimaer and fey called it the human tongue, but it had been declared the Common tongue when human Queens took the throne, as if the name would bring us together.

"Like this one." She grimaced, pointing at Baccha. "But *not so*. Brown-skinned, pale hair but strange. Like a blue or a green. You know how they look—pretty but *wrong*."

So a pretty fey had been here, not as particular as Baccha, but prettier than most if she felt the need to mention it. One with blue or green hair . . .

Immediately I knew who it must have been.

When I last saw Isa at Court, she was with Lord Katro. Lord Katro, with the softly waving green hair, known for his unique beauty and well-connected fey family, but not for his intelligence. Nor was he known for plotting or scheming of any kind.

"Green?" I asked. "Are you sure?"

The barmaid shrugged. "I saw him just once—sent Neshiko to run him off."

I assumed Neshiko was the muscle-bound young man with a dimpled chin and cudgel in hand who sat near the young woman playing a three-string harp in one corner of the room.

"Does she—do you think Lioniten would have ordered the killing of King Lei?"

"Who else?" The girl shrugged. It wasn't much of an answer. To her, the answer to my question could have just as easily been, *Who cares?*

We sat in silence after she left. It felt like there was a lead weight on my chest, but I also felt empty, listless suddenly. Was it that simple? Working to find this place for weeks and immediately having my answer? Katro, one of Isa's known friends at Court? I could make my way to his rooms right now and put a knife to his throat to see what insights he could offer.

I glanced up at Baccha. It seemed he'd had the same thought. He gave me a pleading look. "I'll collect him, Eva. Let me soften him for you, then we can question him in the morning."

If he thought I was going to let him take the reins on this, he was mistaken. "I would rather—"

"Let me do this, Princess. You can't go marching up to this man and expect him to come quietly." His eyes said what both of us knew: it would be too dangerous for me. If Katro had a hand in the King's death, he might think little of hurting me. It wasn't as if I could enlist my guard or Mirabel to help. Whenever I spoke of investigating Papa's death, all their concern became focused on me.

Getting me to talk. Making me practice swordplay, as if that mattered. All foolish wastes of time.

Baccha looked meaningfully toward Aketo, eyebrows wiggling suggestively. I was right to avoid them; I was shifting focus already, worrying about them instead of Papa.

I explained a number of places where Baccha was likely to find Katro, all in the Palace. "Just . . . don't question him without me."

He nodded, face sober. "Of course not." Then Baccha leaned forward, casting his voice low. "Find me in the morning, both of you. Until then, how you spend your time is no concern of mine. I trust you can keep each other safe."

He reached out and tapped Aketo's hand, but when he spoke, he looked right at me. "Good luck."

And then Baccha left the two of us alone.

Aketo's eyes didn't move from his empty cup.

"Let's get out of here." The patrons were eyeing us sharply. We left the tavern and walked in charged silence. My head was so full of him that I couldn't think of anything else.

Time slowed to a crawl while I stared at him. "Aketo?"

He glanced up. "Ah, I'm sorry. It's only I'm considering what to say. Concern will only serve to annoy you, and pity will infuriate you. Tell me what you've been doing, tell me anything."

"There's little to tell," I whispered. *I've just been locked in my bedchamber, crying and reading notes from Mirabel's ghosts.*

I forced back the tears gathering in my eyes. That happened now. I went from fine to tearful with nothing in between and I hated it. I pinched the inside of my elbow; the pain helped.

"I want to understand why you . . . disappeared." He caught my wrist.

I swiped at my eyes. "I'm not going to apologize for it, Aketo."

"I haven't asked you that, nor do I plan to," he said. I could hear the frustration he was trying to hide.

"I wanted to sort out my feelings alone. You and Baccha have ways to understand me that no one else does. I didn't want to see my grief reflected back at me in your eyes." Watching other people wait for me to break was painful enough, but seeing my pain through Aketo or Baccha? Wondering how much access they had to the intimate details of my heart? I couldn't do that. "First it was just going to be until we left Asrodei. But then I couldn't seem to feel any better for weeks. Every day I felt angrier and angrier. It was easier just to retreat from the world."

"When I was a child, I used to run from my mother whenever I was upset. I knew she would find a way to talk me out of whatever bothered me. My mother is very reasonable. It's

266

almost contagious." He smiled slightly. "I'll understand if you want to return to the Palace. I told the Hunter surprising you like this was a bad idea."

I shook my head. I hadn't walked Ternain's streets in weeks. Even the Tiger's Den, with its rows of low-slung apartments and dingy taverns, was precious to me. "I don't want to go back yet. Have you and Baccha been spending much time together?"

"Too much," Aketo snorted. "I wouldn't have come tonight, but the Hunter said he would seduce you in my stead if I didn't join him. I thought such a tragedy should be avoided."

"Yes, um, well, I'm glad you did," I said, cheeks burning. I wasn't sure I could withstand whatever Baccha's attempts at seduction entailed without bursting into flames—or laughing until I cried.

A couple stumbled into the alley, arms wrapped around each other, giggling as they shared a flask. One girl golden-haired, the other dark-skinned, rosy-cheeked, wearing her cap of coils like a crown.

The golden girl grinned, showing all her teeth. "Care for a nip?"

"I think we've had enough," I slurred, pressing against Aketo. "But you have our thanks."

We played the lovers they actually were—Aketo's arm around my waist, my hands against his chest—and I tried not to savor his warmth. This was why I never got close to anyone in the Patch. It was dangerous longing for someone who might change his or her mind.

His fingers slid through mine and he pulled us down the street until they were well away. He drew me close, leaning against a building of abandoned apartments.

I was still thinking of the girls and their easy happiness when Aketo's hands cupped my face.

We stood so close I could feel him breathing.

"Is this your attempt at seduction?" I asked, hoping he couldn't hear the rapid cadence of my heartbeat.

He stroked the warm skin on my neck. "Is it working?"

"Eh," I breathed, "I've seen better."

He leaned back, one hand pressed to the wall behind me. "Really? I thought I was doing quite well."

"You certainly show promise," I said encouragingly. "With some instruction, you might excel."

"I ought to go find the Hunter, then," Aketo said. "He must have some methods from four hundred years ago that we haven't seen."

I looked up to find that smirk of his, only softer this time. His thumb moved over the back of my neck. It was dizzying. "We should go back soon. Just . . . stay with me for a moment."

I rested my head against his chest, and there was only the sound of us together and the steady rhythm of his heartbeat drumming against mine.

Beneath the moonlight and warm in his arms, I felt safe. I wanted to hold on to it as long as I could.

Nearby, a rat ran through a puddle. I jumped and everything came rushing back. Papa, Katro, Baccha—everything.

"Let's go," he murmured into my hair.

When he stepped away, I took his hand and held tight.

✦✦ CHAPTER 26 ✦✦

WE DIDN'T RETURN to my rooms, even though dawn was warm on the horizon and Mirabel would be coming to wake me soon—or make her best attempt at it. Mirabel, who I'd also been avoiding, inasmuch as I could avoid someone who helped me dress every morning.

Aketo lifted his hand to knock, but the door swung open. Baccha leaned against the doorway, giving us an appraising look. I scowled at him and he laughed. "Oh, I've missed you, Princess." His eyes swung back and forth between Aketo and me. "It went well, then?"

"Don't meddle, Hunter," Aketo said behind me. "It's beneath you."

"I doubt that." I shouldered past Baccha. "Very little is below our Hunter."

"*Our.*" He grinned. "How sweet."

"I don't know why I put up with you," I said. "Is he here?"

He tilted his head back, pointing farther into the room.

The room opened into an octagonal shape. Katro sat on a stool in one corner with glowing cords of magick wrapped around his limbs. His brown skin had paled to a dull gray and his wavy green hair was rumpled. His bottom lip was swollen and caked with dried blood. He looked like he'd been pulled right from bed—violently.

At least Baccha was always helpful.

"Lovely to see you, Princess Evalina," Katro said silkily, the effect only somewhat ruined by the tremor in his voice. "Everyone is under the impression that your grief has left you too fragile to attend Court. Good to know you aren't *that* weak, though I suppose it hardly matters, what with your impending death."

I clenched my fists to keep from cuffing him across the mouth. "You will tell us what you know about the Dracolans or"—I pointed at Baccha—"he will hurt you. Again."

Seeing the smug look on Katro's face, I knew I would absolutely hurt him too.

"Stupid girl, I have no idea what you're talking about." Katro laughed and licked at some of the blood coating his bottom lip, and I stepped forward, reaching for the knife in my belt.

Baccha caught my shoulder. "Your Prince can make him talk with his magick. We won't have to hurt him."

I looked over my shoulder and saw Aketo glaring at Baccha, who shrugged and said, "I wouldn't have invited him along if we were going to do this the usual way. Bit cruel to keep someone who can sense emotions around when you're going to torture a man."

I bit my lip, almost breaking the skin. "I'm not sure—"

"I don't know what this is about," Katro said, voice still shaking, "but I won't tell you anything. You're a fool if you believe I know anything about the King's death."

"You are the fool—you were *seen*. Did you think a Dracolan would forget the sight of a fey with green hair? Or were you so confident that no one would ever figure it out? *Your* Princess will love to hear that she chose someone so incompetent for this task."

"My—my *Princess?*" He choked out a laugh. "Oh, Your Highness, you don't understand at all."

Relief coursed through me. At least Isadore hadn't been involved.

Aketo stepped past me and knelt near Katro. He hesitated a moment, one hand hovering over Katro's knee. Right, Aketo had said his magick worked best with touch. "Eva . . ."

"You don't have to do this, Aketo," I said.

He nodded grimly. "I know, but the King meant a lot to my family. I want to know the truth about his death."

"Is he khimaer?" Katro sputtered. That edge of fear in his voice had turned to disgust.

"How will you do it?" I asked, ignoring Katro.

Aketo didn't even blink. "I haven't done this before . . . but I should be able to increase his fear to soften his resistance. And, Hunter, this *is* torture. If this were for anyone but the King . . ."

Aketo dropped his hand on Katro's leg and sort of smiled, showing his fangs. Katro stiffened, testing the bonds on his wrists. They didn't seem to cause him any pain, but he couldn't move even an inch. "Your Highness," he panted, "unauthorized interrogation is—you can't—" His voice cut off as his eyes went wide. His head swung from me to Aketo. "You're going to die anyway. Even if Princess Isadore can't kill you, someone else will. We can't let a mutt—"

Aketo's hand flexed on Katro's knee and he jerked in his bonds, hissing like a wet cat, a cat that wanted to kill me. His body quivered, tremors that seemed to tire him, but he didn't stop straining, trying to get away. I felt too stunned to speak—it *was* torture. I couldn't have imagined Aketo's magick could do this.

And the look on Aketo's face. He swayed, hand still clutching Katro's knee. "Now, Hunter."

"What was your involvement in King Lei's death?" Baccha asked.

"I just found them," he gasped. "The ones that wanted a way back into Dracol since the border closed. That's what she told me to tell them. A way out of Myre and away from magick."

"Who?"

"My mother," he growled. "End this. I'll swear myself to you—tell you whatever you want. *Please.*"

"Lady Shirea? Why would she want to kill Papa?" Was this a plot to crown a fey King? Lady Shirea was actually one of the few levelheaded people at Court. She was military minded; in fact, she and Papa had worked on a number of campaigns together. And if Lady Shirea did want a fey King, her best means of achieving that would be to pressure Mother and Isadore into a marriage bond with one of her sons.

He laughed. It was a ragged sound, raising the fine hairs on the back of my neck. "I cannot tell you."

I pulled a knife from my belt and placed it right against

his neck. Until I could see his pulse tapping against the silver edge. Up close, I could almost smell the fear rolling off him. A tremor shook him so hard that the edge of the knife bit into his skin, a few drops of blood rolling down his neck. "Tell me."

"Tell you what?" he spat, straining against the bonds and the knife even further, forcing me to remove the blade from his neck. There would be no killing tonight. None until I had to kill my sister and then that would be the end of it.

I held my knife over his shoulder. "Why did she have my father killed? Is she behind the attacks on me?"

"I don't know anything about that." He laughed again. He was half wild animal, panicked eyes rolling and showing the whites, and half his scornful self. "My mother only told me to find the Dracolans. You'll have to ask her if you want to know more."

"Is he lying? Can you tell?" I looked at Aketo and Baccha.

Baccha shook his head, unsure. A thin sheen of sweat coated Aketo's face. "I can't be certain. Not while I enhance his fear," Aketo said.

"Stop manipulating his fear, then," I said. Aketo let go of Katro and stood, looking dazed. He looked like he would be ill, but I couldn't worry about that now.

Katro sagged, sucking in gasping, rattling breaths. "Thank you, Your Highness. I was wondering how long you'd let that savagery go on."

I raised the knife to his neck again, though not pressing it to his skin in case he lunged toward me again. "Tell me. Who told your mother to find Dracolans?"

"I won't."

So he did know.

"Just tell me," I said, voice thick with sudden tears. I pressed the knife closer, heedless of my previous worries for him. Why should I hold his life so sacred, when he had a hand in killing my father? "Please just tell me why, Katro."

"I can't. She——" He stopped with a painful choking sound. Then his eyes flickered behind me, to either Aketo or Baccha, I guessed, and then they went strangely blank.

My blood ran cold. His eyes were vacant like Dagon's eyes had been, emptied of any internal will. For a moment, I stared at him in horror. Then the magicked cords wrapped around his body melted away and he jerked forward, burying my knife in his throat.

⇥ CHAPTER 27 ⇤

I CHOKED ON the smell of blood. My eyes were shut tight, my hand cramping around the handle of the knife, and wet. *Wet.*

I was back in Asrodei, my knees squelching in a pool of blood, my fingers brushing Papa's peaceful face as I heard a sound—the rustle of curtains. My mind went crystal, everything drawn into sharp focus as I killed the woman. My hands wrapped around the hilt of Papa's broadsword and I ran, swinging it in an arc that made my muscles burn in protest. Her body fell slowly, hot blood gushing from her wound, splashing me across the face.

I heard someone's voice, drawing me back to the present. "Eva, Eva, Eva." Aketo's voice, I could tell this time. He'd wrapped his arms around me and was still rubbing circles on my back, his mouth against my ear. "It's all right. You're fine."

"Is the body—is he gone?" I whispered into his collar. Katro was dead; no one could survive severing their neck so brutally. He'd jerked his neck onto my knife again and again until I let go and it stayed lodged in his throat. His eyes were still wide and blank as blood washed down his neck.

Then I—well, I didn't know. My mind had gone blank with panic and I found myself in Aketo's arms as he tried to pull me back from wherever I had gone.

"We left the room. I brought you to the other room in Baccha's suite."

And yet I could still smell the blood. I could still feel death hovering all around me. Aketo kept it at bay, but I still felt it. Death and pain and all the things that just wouldn't leave me.

As my panic abated, my awareness of my body and its connection to Aketo's only grew. He was so warm, and with my arms wrapped around him, I could feel all the hard corded muscles in his back. The scales on his neck were soft, almost silky, and I could smell the oil he must have used on his hair, earthy and spicy.

It was disconcerting how comfortable I felt in his arms. We pulled apart and I realized Baccha was standing just a few feet away. I expected an inappropriate remark, but he just looked blank, skin gone white, eyes pinched with worry and exhaustion. Though once he noticed me looking at him, he shook it off. Smiling gently at me, he reached out a hand.

I took it and stood. "Why couldn't you stop him? Why did your magick just . . . melt away?"

"There was a compulsion spell, just like the one on the man who tried to kill you before we left Ternain. It was made to neutralize any magick it met. I couldn't feel it on him. Takes some complex work to cloak that sort of thing; it usually leaves a residue, smells like burning sugar and rot. To use that kind of power, when there was no way to know that we'd even find him . . .

"The compulsion must have been triggered because you were getting close. He was going to reveal something crucial, Eva. Something whoever set the spell needs to keep hidden."

And then he'd died for it, because I'd been so reckless in interrogating him.

"I doubt my description of a compulsion spell will be evidence enough for my mother. I wanted some irrefutable proof." I flinched when my next thought occurred to me. "Perhaps since Katro is dead, we can search his rooms for a connection to the Dracolans."

I glanced up, wondering if they would find such a thing—ransacking a dead man's rooms—in poor taste. Baccha and Aketo were exchanging a look.

"Eva, I don't think that's wise," Baccha said, "considering we'll want to avoid any association with his death."

Something about his tone made me feel panicked. "So now Katro is dead and I have nothing."

I left the room without looking back. Baccha followed me; I could feel him, a worrying knot in the back of my mind, so focused on me and so frustrated. It wasn't a problem, though; for weeks I'd trained myself to ignore him.

This would be more of the same.

✦

I tried to tune out Mirabel's yelling. Baccha had retreated to a corner when we arrived in my bedchamber. After hearing what happened, Anali had gone to deal with Katro's body.

The look of disappointment she gave me right before leaving still cut through me.

I'd never felt more like a child. Unlike a scraped knee that needed healing or a broken toy, the source of my guilt was a body, a life I'd destroyed.

Somewhere there was a Sorceryn guilty of two deaths. And I was guilty of three. Katro was *dead*. Even if I hated him for his involvement in Papa's death, even if he deserved it—he was dead without a trial. I had this memory worrying at the back of my mind of Katro chasing Isa and me through the eastern gardens, his hair cut just above his finely pointed ears. Falun was there too, his hair almost down to his elbows, helping me up into a tree to escape Katro.

At birth my sister and I had been tasked with later having to try to kill each other. Was that what made me such an arbiter of death—or was there some deeper flaw inside me? This violence must have been what the Auguries had seen when I was born. Of course they'd seen fit to lock my magick away.

Mirabel's voice broke into my thoughts. "How, Eva? How could you think this was a good idea?"

"Someone had to investigate Papa's death," I said. On this point, I refused to be chastened. No one else had done anything. When I first returned to Ternain, I spent a week trying to convince Mirabel to act, to just *do something*. I even went to the Auguries to ask about the omens, thinking maybe they were connected, but Sarou turned me away. I explained it to Mirabel over and over again: that whoever orchestrated Papa's death, it wasn't only the King of Dracol. But Mirabel had never changed her stance—saying our focus was my nameday, and that Papa wouldn't have had it any other way.

But I knew what it was really about; Mirabel thought I was too weak and that focusing on finding out who had ordered the killing would only worsen my grief. But what did that matter?

"I was investigating Lei's death, fool girl!" Mira snapped. "I connected Lady Shirea and her sons to the Dracolans days ago. The Captain and I have been watching them—waiting, and planning on what to do with that information *after* your nameday."

"What?" I gasped.

"Yes, child. If you had just had a little patience, or could trust the people who mean you well, a man wouldn't be dead—and you wouldn't have destroyed our only connection to the truth."

"Don't you mean if you had trusted me?" I said. "How could you not tell me this? How dare you?"

"Because you don't sleep at night and can barely get out of bed in the morning. You've shut everyone out." She shook her head. "You weren't ready. And you have so much more to prepare for. You didn't need this as well."

"I did need it," I whispered, because if I didn't whisper, I would scream. "Caring for Papa is the only thing keeping me sane."

Mirabel reached for me, but I backed away. She should have known I didn't want to be touched after weeks of me flinching away from any sort of comfort. "Eva, your father is dead. He doesn't need you to care for him. But I, and everyone else, need you to care for yourself."

"I tire of you deciding what I should do, what I should want, what I should *know*. You and Papa, you want me to be

Queen, but you trust me with nothing. When you lie to me, why are you surprised that I do the same? I'm exactly who you taught me to be."

"Eva, please," Mira said.

"I need to be alone."

Mirabel faced Baccha, pointing a shaky finger. "What about him?"

"I have to speak with the Princess, Lady," he said sheepishly. He glanced in my direction. "About her lessons."

Mirabel turned her sharp gaze on Baccha. "My trust is wearing thin with you, Hunter. How could you let her do this after finding her outside of the Palace?"

"My apologies, mistress, but I couldn't very well throw her over my shoulder and run," he said, bowing his head.

She huffed and stalked out of the room.

"Turn around," I told Baccha, then proceeded to strip to my underthings. Once I was down to just a chemise, I slid under the blankets and pulled them up to my neck.

"What do you want, Baccha?"

"You have to start training again," Baccha said. "You have to get used to violence again. You completely crumbled today. You just went blank. If your sister challenges you and you react the way you did today, you will die. I've waited long enough; it's time for your final lesson."

I looked away from him. "Before my father was killed, he told me the Sorceryn who placed my binding is dead. I never told you, but it's grown worse. The binding grows tighter and tighter every time I use magick. That bit I called up earlier is the best I can do—and even that pain is difficult to bear for long."

"And what?" he asked. "Does that mean you're ready to give up your life?"

No, I was prepared to endure whatever I must to become Queen. The binding could not compare to the pain that had become my constant companion since Papa's death. But I wasn't going to spent the little time I had left before my nameday on a futile lesson without getting something in return. "I'll do it under one condition, Baccha. You have to tell me the truth, about your past and why you came here."

"Perfect, because that is exactly what I'd planned to do." Baccha looked quite satisfied. "I thought it would take more to convince you than that. We have a deal, then, Princess. I'll expect you at the Little Palace in the morning."

With that, he turned on his heel and left my bedchamber.

I doused the lamps and climbed back into bed. When I closed my eyes, I saw Katro's eyes, wild with the fear I'd asked Aketo to torture him with. I told myself he deserved it as tears wet my face, but I knew it was a lie. I didn't bother wiping my face. I was used to sudden tears and sleepless nights, and wondering when, or if, this grief would end.

I stared down at the cup in my hand and tried to remember the last time my father had been in Ternain. The thin porcelain had a crack down the side, but none of the muddy dregs of kaffe left inside had spilled from it. Was it two years? Three? How long ago had someone—likely one of the men in his Kingsguard—brewed this draught for my father? Long enough for the leftovers to have dried to a tar-like sludge at the bottom. I set the cup down and backed away from Papa's desk.

I'd arrived at the Little Palace at the crack of dawn, hours earlier than Baccha expected me—timeliness was an unexpected advantage of not being able to sleep through the night—and had gone to the office where we had our first lesson. I was attempting to clean the desk while I waited for my escort, Falun, to retrieve the Hunter.

This was my first time visiting the Little Palace since returning to the capital. I'd planned to begin going through his possessions as soon as I was back in Ternain, but every time I began to consider it, some other meaningless task drew my attention. It was the sheer volume of objects my father collected that daunted me. There were rugs from the weavers in Korsai; sculptures of Godlings and magickal charms; *cherik* game sets and weapons of every sort. It would require a year just to take stock of it all and decide what I wanted to keep and what to send to his family's home on Arym Plain.

I didn't have a year.

With just two days left until my nameday, I might not even have a week.

After my nameday ball, I doubted Isadore would wait long. Tradition would hold—there were never challenges on an heir's nameday—but a reprieve of just one day held little comfort. I'd started to imagine when and where she would do it. At Court in the coming days, most likely, so we could put on a grand show.

My only choice for now was to avoid her. I could challenge Isadore, but only a fool rushed death. However our fight began, it would end with one of our lives cut short. I couldn't best my sister yet and I needed to live to find out who else was involved in Lady Shirea's plot. I would avenge my father.

After that I could become Queen.

A knock sounded at the door, but Baccha never waited for permission to enter a room. He strode inside, wearing leather breeches, knee-high, gold-tooled boots, and a white cotton tunic. His golden hair had been woven into a loose braid and he drank from a steaming mug of tea.

He said nothing as he walked to the table in the center of the room and collapsed into a chair, his limbs splayed out like a well-fed cat. "Aren't you going to join me, Princess?"

I sat across from him and folded my arms across my chest. "I'm waiting, Baccha."

Baccha let out a bark of laughter. "Is that any way to greet a man who spent the last four weeks trying to think of a way around an oath that has held for nearly two hundred years?"

"I don't yet trust that you'll hold up your end of our bargain."

"Well, be assured I have found a solution. The oath forbids me from speaking of it, but it can't interfere with my thoughts." At my blank look, Baccha simply smirked and shut his eyes.

Then I understood—our mindscape. At the lake we could speak freely without ever saying a word.

When I appeared on the shore, water lapping at my toes, Baccha wasn't in his usual place beside me, but his voice rang clear in my mind.

I was born far north of here, in the forests of the A'Nir Mountains.

Where are you? I wondered. I left the lake and walked toward the treeline.

Baccha's tart annoyance came through the bond. *I am in my region of our mindscape. You're free to join me, if you can. Do you want to hear the story or not?*

Get on with it, then. I entered the woods, searching for signs of movement. Every step I took seemed to span miles, the trees blurring around me. It was like running with the wind, but smoother.

I was born at the base of a nameless mountain. My mother and father, whoever they were, must have been too preoccupied to care for me. I didn't leave the forest on the side of that mountain for the first hundred years of my life. Instead I wandered and tested the limitations of my magick, until a khimaer magick-worker from the South camped near my home. He sought me out just like you did, by sensing my magick. He was not what anyone would call a positive influence. He taught me about Akhimar and how to fight and to learn other magick, and told me that I was not like most people who lived in the realm. And that most of the ageless ones, Godlings like me, had either died off or worked for the Queen in the South. He said the Queen wanted him to work for her as well, because she wanted every powerful magick-worker in the Queendom under her thumb. We formed the Hunt together to reject the Queen's rule. It lasted for a hundred years until we were caught. The Queen at the time was named Onaye. She was from the ibasi tribe, had wings like an eagle, and she could call fire. Onaye was fearsome; even the Hunt could not stand against her. To pay for my crimes, she gave me a choice: I could return to my mountain in exile, or pledge my sword to the crown. Unwilling to return to isolation, I swore on my blood that I would follow her and every rightful Queen that came after. An oath that would cause my magick to betray me if broken.

Did you hate her for it? I asked. I was still roaming the trees. Unlike when we hunted the antelope, in the mindscape sunlight pierced the canopy of branches overhead, and the loamy forest floor was soft beneath my bare feet.

In the beginning, no, Baccha continued. *I'd tired of the constant violence of the Hunt. Traveling the realm taught me there was more to living than hunting prey. I believed that if I fought for the crown, it would feel . . . cleaner. But it was worse. I cut more throats for the Queen than I did with the Hunt. I fell in love, had a daughter, and learned to mourn, all while straining at the bonds of my service. By the time I met Raina, I hated the Queens.*

I took one last step and came to a clearing. At its heart was a huge tree, with hundreds of spindly, leafless branches all answering the wind's call to dance. Baccha lay beneath it, his golden hair spread out beneath him. He didn't stir at my approach and continued his story as I joined him.

There was one lie I told you, Eva. I learned of Raina's plans days before I brought her to the Palace. I believed my oath would end without a rightful Queen. I only changed my mind when I realized Raina's intentions weren't just to exact revenge, but to claim the throne. I couldn't risk a woman as cunning as Raina controlling Myre's fate, but I failed to thwart her plans. That night after I found the dead Queen, I confessed my betrayal to her daughter. She asked what I would do to repay my sin.

She asked me, Would you serve us again, Hunter? You won't be working toward a Queen's ends this time, but for the preservation of our people. I agreed, not realizing that she had a different oath in mind, one not susceptible to betrayal. The oath was sworn thrice over in blood: mine, that of a descendant of Queen Onaye, and in the blood of one of my grandchildren. I swore to never speak of our agreement and to follow the descendants of the last Queen until they could retake the throne. That is all I have done since the Great War: follow orders I did not agree with and could not explain to anyone. Until now.

Baccha sat upright. *What do you think of my legend, Princess? Did it live up to your expectations?*

His voice in my head sounded deceptively light, but I could feel grief to match my own through the bond. Both grief and a rage so potent it made my teeth ache.

I'm sorry. It was all I could offer, but not nearly enough. *The khimaer Queen's descendants, they still live? In the Roune Lands?*

Baccha nodded.

What was the order that sent you back to Ternain? I held my breath. I was certain I would not like Baccha's answer.

Sure enough, he wouldn't meet my eyes, and his voice in my head was like a whisper. *I was sent to gather information on the Queen.*

I opened my eyes and was back in my father's office. I clenched shaking fists. "I knew it. I knew I couldn't trust you."

A moment later, Baccha's eyes flew open. "You can trust me, Eva. I swear that I will not let any harm come to you from my actions."

"That isn't your decision, though, is it? What if they ask you to kill me next?" Baccha hung his head but did not answer. Just as I expected. He couldn't control his fate or mine. "Did I really stumble upon you that day, or did you plan it, Baccha?"

What better source than a desperate Princess cursed with the rare magick he possessed?

He shook his head. "I'd planned to keep my distance from anyone connected to the throne. I was told not to risk discovery. Believe me, you were an unexpected complication. One that will likely result in pain for me."

That gave me pause. "They punish you?"

His expression softened. "It doesn't matter. There is nothing you can do to change it."

"Couldn't you just . . . stay here?" I hated the small hope in my voice. "Remain in Ternain after my nameday. Help me win the throne."

"It is not as simple as that, Princess. I've been locked in dungeons and sailed to the lands beyond the Isles. I've even infiltrated Dracol's Court. Built into the oath is the ability to summon me from anywhere. When they call, I must answer."

I understood. I didn't even blame him. Not for this betrayal and not for what he'd allowed Raina to do. Surely he had already paid that debt with his enslavement. But the meager trust we had built in the past weeks was gone. Even if he hadn't used me intentionally, I'd brought him to the Palace and with me to Court. I'd given him all he needed.

"Despite myself, I believe you don't mean me harm, but if you try to leave Ternain, we will see how long a dungeon can hold you." I stood and made to leave.

"What about your lesson?" Baccha called when I reached the doorway. "You need to practice using blood and marrow magick in tandem."

"I think our lessons are over, Baccha." Besides, he'd already taught something important today: to trust no one but myself.

✤ CHAPTER 28 ✤

WHEN I WOKE the next morning, Mirabel had news. Katro's mother, Lady Shirea, and supposedly both her sons had left Ternain suddenly to vacation in the North. Though I knew one was dead now. It was as clear a confirmation of their involvement as anything. Certainly they knew someone was coming close to learning what they'd done—and so they fled. There was also a card waiting in my sitting room. I nearly threw it away, thinking it was an invitation to some courtier's event, but opened it when I saw the cobalt dagger, the sigil of House Killeen, painted on the back.

> *Evalina,*
>
> *Your absence at Court is keenly felt. Many worry that you are not fit to compete with your sister in the coming weeks. I admit, I have the same concerns and I would hate for your few allies to turn away from you now. I have sent*

Isadore to check in on you. I know you grieve
your father most deeply, having found his body,
but it will be easier if we all bear his absence
together.

She hadn't signed it, but I knew Mother's elegant script well enough. I crumpled the note.

I closed my eyes for a moment and pressed my hands against my thighs until I felt sparks of pain. I pushed harder and harder until I was sure the skin would bruise. When I pulled away, I could feel my pulse in every part of my body down to my fingertips.

We didn't meet in my rooms. That would have felt entirely too intimate. Instead, my guard escorted me to a nearby sitting room where Isadore and her guards were already stationed.

Light filtering through the latticed windows created a lace of shadows, making the dress Isadore wore all the more ornate. It was hardly mourning white. The white brocade was thick with lace and cut expertly down the subtly curving lines of her body. Her dark gold hair was pinned up, showing off the elegant tanned length of her neck.

It was a mourning gown fit for a ball. Or, alternatively, a mourning gown meant to outdo every single person at Court.

By comparison, my dress was simple. A white cotton sheath falling straight to the floor, like the strips of white hanging from nearly every window in Ternain, bright against the city's many colors.

I could not begin to compare to my sister's magnificence.

Well. That would always be true. To each their strengths, Papa would say.

Why pretend I was anything other than what I was, when she was alone and couldn't yet hurt me with guards just feet away? Why hold anything back?

"What do you want?" I asked.

She leaned away and her expression dropped into a scowl. "Didn't you read Mother's note? She worries, as do I." She waved a hand in my direction, lips curling. "And clearly we have reason to. You haven't been to Court since you returned to Ternain. Surely Papa wouldn't want you to retreat before your nameday."

I didn't flinch at the mention of Papa—a small victory— though the bloody mess of him flashed behind my eyes.

"Court is your domain, Isadore." I folded my hands on my lap. "I have no interest in it."

She wrapped a lock of hair around her finger. "Even if by some stroke of luck you manage to be named True Heir, the Court will never follow you if you refuse to take them seriously."

Why didn't I just send her away? She had come here to torment me. And what was I supposed to do, just take it?

"They aren't the only ones who matter, Isadore. And besides that, they'd follow anyone with a crown."

She glared at me, eyes flinty with annoyance. "If you think that, you're truly a fool. They, we, *rule*; we aren't the only ones who matter, but we matter more than most. You'll never be Queen if you can't understand that."

I met her eyes and remembered the cake shared between us as we spilled crumbs all over her bed. Had she abandoned me, or had she prepared me for the loneliness that would be my constant companion?

I must have gone quiet for too long, because Isadore sneered at me, leaning forward. "I see you've given up, without Papa to push you. I'm not surprised."

I shook my head, refusing to take the bait. "I'm not going to trade petty insults with you. What would be the point?"

Isadore's face flashed through so many emotions. Disbelief and regret, I thought, and then anger. Finally, grim determination settled on her face. "Why is it you never wrote me back when you went to Asrodei?"

Because I spent all that time waiting for her to apologize just once in those letters, and she never did. "Why is it you decided to hate me when I came home?"

"It wasn't difficult once I realized that you could keep me from what I deserve."

Except Myrean Queens didn't deserve crowns—they earned them.

"And you've never regretted it?" I added.

Isadore straightened her spine. "Maybe I did once. But now that I know who you are, I'm grateful. You're not fit to be a Queen, Eva. You never were."

My heart felt cracked in half—one half hating her and the other half trying to understand.

But she was wrong. She was so wrong. I could be a better Queen than Isadore. I had to be.

I'd expected to feel anger at Isadore, for all the rage I'd been feeling these last weeks to rise up in me until I was burning inside. And there was that. But there was also pain. An ache had settled into my bones the moment I saw her. I didn't want to kill her. I wanted to dig every bit of her out of my heart and mind, and just *forget*.

How cruel was my heart, that it still loved her?

I leaned forward, cupping her cheek. "Isa, I have given up nothing and you will not have Myre without a fight."

She jerked away and stood. Her eyes were sharp glittering jewels as she glared at me, the fire of them bearing down on me. "I look forward to it, little sister," she said. The smile she gave me felt as deadly as a razor's edge pressed to my neck, but my flesh wasn't hers to cut.

I felt no fear of her, only certainty. It hit me like a punch to the stomach. We were lost to each other now and we always would be. As many times as I thought it, it had never felt truer. We were rivals and would never again be anything but that.

She was half to the doorway when I spoke. "Do you care that Papa is dead? Do you care at all?"

I couldn't see her face, but I watched her shoulders draw together. For a long moment, Isa hesitated. "You have your pain and I have mine." Her voice was thick, like she could hardly say the words. "Just because I don't wear it like an accessory, demanding that everyone see it, doesn't mean it isn't there."

I was certain she lied, but I still felt ashamed somehow. Of what, I couldn't fathom. "Until my nameday, Isa."

"Yes, until tomorrow. Goodbye, Eva." She swept out of the room, all silver, emerald, and gold.

She looked like a Queen, shining and sharp as a diamond, and without flaw. But I knew better now. Papa's death had taught me no one was unbreakable.

Isadore could die just like anyone else.

⤛ CHAPTER 29 ⤜

THE NEXT AFTERNOON, I let Mirabel pretty me to her satisfaction, and once she was done, I had her leave the dress on my bed. I marveled at the wonder of it once the door shut behind her.

I hardly remembered sitting down with the dressmaker months ago to discuss what I wanted, so it was mostly a surprise. I'd chosen a *kinsah*, a dress with a long, layered silk skirt and a detached and elaborately embellished bodice. The skirt held all the colors of the horizon, orange, gold, palest pink and lavender, pale and dark blue. The detached bodice was all night sky; black pearls and tiny diamonds. They clashed, and made sense. They fit, but also didn't.

It was perfect.

Before she left, Mira gave my hand a squeeze. "It is queenly. As," she whispered, "are you."

It was the best thing she possibly could have said, as I hadn't known anything queenly could seem like me at all. I would look more than beautiful in it; I would look powerful—like a force of nature. And it would be the first thing I'd worn outside of mourning white since Papa's death.

I slipped out of my robe. Though this dress was so much more ornate, its bodice was similar to the tops I wore to the Patch, and even more revealing—baring my stomach and cut wide around the straps to show a glimpse of the sides of my breasts. The bodice didn't close fully across my back, just a lacing of gold ribbon, and the way the beading was laid over sheer fabric made it impossible to wear anything beneath. I stepped into the skirt and spun around once, the hem lifting off the floor in a bell shape.

I stared at my reflection in the standing mirror in my dressing room and a breath came rushing out of me. I ran my hands over the beading, the chain of firestones I'd hung low on my stomach, and the sturdy wings of my hips—both intrigued and impressed with myself. My hair was a frothy cloud of curls—Mirabel having spent hours making sure each spiral fell perfectly—and my nails were sharp and bright as blood. Even my summer-dark complexion held a glow. I looked a bit thinner and sad, somehow, though. Tired. But the dress made up for it, I hoped. Still there was something missing.

I picked through a few chests of jewelry. Nothing satisfied me—everything either too encrusted with jewels or too plain—until eventually my eyes fell on the horns, hanging on the back of the door. I blinked and was standing before them, my fingers just an inch away from their sharp ridges. I hadn't touched them since returning to Ternain.

I wrapped one hand around the base of each horn and

energy pulsed through me. I felt a pressure behind my eyes and the longer I held them, the more insistent the pain became. I held on until I could feel consciousness slipping away.

I let go, bending over to catch my breath.

I closed my eyes and my bare feet were pressing at the damp edge of the lake. It was utterly calm, no ripples, no movement.

I jumped in and sank like a stone.

I gasped and water sucked up through my nose, choking me. *Just your mind.*

It's all in your mind. You can do this—you have to do this.

Panic burned within me as I coughed and sputtered, fighting the water, trying to drag myself back to the surface. A tendril of something wrapped around my wrist, pulling me to the bottom. I screamed and thrashed, swallowing more water.

I came back to my body, took a deep breath, and then closed my eyes again.

My toes pressed into the damp dirt. *Just dive.*

I jumped. My arms cut through the water and I kicked toward the bottom, reaching, stretching until I was sure I would feel it in just a moment. The water pushed back at me, but my arms cut through it like blades. The water started to thicken, but I was close. I could feel it, from the hot knives stabbing at the base of my neck, and impossibly I just *knew*. I felt power, the pressure of it—a weight like nothing I'd ever known.

I reached out and my fingertips brushed the bind. A shock went through me. It felt as light and delicate as gossamer. I opened my eyes to the dark of the lake and found it spreading out below me, a shimmering film over the glowing embers beneath.

My hand curled around the bind and my vision went white. I couldn't feel the lake or my body. Only pain spreading from my mind into every part of my body, licking flames burning me down to a column of ash.

I dropped the binding and the pain fell away. I reached for it again. If I could just tear it before the pain blew through me, I could be done with it. But when I grasped the binding again, the pain hit me like a wall of fire. Not spreading, but all encompassing. There was no beginning or end to it—it just was.

I floated, too stunned to do anything, and the binding became just a glimmer in the distance. I screamed in frustration, choking on the water again. The tendrils from earlier pulled me away from the binding—my magick, trying to save me from this pain. But I thrashed again, fighting them.

I had to end this.

But the pain left me stunned and sluggish. And the memory of it floated just at the edge of my thoughts. *No more.*

Evalina. Baccha's voice was sharp, like he was right next to me, breathing down my neck. *Come back.*

My eyes snapped open, expecting to find Baccha standing over me. Instead, I found that I had slid down to the floor, the beautiful skirt in a tangle around my legs.

I climbed to my feet and snatched one of the pillows off my bed. I pressed it to my face and screamed until tears were smarting in my eyes, until I could pretend the rawness in my throat had come from this, instead of from the impossibility of drowning in magick.

I couldn't do it. I couldn't even close my eyes and think of the lake; the residue from that pain still lingered in my body and the thought of returning to it made me want to vomit.

I couldn't do it. It was impossible, that pain.

I just couldn't.

A knock sounded at my door and then Mirabel's voice came through, asking if I was well. I called out some excuse.

But if I let my mind focus on this failure, I would never leave. Mirabel would find me still standing here, screaming or worse. I couldn't let this stand. I couldn't be some fragile, foolish thing. I had to be Princess Evalina now. Princess Evalina, who Papa and Baccha believed would be Queen. Or Princess Evalina, who would never be anything more than this?

I dropped the pillow and started toward my dressing room, but my eyes fell to the table near my bed. My music box, an old gift from Papa.

I cracked open the delicate crystal casing and spun it in my hands. Isa's music box held only the Palace, but inside mine spun the entirety of Ternain, made from tiny bits of gold and brass and diamonds. He'd sworn to have one created for every great city in Myre, but never made good on that promise. The Palace was there in the center, rendered in exquisite detail, but if I looked closely I could also find the Patch, the Sorceryn Temple, and all the fashionable fey shops on the edge of the Red River. I curled my hands around it protectively, the sharp edges digging into my palms.

Seventeen is of age, I heard in Papa's voice. I could remember the first time he said it—when I arrived at Asrodei with

Mirabel and he was forced to finally explain everything being a Rival Heir entailed.

Seventeen is old enough to kill, I'd said years later. *And old enough to die.*

I put down the music box and walked to the dressing room to see if this dress might have some places to hide knives.

⤔ Chapter 30 ⤕

I STOPPED AT the threshold of the antechamber leading to the balcony where I would be presented. Isadore's name had already been called. Mother stood just a few feet away, waiting for the crier to announce her.

I hadn't seen her since a few days after Papa's funeral. It was my longest and most successful attempt at avoiding her.

"Mother," I said.

She gave a start when she saw me.

I walked farther into the room and stood beside her, the cloud of her sea-salt perfume reaching my nose. Once I had loved the scent, how it somehow carried the bracing feel of the ocean, but somewhere along the line my mouth had started twisting whenever I caught the edge of its corrosive salt.

She gave me a cold look. "Glad to see you've finally grown out of that tantrum you were throwing. I had some worry that you might miss your ball."

"A tantrum?" I leaned back, too shocked to curb my reaction. "That's what you call grieving? Forgive me for not following your lead by pretending that nothing had happened at all."

She sighed. "I know it hasn't always seemed this way to you and your sister, but you've always been more like me than Isadore is. And she's always been more like Lei—a great deal more charming and much more pragmatic. We, on the other hand—"

"I am nothing like you."

"Evalina, I do not care how deeply you grieve your father. You will not disrespect me." She started to spin the big blue bauble on her finger. I stared at the ring, too large to fit her. It was Papa's. "When I was your age, I almost always reacted according to my heart and not to the wisdom of my mind. Fortunately, I learned that the heart is not to be trusted and that emotion, while telling, can often lead you astray. You haven't learned that lesson, sadly. I regret it."

If her feelings were so profound, how could she keep them so orderly? How had she severed herself from them? I almost—*almost*—wished I could do the same. "You know nothing of the emotions in my heart and the wisdom of my mind. You've never inquired as to either."

"Alas, I do not have to. I see you and I see them." She closed her eyes for a moment and it was pain that met me when she looked up again. "You know your child even when you do not wish to."

"Papa told me about the omens, Mother."

She shook her head. "And what of them? Did he tell you to hate me for doing nothing when I learned of them, instead of meddling like he did? Which do you think served you better?"

I squeezed my eyes shut, willing back my tears. Gods, how could she insult Papa like this, today of all days, when he should have been here with us? "I wondered if that was why you chose Isadore over me. Because you already knew I was fated to die."

"How could you think that? I . . . chose Isadore because she was first."

"And what about me?"

"You had your father."

I laughed bitterly. "And now he is dead."

My breath caught. There were tears dampening her cheeks. How strange a thing it was, to see my mother crying. I reached toward her, but she snatched her hand away. She looked down at it, as if it was poisoned. "You . . . you look just like him—just like him."

"Mama?" I whispered, the word foreign on my lips. I hadn't called her anything but Mother or Queen in so long.

"Mama," I whispered again.

"I've been waiting for you to come out of hiding so that I could give you this." She pulled off Papa's ring and offered it to me, but something about the way she held it wasn't quite right. She held it toward me pinched between two fingers, like she wanted it as far from her as possible. I couldn't understand why she'd been wearing it in the first place, but it was clear she didn't want it. She didn't want anything to do with my father; she hadn't for years, so I couldn't say why it still hurt me.

The booming voice of the crier came as I pulled the ring from her hand. "Her Majesty Queen Lilith, her magick of air and sea."

Queen of Storms, they'd called her when she was first crowned, for the tempests she called up from the sea. When and why had that stopped?

Mother wiped her face clean. "Finally."

"Her Highness Evalina Grace Killeen, her magick of marrow and blood."

I stepped through the doors onto the balcony overlooking the ballroom. I smiled as shocked silence swept through the room. Isadore stood a few feet away.

As the attention of everyone in the ballroom focused on me, my chest tightened with nerves. I wanted to flee. Nothing, nothing was right about this moment.

I slipped Papa's ring onto my thumb. The warm, heavy gold was inlaid with small blue stones for Mother—it was the ring she'd given him when they wed.

I knew I looked magnificent. My eyes were the color of bright poppies and lined with kohl, and my lips were bare but full. I hoped my smile looked exactly like my father's. I hoped I reminded them of him.

I was like Mother, pretending I was fine even though I ached inside. I couldn't even regret it. This skill that I'd learned from Mother kept me on my feet, but knowing Papa believed in me was keeping me alive.

I stretched out my hand in greeting, like I'd seen Mother do hundreds of times.

A sigh of rustling fabrics eased through the room as row after row of courtiers, nobles, and guests fell to one knee.

Time slowed. This was the first time the entire Court had bowed before me. Suddenly the weight of what would begin tonight hit me with renewed force.

I gestured for everyone to rise and my eyes slid to my left, where Isa and Mother stood.

"We will begin," Mother said in a sharp whisper, then gestured for us to step forward.

I searched the crowd from the edge of the balcony. There was only a sea of faces, expectant, scrutinizing, watching like hawks.

Only Mother's sharp glance in my direction drew me away.

She had a trick of using her air magick to make her voice carry. Sound erupted from Mother's throat, echoing through the ballroom. "Today we gather for a momentous occasion. Today my daughter Evalina comes of age to become a true Rival Heir. From today on, Princess Evalina and Princess Isadore will engage in combat." She paused. "As a mother, I have come to dread this day. I cherish the lives of both my daughters more than any of you know, but as your Queen, I revel in the contest of heirs. Not for bloodthirst as the Dracolan Kings accuse, but for Myrean strength. The Rival Heir who takes my place will be stronger for the things she has had to endure—strong enough to defeat whatever threat Dracol presents. Though all of Myre is still mourning the loss of our King, I ask you to celebrate tonight. Celebrate Princess Evalina's nameday foremost, but also celebrate the strength born from our daughters, and await the ascension of a powerful Queen."

I held my breath. Though I could see Isadore beaming, I

couldn't smile. There was some smattering of applause, but mostly tension filled the room.

"To Evalina! To Isadore!" Mother called. "To Myre!"

Her words echoed in my head as the Court lifted their glasses to me.

Two Sorceryn stepped out of the antechamber— Sorceryn Tildas, chosen by me, and Sorceryn Arinel, Isadore's choice. I owed a debt to the lawmaker who had established that two Sorceryn, one chosen by each Rival Heir, would complete the spell. Because I had felt sure Isadore and two Sorceryn loyal to her could come up with some simple way of killing me right here and now. Arinel might've been Isadore's co-conspirator. The only reason I trusted Tildas was that he and my father had grown up together.

"Welcome, Sorceryn Arinel, Sorceryn Tildas." Mother's lips thinned. "Each Sorceryn has been chosen by one of the Heirs to complete the Entwining."

Arinel used a similar trick, his low voice booming across the large chamber. "Princess Isadore and Princess Evalina's fates have always been entwined, but today we twist their lives together with magick."

Tildas stepped forward and intoned in the same booming voice, "Once the Entwining is complete, a Rival Heir can only be killed by a weapon or magick wielded by the other."

Isadore and I stayed in place while everyone else stepped back. We both knew our parts. As Tildas and Arinel began to hum low within their throats, Isadore and I turned to face each other and joined hands.

Out of the corner of my eye, I could see both Tildas

and Arinel, their fingers moving in complex, impossible-to-follow motions. Both lifted their hands and drew their fingers down a braided tattoo on their necks.

The humming stopped and threads of red magick sprang from their fingertips, like ribbons, but sucking up light around them and pulsing rapidly. They wove through the air until they became one. As the ribbons settled around our throats and our joined hands, they gave me only a light sensation of warmth. It was almost pleasant, but then both Sorceryn slapped their hands together, the sound crackling through the ballroom like lightning, and the ribbons became like hot irons, driving straight into my heart.

I squeezed Isa's hands, bearing the pain with her. It was deeply unsettling, seeing everything I felt mirrored in her eyes—fear, pain, and trepidation—both of us unmasked. There was no hiding in the midst of this. The pain intensified as the ribbons cut through every bit of my body—blood, flesh, and bone.

The Sorceryn rubbed their hands together and the pain abated. Together, Isadore and I sucked in a breath, and then realized we still held hands and jerked away from each other. I felt no different, only out of breath. It seemed there should have been a sign, a physical representation of the way we were twisted together, but there was nothing—only Isadore standing across from me, watching the tattoos on my arms, expression eager.

Isa's quick slice of a smile stopped me. "So it begins. Happy nameday, little sister. I hope you savor it."

✦→ CHAPTER 31 ←✦

THREE GLASSES OF wine later—unwatered, sweet, high-summer wine downed in two gulps and chased by flaky fruit-stuffed pastries—I'd danced with a great many men. Some lovely looking, others plain, one toadish in a way I found charming, and all connected by two things: the overblown ambition of becoming King, and their general disinterest in me. I found this interesting, if a bit mystifying. One would think the surest way to fulfill that ambition would be to impress me, flatter or charm me, and find some way to make an impression on *me*. Because in these fantasies in which they were King, I would be Queen—they would be mostly ornamental unless they had something exceptional to offer. Alas, there was nothing even remotely exceptional among this bunch, besides their clear detachment from reality.

The fools were a welcome distraction from my looming demise, along with the wine. I felt like I finally had a firm grip on myself. And if I hadn't yet accepted my fate—ending up magick-less and dead, never to have a ball in my name again—at least I stopped despairing over it. Besides, I didn't need to worry tonight. There were never challenges on the first night after the Entwining.

Eventually I was spun into Falun's arms. All his hair, save for the bright little tendrils on his brow, was braided back in a complex pattern that lay flat against his scalp, mimicking a shorter style. Without all the hair to distract from his face, he looked terribly handsome. But when I smiled at him, he frowned back at me.

"Did you tell him not to come?"

"What?" I blinked at him as his hands settled on my hips for a spin. "Who?"

"I knew you were upset when we left the Little Palace a few days ago, but what is the point of shutting him out now?"

That answered my question as to whether things were still going well between the two. "I'm not . . . angry at Baccha." I had given one of the guards sent to watch his room an invitation for Baccha, though I didn't expect him to come. A nameday ball didn't exactly seem like something he'd be interested in, unless he planned to use it to gather more information. And he might not be pleased with the five guards I'd ordered to watch his comings and goings. "Did he tell you what he told me?"

"No." Falun frowned. "But he told me that you would."

"Tomorrow," I promised. I switched my grip in Falun's hands so that I led. He rolled his eyes but went along with my direction. "This party is for me, if you didn't notice."

"Happy nameday," Falun said, voice flat. His blue eyes were round with concern. "I had an idea. What if we all moved to the Little Palace? You and Mirabel and the entire guard. That way, until we have a plan, you won't risk running into Isadore in the Palace until you are ready."

"I can't move into my dead father's house," I snapped.

"All right. It was a silly idea. Half the guard would have to sleep in the stables."

I laughed softly at his attempt to defuse the moment, cursing my sharp tongue. It wasn't silly. It was smart, but I couldn't do it. The rest of our dance passed in uncomfortable silence. But when we embraced, it seemed all was forgiven. Falun never could hold a grudge—even when I deserved it.

I slipped through the crowd, searching for Aketo. My hands started shaking when I realized I couldn't find him— he'd gone before I even had one dance.

Someone cleared their throat behind me and I braced myself for another one of the dull, insulting would-be suitors. I spun and found Aketo smiling down at me.

He bowed slightly. "Can we share a dance? Or do you have other partners lined up?"

I looked past his shoulder to find Mother glaring at me. Certain it was fury keeping her back ramrod straight, I took Aketo's hand. If the look on Mother's face was any indication, she knew who he was, and the preferred ratio for dances at my nameday ball was at least one hundred human lordlings for every khimaer Prince.

"Aketo," I said, breathless with relief. "Can we get a drink first?"

He laced his fingers through mine and guided me toward the long table where the wine and sweets were being served.

As he passed me a goblet, I took the chance to get a good look at him. He wasn't wearing his soldier's uniform tonight and the difference was significant. His trousers were black and fitted quite well to his long legs. His jacket was also black, though the lapels were crowded with gold knots like the scales on his neck.

Along the edges of the gold embroidery, more knotwork tracked up his shoulders in bright orange and cobalt—both colors for me.

He took a sip of his drink and paused with the goblet pressed against his bottom lip.

Warmth licked up my body as he lowered the wine and traced his full bottom lip with his tongue. "Eva."

I shivered as I reached past him to grab another glass of wine. As I pulled back, my arm brushed his, raising gooseflesh.

"Lord Prince, you look terribly handsome."

"And you are more beautiful than I ever could have prepared for, *Princess Evalina*." He grinned. "And is it so terrible?"

"Yes, it's terrible how much I like your face."

He leaned close. "I'll allow that. In truth, I'd allow *anything* from you tonight."

I choked on a swallow of wine. "That dance you mentioned. Shall we?"

Aketo's hand was warm and electric in mine, but even he couldn't drown out the weight of everyone's attention. "They're all watching."

The hand not holding mine settled against my waist. His

thumb rubbed over the firestone chain and my breath hitched. "Somehow news of who I am has spread. I don't mind the attention, but if you do . . ."

Gods damn it. I needed to ask Anali to have guards with him at all times. "I'm fine." He watched me. "I don't *mind* being around the Court. I just find them tiring. I haven't missed being in the Palace at all."

"Did you have to spend time with them often?" The lightest flexing of his hand drew me in and away, the pair of us twirling the entire time like a spinning top. He put pressure in the hand at my waist, nothing like the polite, barely touching suitors earlier or Falun's mechanical movement. For a moment as Aketo twisted, his palm stretched wide and his thumb brushed the bottom edge of my breast. Protected by the heavy beading at the bottom of the bodice, I shouldn't have felt it, but I did, like a small shock. I'd been feeling hands on my bare waist all night; his touch shouldn't have felt more drugging than the wine.

But it was.

"I attended Court three times a week, or only twice if I could get away with it, though that wasn't often because if I skipped it altogether, either my mother might decide to pay attention to me or people would talk. Mostly I . . ." The music shifted to a quicker tempo and Aketo slid his hand up the side of my body and down my arm to take both of my hands. "Mostly I sparred with my guard, read, and tried to avoid my mother and sister. I spent most of my days alone."

"Solitude sounds lovely. In our home, there were always people. It never stopped."

We spun and I was glad I'd been saved from answering. Papa had been one of those people frequenting his home. "Have you danced with anyone else tonight?"

"Anali danced with me, which was a bit awkward, and some of the guards." He flushed. "I also danced with your sister."

I froze and we stood pressed together. His body was so familiar. I could have gotten lost in it, if not for the fear racing up my skin. Why would she dance with Aketo? Why would she know anything about him?

"Isadore is quite the accomplished dancer. I'm sure it was lovely."

"As are you, but she seemed less inclined toward dancing and more toward investigating why I'd come to Ternain."

"And what did you tell her?"

"That I came to protect you." He held my eyes for as long as the music allowed.

"Did she ask anything else?"

"She asked about Baccha and she wanted to know more about . . . us," he said hesitantly. "I told her nothing, but she seemed to have made some assumptions."

I flushed under the weight of his gaze, and everyone else's. "I think I do mind the audience."

"There is something I wanted to give you." He pulled me through the twirling couples until we reached a spot behind two large pillars in the corner of the ballroom that created a semi-private nook.

He held up a fine gold chain; hanging from it was a dark stone about the size of my fingertips, cut into a teardrop. As it twisted in the air, the colors shifted, from bloodred to black and then to a blue sparkling with an internal light. I'd never seen anything like it.

"Baccha told me it worked like this. A suitor's gift, the first of many."

Our Hunter meddling again. "But, Aketo, I might die."

He caught my chin in his fingers so that I would look up at him. His eyes were safe.

The words spilled out of me before sense could take hold. "Prince Aketo, I accept your suit."

We stood there for a moment, just staring at each other as he fastened the pendant around my neck. Aketo shifted his weight and I burned at our closeness. His face hovered inches above mine, the entire line of his body pressed against me, with one of his hands resting against my waist with the same insistent weight as when we danced.

He bent close enough for his lips to brush mine. Heat scorched an unforgiving path up my thighs, to my waist and my mouth. His mouth met mine, lips soft but insistent. He deepened the kiss, tongue sliding over my bottom lip. I knotted my fingers through his hair, drinking him in with my mouth and my hands.

He pressed me back against the pillar and I pulled him closer. I forgot where we were, forgot everything but the trails of heat left in the wake of his fingertips and the taste of his mouth, like sunlight and caramel.

My tongue caught one of his fangs and a sigh shuddered through him, raising gooseflesh everywhere we touched. "Careful," he whispered.

I pressed my mouth back to his and we twisted so that his back was against the pillar. I crushed myself against him and pulled at his lips with my teeth. His fingers tested the edge of the skirt, dipping beneath the waistband.

I was gasping against his mouth when Aketo leaned away from me and rested his head against my neck, breathing in my scent. "We should—you should get back."

I shook my head. "Let's not. The night's almost over anyway and I've had enough dancing. We can just slip up to my room and the guard will follow eventually."

Emotions flashed across his face so quickly that I could hardly follow. Desire, confusion, regret, frustration. "We can't." I opened my mouth to protest as Aketo took a half step away from me. "And you're . . . we've both had wine tonight. Perhaps another time would be—"

My stomach gave a lurch. I shoved him away. "If you don't want to be alone with me, say so. No one is going to attack me tonight, and even if they try, we'll be together."

"I don't trust myself to protect you tonight. We've both had more than our fair share of the wine. Who knows what plans your sister has?" He stepped forward again, eyes softening as they took in my face. "We can spend more time alone when it is safe. *And* we're both in full command of ourselves. I would never want you to regret anything. It was just last week that you weren't speaking to me."

"That has nothing to do with this. I was *grieving*." I hated myself even as I said it. "I thought you understood."

"I do understand, Eva. You still are grieving," he whispered, turning away. "I can feel it all the time, even when you're with me now, you're still—you're still in pain."

I jerked away from him and wrapped my arms around my stomach.

My pain was my own. For him to throw it back in my face, when it had no bearing on this at all . . . It felt unreasonably cruel. I'd managed to forget my father for a few hours. Why did it matter that I'd done so with the assistance of a few cups of wine. The forgetting was the important part. I thought he would want to help me forget.

He reached toward me. "I'm sorry, Eva. I shouldn't have . . ."

And I thought he wouldn't use my own heart against me. I thought he was safe. *Fool, fool, fool.*

"I need to leave. I need Anali and I need to go," I said. He stepped closer and I backed away. "Please don't touch me."

He nodded. "All right. Well, you shouldn't be alone."

I stared down at the marble floor. "I'm not so helpless that I can't be alone for a moment."

He hesitated and the need to hurt him back rose in me. "I don't *need you*, Aketo. At all. Please go."

I pushed past him. When I was far enough away, I wrapped one hand around the pendant. It wasn't nearly as warm as he was.

I moved through the press of bodies, searching for Anali. I found her at the edge of the ballroom, in the same antechamber where I'd spoken with my mother. She didn't ask why I needed to leave, only went to find the rest of the guards so that I could return to my rooms.

"Where is Aketo?" Falun asked when he came up to the room. "I saw you two together. I thought . . ."

I didn't answer, just held on to the pendant tighter and tighter. I should have been making myself less attached to it, because I would need to give it back to him—but I couldn't let it go.

When Anali returned, she had the same question.

I looked away from all their expectant faces. "He should be in the ballroom."

"Well, we have searched and we can't find him. He wouldn't leave, unless . . ." Anali cut a suspicious glance in my direction. "Did he have some reason to leave?"

Our argument wasn't cause enough, and I didn't care for the look Anali was giving me—somewhere between accusatory and concerned.

Maybe he had reason to leave. My mind played back our conversation, hesitating over one detail.

She wanted to know more about . . . us.

"Is Isadore still inside?" Unease pulsed beneath my skin.

It took hardly any searching to confirm it. I knew with a certainty, felt it deep in my bones. I had left him, even though I knew Isadore had noticed him. I thought of every treat and trinket, every friend and gift she had coveted, then taken.

I knew.

And now Aketo was gone.

❯❯ CHAPTER 32 ❮❮

I RAN.

Through deserted hallways, down winding staircases, my slippers alternately slapping the marble and skidding when I made too quick a turn.

Someone snatched at my arms—guards, maybe Falun or Anali—but I kept running. Even when I reached the door to Baccha's rooms, I didn't stop. I kicked the door and it swung open, unlocked.

I ran into his bedchamber and found another unlocked door. He wasn't inside and finally I stopped.

I crouched, burying my head in my knees as I screamed in frustration.

Then I stood and found all the guards standing around me, weapons drawn, looking between me and Anali, unsure of who they needed to be fighting, but certain weapons must be necessary by now. They all looked winded, but I didn't feel tired. I felt like a flare, burning in the sky.

"Eva." Anali reached toward me, the way you might

approach an untamed dog. "Wait for a moment. There's no proof your sister took Aketo."

Your Highness, I wanted to say. Why couldn't anyone respect me when I needed it?

I shoved past her and the rest of them, moving out into Baccha's suite. I was going to start running again, this time for my room and my weapons, when the door to the sitting room creaked open.

Baccha stepped out. "If you've come to ask me to be your escort to your party, this is too last-minute."

I crashed into him, but Baccha caught my fists before I could hit him. "Why would you leave your door open? You fool, I thought she had you too. I thought—"

"Princess, love, what has happened?"

I grabbed his arm and started running again.

I changed while someone else explained to Baccha and Mirabel. I hesitated over my swords, but eventually belted the Khimaerani blade around my hips. I'd killed somebody with it and I felt more murderous than ever now. Besides, it was another piece of Papa that I could carry. The knives I'd strapped to my legs earlier stayed and I added two on my wrists. I also hung the horns around my neck.

When I left my dressing room, I called Baccha, Mirabel, Anali, and Falun into my room.

I pointed to the hatch Mirabel had boarded up. "I need this removed. The best way to get to Isadore's room without alerting her is through the passageways."

Mirabel snorted. "I'm certain your mad sprinting through the Palace has alerted her enough. I wouldn't worry about that."

"I wasn't asking." I pointed again. I turned to Anali. "Only Baccha is coming."

She sputtered, stepping closer to me. I willed myself not to step back. "Eva—" she started. I cut her a hard glare. "Your Highness, Prince Aketo is important to me, as are you. I would ask that I accompany you."

"This is my fight. It isn't about Aketo. She's just using him to draw me to her." And I was going to kill her for it, if I could. She'd taken so much; she couldn't have him. I refused.

"I know, Your Highness, but *you* are my fight and Aketo is my Prince. Rival Heirs have done this many times before, and often those they take are killed. Princess Isadore would likely face no consequences for his death. I cannot let that happen."

I opened my mouth—a yes perched on my lips—but an edge of panic scattered my thoughts. I needed someone to make certain Aketo was safe, but Anali could be used against me. I couldn't offer Isadore another weapon. I'd seen Baccha withstand her magick. He was the only one I could bring.

But even more than that, I needed to do this without her. I didn't have time for Anali to question me or worry about my welfare. This wasn't just about me anymore and, despite her words, I wasn't certain she would see it that way.

"I'm sorry, Anali," I said, voice fraying. I pressed my lips together and shook my head until I had control. "Captain, I'm sorry, but no. You will stay here with Falun and the rest of the guards. If we do not return in an hour, it will mean that

I am likely dead, but you still must bring everyone you can to Isadore's rooms and save Aketo. And Baccha, should he require saving."

"Evalina, Falun and your Captain should go with you," Mirabel said.

"I'm sorry. They both have to stay safe," I whispered. For the first time, I felt emotion seeping through the cracks in the steel fortress I'd erected around my mind.

I stumbled toward a chair as the room swam. I curled my hands into fists. I didn't have time for this. I had to save Aketo.

"I have to do this," I said. "Baccha will be with me. I won't be alone."

"Evalina," Anali said, her voice thick with an emotion that I had no time to understand. I thought she would argue, but she just squeezed my hands and said, "You have an hour."

Falun pressed a kiss to my cheek; his face was wet with tears. "My Queen."

Mirabel set someone to pull up the boards on the hatch and then pulled me to the side.

She glanced down, and when she looked up, her eyes had filled with tears. "Your father would be so proud of you."

"Proud of what?" I asked. I itched to tell her I had no time for this.

"You've feared facing your sister since you first learned of this. You feared your place in this world and your magick—your very self. It takes a great deal of strength to face your fears." Her eyes went distant, recalling something other than this moment. "Even your father, great man that he was, never mastered that."

She pulled me into an embrace, but I could hardly wrap

my arms around her. I couldn't put all the battling fears inside me into words. At least not ones I was willing to say aloud.

This could be the last time I would see her, Falun, and Anali.

I wiped my wet eyes and followed Baccha down the ladder. I couldn't even manage to tell them goodbye.

As soon as my feet hit the floor, the hatch closed, leaving us in the dark. "I will challenge Isadore and you will take that opportunity to free Aketo."

"You should avoid challenging your sister, if you can. You're not ready yet," Baccha said. My eyes hadn't adjusted, but I could see his, luminous in the dark. "Distract her as long as you can. We will see to Aketo."

I started down the passage, resting my hand on the bone hilt of my sword.

"I have to challenge her," I said. "Why wait?"

"What about the binding?" he whispered, near my ear.

"I already tried," I said, casting my voice low. Mirabel and Anali still didn't know about the binding. Baccha blinked at me. "I couldn't do it. I will have to try to kill her without magick."

Baccha let loose a string of curses. "I would have told you the key to breaking it if I'd known you'd do something as stupid as to try on your own."

"What else was I to do? Wait for you to fix me?" I laughed. "It's not worth discussing anymore. I tried. I can't break it and I can't use my magick." I was back where I started, only now I'd had a taste of my magick. I knew its power and I'd lost most of my fear of it. Yet I was here still and I would use what little magick I could.

"What did you do, exactly?"

I explained, though I didn't want to. We were close to Isadore's rooms and I wasn't going to hope Baccha could fix it.

When I finished, Baccha was muttering under his breath.

"The problem is, you don't know the most important part, Princess." He shook his head.

I stopped. "What is it?"

"The key to removing a binding is wanting your magick. And not just as a tool." He stopped me with a hand on my shoulder. "Magick is a vital part of who you are. To break the binding, you have to accept yourself. Even the parts you don't like. That is why the binding has gotten worse after your father's death—because you resent yourself."

I stepped away from him with tears in my eyes. It took only a moment to steel myself against it. I twisted Papa's ring on my finger until I felt barely anything at all.

I stepped back and pulled my sword from its scabbard. "Draw your weapon. We're close now."

Just walk straight to the right, I'd told Anali. *When you see blue tiles and a ladder, climb.*

We walked right under the hatch, a square slab of sandstone rimmed with light. It could have led anywhere, but I'd sat here before, dozing while my fingers traced the cobalt tiles, waiting for Isadore to let me up. I knew what awaited me.

Our suites mirrored each other, Isa's in the east wing of the Palace and mine in the west. They were so similar. When we were children all the furniture in our rooms was the same, down to the hand-painted doves on our bedposts.

Even the hatch was the same, like the placement of these rooms had been designed to keep us connected.

Baccha took a step toward the ladder and my mind suddenly went clear as crystal. Aketo had been taken because of me. This was my fight. And I wasn't going to put anyone, not even Baccha, in danger.

Before he could realize what I planned, I sheathed my sword and jumped in front of Baccha. I started climbing up the ladder.

Instead of pushing it open, I banged on the hatch. "I'm here, Isadore. I've come to challenge you, on the condition that you let Prince Aketo go."

There was no answer. I said it formally. "I've come to challenge my Rival Heir, Princess Isadore, her magick of light and persuasion. I've come to challenge you, Isa, just as long as you return my Prince!"

For a moment, I thought I was wrong. Isadore had taken Aketo to another place. Maybe she was going to kill him, just to see how it would weaken me. Maybe it was someone else who took him, because they didn't like the khimaer Prince dancing with their Princess.

The hatch swung open and a guard with fey-sharp ears was silhouetted in the light. He reached for my collar, but we both knew he couldn't hurt me.

"Her Highness awaits you in her sitting room. I will gladly bring you and Lord Hunter," he said.

I glanced over my shoulder at Baccha. He nodded. "By all means, show us the way."

✦✦ CHAPTER 33 ✦✦

THERE WERE TEN guards in the room, half human and the other half fey. Even knowing none of them could harm me, my mouth still went dry. I could feel my heartbeat in the fingers curled around the bone hilt.

None around us moved as Baccha, keeping his knife in place, bent the guard's arms behind his back.

"As you said." Baccha pushed the man forward. I walked a few steps behind the two, my sword pointed straight ahead.

We made our way around a large four-poster bed, past a table strewn with what looked like invitations—the gold-and-poppy-orange invitation to my nameday ball in the center—and past an empty dress form.

It was eerily intimate, and wrong somehow, even with all these guards watching us. Challenges were meant to be at least somewhat public, as well as not held on the night of a nameday ball. Isa's guards didn't seem to care. Their faces gave no impression that they thought there was anything wrong with kidnapping a man in order to force a challenge between Rival Heirs. We reached the door and Baccha gave the guard enough slack to pull it open.

I turned to watch our backs as we left the room, but still none of the guards moved toward me, as if their instructions had accounted for every moment of this.

When the door swung closed behind me, I spun around. Another line of guards, five this time, pointing toward a door to the left.

"Baccha," I whispered. "Call to the wind and the wolves when we go into that room."

By design, the abundance of guards expecting us had set me off-balance. This moment had been planned carefully. The invitation felt like a taunt, and all these guards, a show of power.

Well, Baccha had enough power for the both of us.

"As you wish," Baccha murmured.

I stepped in front of him just before we reached the door. "Leave the guard."

I pulled open the door and stepped inside.

The stirring wind lifted my hair off my neck as my eyes adjusted to the dim light. Isadore sat on a narrow bench in the center of the room and Aketo sat next to her, his hands and feet tied with rope. No one else was in the room.

Isadore smiled at me, looking so like her childhood self, as if I was the trinket or candy she'd requested. Aketo seemed calm, at least until he saw my face. His eyes rolled over to Isadore and he glared at her.

Isadore shivered, her hands curling into delicate fists, and she laughed. "Are you really going to try to use your magick again?" She twisted toward Aketo and grabbed his chin, forcing his eyes to hers. I could feel her magick, pulling at me. She was beautiful, heart-achingly so. "Do you love her? I could convince you to love me, if only I had use for a powerless khimaer."

"Stop," I cried, but didn't step forward. That sucking void of her power filled me with dread.

Aketo growled low in his throat and opened his mouth, fangs bared. "Let go of me, Princess Isadore."

"Let him go, Isa, so we can end this."

"End it?" Isadore laughed again and rose to her feet. There was a knife in her hand and I wasn't sure where she had gotten it. "We've just begun, little sister."

It was my turn to laugh. "We began the first time you tried to kill me, Isadore."

She tilted her head, giving me a strange look. "You're still going on about that, Eva? It's been years."

A shiver went up my spine. The pitch of her voice was high and wrong, her frozen smile.

"Are you all right, Isadore?" I asked, inching farther into the room.

She shrugged, casual as anything. "I will be. I'm about to become Queen."

"Even if you kill me, it'll be years yet until Mother gives you the crown."

"No," Isa said, grinning widely enough to show all her teeth. "I know how to force her hand. I know all of her secrets."

I froze. "Speak plainly, Isa. What secrets?"

She giggled softly and shifted on the couch. I caught a glimpse of polished steel. "You and me, Eva. We're only half sisters and Mother hid it from everyone."

"Liar," I growled.

A look of murder flashed across her face. "You are the liar." She took a half step forward, but then turned back to Aketo. "Did you use your magick to make her fall in love with you? It seems a waste. You should have saved yourself the effort. If Eva can kill me, there will soon be a khimaer Queen on the throne."

Aketo froze. "What are you saying?"

Had they been chatting this way, Isadore rattling off these ridiculous ravings, and Aketo enduring it, since he was taken?

"He doesn't know?" She blinked at me. "Oh, Eva, you didn't even tell him? What about . . ." Isadore's wild eyes latched on to Baccha. "You knew, didn't you, Hunter?"

Baccha went still next to me.

"Knew what?" Aketo asked.

Isadore let out a stream of hysterical laughter. I wanted to grab her shoulders and shake her until she started speaking with sense. "Oh. She still doesn't know."

I'd lost all patience with this. "*Know* what?"

"Mother was engaged before she and Papa were married. When she became with child"—Isa's voice took on a bitter tone—"her betrothed fled Ternain. For some reason, he didn't want to become King. Papa was just a replacement. He was a rising star in the Queen's Army from an unknown House and a perfect pawn for Mother to manipulate. But that isn't even the best part."

"Isa, I know you and Papa weren't close but this is ridiculous. He was your father as much as he was mine."

Isadore ignored my words. "The best part is Papa tricked her into thinking he was human. Papa was khimaer. *You* are khimaer."

I shook my head. This—that couldn't be true. Papa would have told me if he was khimaer. Besides, if I was khimaer, Isadore was too. "But you—Isadore, no. Papa wasn't khimaer. Who told you this? Isa, it can't be true."

"It's true." She wiped at a single tear falling down her face and folded her arms across her chest.

A horrible thought occurred to me. "Did Mama tell you this? You know she hated Papa. You can't trust what she said about him. Our father kept secrets, but he couldn't have hidden something like this . . ."

"He was not my father." Her voice shook and she pointed the knife toward me. "He was a beast and a liar. And you are not my sister, not really."

"Please, Isadore. This can't be true. Tell me who told you this. We'll make sense of this together." I recognized the taste of salt in my mouth. I was crying and I couldn't even lower the sword to wipe my eyes for fear that she'd attack me.

"Baccha," I said. "She's lying, isn't she? Someone told her this and she just . . ."

"Princess, no matter what your sister says, you came here for a reason," Baccha said slowly. His eyes were shiny with tears. "This is still your fight. End it."

Then I realized—the binding. Papa had said that it was created to lock only a portion of my magick away. What if it was khimaer magick? It had never made sense, my father

329

binding my magick just because of the word of the Auguries. But if he had known there was something I needed to hide to grow up safe in the Palace . . .

It is true.

My father was khimaer and I . . .

My blood raced beneath my skin. I closed my eyes as the room spun. "But how could he lie? How could he . . ."

It takes a great deal of strength to face your fears . . . Even your father . . . never mastered that.

And wasn't the truth impossible to face?

My sword rang as it hit the floor and I met Aketo's eyes, so beautiful and so wide with confusion. He didn't know, but Baccha did. Baccha knew the truth, and Papa had *lied*, spent his life lying. Like a flame under a strong wind, my vision wavered, then blew out. When I opened my eyes, I found the dark, damp dirt on the edge of my lake.

I lay on my side, finger dipping beneath the water. I stretched toward it and reached for the truth.

The water felt warm and welcoming as I kicked to the bottom. Tendrils snatched at my arms and legs, but it wasn't magick—it was fear. I let my desire for the truth fill me up, because that was what this binding kept trapped. All the magick I feared was part of the whole truth of me and I wanted it.

I wanted me.

When I reached that shining barrier, I stretched out a hand and cut through it like a knife. I gasped in wonder as warmth enveloped me and golden light blew through my mind.

Pain lanced through my limbs, like my bones were growing too quickly for my body to contain.

I felt small as a child growing in my mother's womb, but also large and infinite—layered, feathered, scaled, and furred. I rolled around in the allness and felt warmth and comfort that had been trapped inside me along with this magick.

I felt wholly different, but whole for the first time. I had only my mind, and in my mind I could become all manner of things. No, I *was* all manner of things.

A sound pricked my consciousness and I chose, understanding that choosing was now a part of me.

I opened my eyes to find Baccha standing over me, soft wonder on his face. I'd curled up on my side and I looked down at my fists clenched so tight. I relaxed them and winced, feeling as if I'd just pulled pieces of glass from my palms. Then I screamed.

CHAPTER 34

BLACK CLAWS CURLED over my fingertips, wet with my own blood. A growl vibrated through my chest. I tried to sit up and realized my head felt heavier than it usually did. Tentatively I ran my fingers over my face—no changes there—then over my scalp, and I jumped as the claws scraped against horns. Like the antelope horns, these spiraled up to sharp points. Unlike the antelope horns, they forked at the midpoint, stabbing backward. I felt up to the top, not breathing the entire time. My claws clicked against them and I snatched them away, afraid I would cut them.

Another scream built in my chest, making it impossible to breathe.

"Eva?" Baccha reached toward me.

I flinched away.

A strangled noise from the other side of the room made me look up. The sound hardly escaped Isadore's mouth before I shifted into a crouch. She stood next to Aketo, the point of her long knife pressed to his throat.

I made a noise between a whine and a growl. "Let go of him."

"You stay back," she said, "or I will kill him."

I glanced at Baccha. He nodded and reached for my hand. My claws slid along his palm when I let go, drawing blood.

I jerked away from him, but Baccha just shook his head and dropped his hand so that one of the wolves could lick his wounds.

Nothing made sense—who or what I was, *why* I was—but I understood that knife against Aketo's neck. I understood that it was there because of me.

My sword was only a few feet from where I'd fallen. I picked it up and leveled it at my sister once again. "I, Princess Evalina, challenge you for the title of True Heir."

Isadore bent down and reached under the bench to retrieve another long knife.

She didn't smile or gloat. All the wind had gone out of her sails. She looked hollow, broken somehow, and she would look at me only out of the corner of her eye. Even so, there was steel in her voice when she said, "Let's begin."

I let out a breath, and then Isadore shifted her blade and stabbed Aketo in the chest. He and I screamed as one.

In that moment of distraction, Isadore struck, lunging forward with both of her knives outstretched.

If she had any fear of me, of this new version of me, it didn't show. When I blocked the strike of her blades, she spun, one blade striking me across the stomach, raising a line of fire.

I hissed and danced out of her reach, looking for Baccha and Aketo. I glanced over my shoulder, even though I knew it would cost me. Baccha had pulled Aketo from the bench and was busy cutting him free. His eyes were only half-open and blood spilled down his clothes like a splash of crimson paint.

Red washed over my vision.

"Go," I called. "Get him out of here."

With my back turned, Isadore's knife bit deep into my shoulder.

I swung the sword as I spun, but Isadore avoided the blade, using the guards on her knives to shove me away.

Isadore came toward me again, but I ducked her blades, slamming the pommel of my sword into her stomach. I twisted my sword upward, striking just where I knew she would be. She raised one knife, holding me just inches from her neck.

I could hear her heart beating and knew I was stronger. I flexed my arms and pushed her own blade down to her flesh. Isadore bared her teeth in a grin. Her eyes met mine—flaring so bright that light emanated from them—and I was lost.

Every bit of my will melted away as she pushed her desires into my head. She blew through me like a scorching wind, like a storm. In the haze of her power, I realized she'd been holding back for years. The beauty she displayed at Court had been a parlor trick. This was a crushing, expansive power—poison coaxing me toward death.

When I looked up, a crown rested on Isadore's head: sharp red rubies like tiny hot knives, her golden hair falling like flames around her delicate face. She glowed from the inside out, looking like Mother, but so much more.

She was the Queen. How hadn't I seen it before?

I lowered my sword and fell to my knees, swaying toward her like a flower in the sun.

I gasped as she gripped the back of my neck in an iron grip. Her other hand went for my throat, gentle yet holding a blade painted in blood.

There were tears in her eyes, glittering like diamonds.

My beautiful sister, why should she cry?

Suddenly howls rent the air, shattering Isa's voice inside my head, and I remembered myself.

Isadore's hold on me broke. My claws raked down her arm and she stumbled back.

The wolves surrounded me, their howls mournful and aching. One voice rose above them all, Baccha screaming my name. "Eva, your magick!"

"Call off those beasts, Eva. This is a fight between you and me."

I climbed to my feet and lifted the sword again, the hard edges of the bone hilt cutting into my palms. I stepped away from the wolves.

I already had Isa's blood dripping steadily from my fingers. And the antelope horns I'd claimed still swung from my neck. Could I even use marrow and blood magick? I had removed the binding, but doubt still lingered. Magick had never come easy to me.

I ripped my sleeve, reaching for a blood magick tattoo.

I wiped the blood across the tattoo and my arm burned with it, every tattoo feeling warm and alive. But I wasn't quick enough. I lifted the sword in a two-handed grip as Isadore spun toward me, blades flashing silver and bright. I couldn't risk her magick again. I shut my eyes and listened to the whistling of the blades, the off-kilter beating of her heart.

Soon as I felt her near, I pivoted, bringing the blade low. Her knives struck with my sword in a jarring impact. Using the hilt, I pushed her backward, then kicked her in the chest. I reached for the energy in the horns as I heard the welcome sound of air being shoved from Isadore's lungs.

She bent over, coughing, and I swept her feet from under her. She landed on her back with a yelp, but was on her feet again in a moment, circling.

The warm buzz of the horns' power surged through my limbs.

My eyes fell shut and I found myself back at the lake, now choppy with energy. When the blood magick rose from its depths, I took it in my hands and threw my consciousness back toward my body. I opened my eyes to find Isadore's blades just inches away. Quick as a flash, I caught her wrist and held on even as her knife bit into my arm.

"That's enough, Isa." Isadore watched in horror as the crimson power on my hands crept over her skin. "Drop your weapons."

I hissed in pain as she pulled one of the blades from my arm and waited till both fell to the floor. I kicked them far out of her reach.

I could see how I could easily kill her. I could bleed my sister dry with just my bare hand on her wrist. The world narrowed to nothing but her pulse beneath my fingers. It fluttered, quick and delicate as a bird.

Memories flooded me. My mind flashed from Isadore's

bruise blooming at my touch and her hands wrapped around my throat, to dipping our feet into the Red River, clasping her hand in mine as we were chased from the Palace's kitchens.

"Do it," Isa said, her face carved in rage. "Just kill me, if you can."

Well, she'd always wanted to see my magick. *Bleed.*

Blood sprayed as four long wounds opened on her arm, but Isa only laughed. "Is that all?"

"How can you want this? Is the throne so important that you would race toward death?"

"I did what we were born to do tonight, Eva. Should I have waited until you felt strong enough to challenge me? I'm not some bloodthirsty monster. I want to live. I want to become Queen—you hardly care." She shook her head and spat out some of the blood. "I told you the truth that day at Court. I don't know who was trying to kill you, but it wasn't me. Probably someone who knows you're part khimaer and thinks it's their duty to kill you, just like it is mine."

But she failed and here I was, about to kill her.

Tears rolled down her face. "Just end it, Eva. Kill me cleanly if you can manage it."

I needed her to stop speaking before I accidentally killed her. It was becoming harder and harder to resist, when her words made me want to hurt her. But as I imagined the blood that would spill from Isa's neck, Papa's broken body flashed through my mind. The coppery tang of blood and stomach-turning reek of gore filled my nose.

I shook my head, dispelling the memory, and ground out, "Who told you about Papa?"

"Just kill me, Eva. One of us has to end this. Although," she sneered, "there's no way you can be Queen now. They'd have to break the crown just to fit it on your head."

Despite her words, I saw the pain and regret in her eyes. The fear.

No, a voice whispered in my mind. No more killing, no more death.

Just as Anali said weeks ago, we decide how to use our gifts. Regardless of the crown, the law, and the throne, this was my decision. One I would have to live with for the rest of my life.

"Don't you know that crown was made for khimaer Queens?" I smashed the pommel of the sword over her head.

Isadore's eyes rolled back and she fell to the floor.

Someone's hands closed around my shoulders. "She'll survive," Baccha said.

"I nearly killed her. I almost wanted to do it. Baccha, why didn't you tell me? How could you have known?"

Baccha hesitated before spinning me around. His eyes held steady with mine. "I wasn't certain. I suspected it when we found the binding, and I knew if anyone found out, you would be killed. I couldn't let you break it."

In the silence that followed his words, we heard the sounds of swords striking each other. Only a moment later, the door crashed open.

Anali had a bloody smear down the side of her face, but when she saw me, her face went completely blank. Her gaze tracked to Isadore's fallen body. "Is she . . . Is Princess Isadore dead? We've taken care of her guards."

Falun stood in the doorway behind her, eyes wide as he took in the scene. It was me he stared at the longest.

Baccha spoke, so that I didn't have to. "Someone must see to Prince Aketo. I healed him as best as I could, but he should still see a true healer. And we need someone to carry Princess Isadore. She will be coming with us." Baccha's eyes slid to me. "Also, we need to get back to Eva's rooms immediately. Unless you'd like it to get out that the Princess is khimaer."

⇥ CHAPTER 35 ⇤

"TELL ME."

Mirabel sat down heavily, patting the bun her hair was twisted into. I couldn't stop pacing across my bedchamber, cringing each time my nails rasped against the marble. There were claws on my feet too, which I hadn't noticed until I walked into my room. Strange, silly things kept occurring to me. Bits of lacquer still clung to my claws, which struck me as both macabre and amazing, but mostly nauseating. All my slippers would be useless and I'd need new boots, but wouldn't the claws shred through everything?

I turned toward her. "Isadore said that Papa was khimaer. She said Papa wasn't her true father. And I . . . well, obviously there was truth to what she said."

"It . . . oh, *a'daya*," she said. My daughter, in Khimaeran. "Your father wanted you to be named True Heir before you learned who . . . what he was. He didn't want you to have to cope with both at once."

"So it's true." I pressed my palms to my eyes and stumbled toward my bed. When I saw Isadore there, blond hair bright against my dark bedspread, I paced away. Mirabel had forced a sleeping draught down her throat when we returned to my room. But I wanted to wake her so that we could question her. Who else had she told?

My panic spiked; I began twisting Papa's ring. "Papa told me that he placed the binding on me because of the omens. Was that a complete lie?"

"The omens only confirmed what he knew. If your khimaer magick was ever discovered, you would have been in danger."

"How does this work, Mira? I thought bindings trapped *magick*, not—not your entire being."

"It *is* your magick, Eva. Khimaer magick is more intrinsically connected to the body—so the bind held back magick along with your form. I don't know very much about it, so it's best you ask Lei's family about that."

"But you knew? You knew all this time that I was khimaer?" I closed my fists, my claws dragging against my palm.

"Your father made me swear, Eva. He feared placing so much on you. I knew he was wrong, but I listened." She drew in a shaky breath. "I thought he knew best. He was your father and I'm only . . ."

"Did Papa only marry Mother to put a khimaer Queen on the throne?"

"I believe there was some sort of plan, but I never learned the details. I know whatever plans were made, he did love your mother when they were first married."

"Who else knew? Anali?"

Mirabel nodded. I wiped at my eyes, but they were dry—blessedly dry. "Aketo?"

"No."

Well. There was that at least. But still, Baccha had suspected and all the people who raised me who had known the truth. And yet no one told me. I had never even suspected, but there were things I'd always found peculiar. Like why had Papa assigned me a khimaer nursemaid and Captain when it made Mother so angry? And why did Papa spend so much time at the Enclosures?

And why had I never known his family?

"We have to start packing now. We have to hurry. It's late already and—"

"Slow down, child. Packing for what?"

"We have to leave Ternain. You have to come this time too, Mira. I wish we had more time, but—" I cut myself off, rambling again. "I have to leave Ternain for good. Isadore isn't the only one who knows about me and until I know who else does, I'm in danger. And we still do not know who sent the assassin and Dagon, or who else was involved in my father's death."

"Your sister won't tell you a thing, not even because you've spared her. She is still her mother's child. Don't forget that, just because you couldn't . . ."

There was a hint of disapproval in her voice. More than a hint, really. "Mirabel, I couldn't. She is my sister and I love her. I won't kill her just for a crown. And while we're outside Ternain, there will be no one forcing us to."

Her eyes met mine and I could tell she was deciding how much to say.

"I know you have to leave, *for now*. But there's no time tonight. The sun's nearly risen. Everyone in the Palace will be up in a few hours. We'll plan; we'll keep you secluded and pray no one notices Isadore's disappearance. Then you can leave."

"Then *we* will leave."

"No, my place is here in the city, so that I can get word to you about whatever is happening in Ternain. Have you decided where you'll go?"

"I'll cross the Arym Plain to finally meet Papa's family and then I'll go to the only place I'll be able to blend in—the Enclosure."

"Ask the King's family for advice. They've been hiding for generations; they're quite good at escaping notice. And . . . they'll know more about your magick."

I wasn't too worried about that. Baccha would help me with my magick. Mostly I wanted see Papa's family so I could understand why Papa had married Mother in the first place, and how Papa's family came to pretend to be human. And how they managed it without being caught.

Mirabel pulled me into an embrace. I thought, for a moment, that I felt too numb to cry. But then Mirabel whispered into my ear: "You look so beautiful, so very beautiful."

My head tipped down with the weight of the horns, neck straining to hold them up. It was as if I wore a heavy crown, a crown not made of gold and silver, but something heavier, older, spiraling up and up.

Everything, all the rage and fear and confusion poured out of me, onto Mirabel's shoulder as I wept.

*

"Please, Mirabel, I only want to see her. *Please*."

I turned over, neck and shoulders aching greatly, and saw Mirabel standing in the doorway. I could see Aketo behind her, staring at me, his expression torn between alarm and shock.

"I've told you she is resting now and you should be too."

"Aketo," I whispered, trying to sit up.

"Please?"

She sighed and let him into the room. "I'll give you a few minutes."

I blinked a few times and Aketo was standing by my side. His eyes swam as he looked at me.

"Aketo." I touched his face; a tear fell onto the tip of one of the claws. Claws I hardly recognized as my own.

One nail caught the edge of his face, drawing blood. I wiped it away with the back of my hand and mumbled a useless apology.

Aketo grasped my hands. He leaned forward until he was inches from my face, gold eyes like coins, lashes casting shadows on his cheeks. "Please, please don't apologize."

"I'm sorry she took you. I shouldn't have left you. I just . . ." How many times did I need to say sorry? What could be enough, when he'd been taken and hurt because of me. "I am so sorry."

"I felt you change, Eva." His voice took on a fervent tone. "When I saw you, I thought I was dreaming—or that when your sister stabbed me, I died."

I turned away from the intensity in his eyes. He cupped my face. So close, I couldn't look away from him. We didn't kiss exactly, but my mouth rested against his. His fingers skated over my cheeks and slid into my hair, drawing a sigh from my lips that spilled right into his—carrying something in me, not love but a kin closeness. A bond of survival, forged twice over now. It tumbled from my heart and poured right into him.

His eyes moved over my horns. His hands were still in my hair, his thumbs close to the base of my horns. I pulled away, shivering. I didn't want him to touch them—I didn't want him watching them like some kind of marvel, like I was changed.

I looked away from him. "I know it's different. I'm not . . . the same."

One of his hands moved from my hair to my chin, twisting it so that I faced him. "It makes no difference. Whatever outward changes, you're the same. You feel the same." He pressed his lips hard against mine. He whispered against my ear, "You taste the same."

I laughed until his lips captured mine again and I became lost in them. He tasted of my favorite mint tea, steeped just a bit too long, and sweetened with two spoonfuls of honey. Bitter and achingly sweet—just right.

But still the thought came to me. *Are you the same? And if you're khimaer, are you still a Princess?*

"I should let you rest," Aketo said, sensing my torment. We shared a breath and he turned away.

I grabbed his wrist. I didn't want to be alone. "Stay."

"Are you sure?"

No, I wasn't, but I was tired of spending every night alone waiting for my nightmares to find me.

When Aketo crawled beneath my blankets and draped an arm around me, I let my eyes fall shut. Soon I would cross the Red River, under the cover of Baccha and Falun's heavy glamour, with this Prince beside me. I felt so many things at once, but one won out: hope.

Once I left Ternain, I would know something akin to freedom, the likes of which I'd never felt before.

⇥ Epilogue ⇤

Queenmaker

A KNOCK SOUNDED at the door. Baccha swore—*rot and thrice-damned magick*—and lifted the pen off the paper. A drop of ink fell from the tip, ruining the page.

He frowned. He'd only written her name so far, but words to suit this occasion floated at the edge of his thoughts.

My apologies, Evalina, I'm breaking what little trust is left between us. Best of luck, love. Remember at coronations red is best. Reminds them of all the blood you've spilled to get there— and all the blood you'll spill should anyone cross you.

No, that wasn't right.

Having decided against throwing the table into a wall, Baccha crumpled the parchment and strode to the door. He hoped it wasn't one of guards the girl had sent to watch over him. The fools thought that if they knocked every so often, to remind Baccha of their presence, he would stick around.

Luckily it wasn't them. It was the boy, the Prince. He still looked dazed from last night, but some small happiness hung about his face. He'd seen her, then. He smelled like her—

crushed roses, blood, steel, and a bit of Baccha's own scent, the result of the coalescence.

Baccha let him into the room. "How is she?" he asked in Khimaeran, for the boy was freer with his words in his native tongue.

Aketo rolled his eyes. "Come see for yourself. I doubt you'd like my assessment anyway."

True enough.

"So you've come to hurry me along." The news that they were all leaving Ternain hadn't come as much of a shock, though Baccha had hoped that Mirabel would force her to mull it over for a day or two, giving him time to leave before Eva could notice. Unfortunately not. And he hated making escape plans under such a tight deadline. "Running errands for her now?"

"She's anxious. She was going to send Falun, but I figured he would only slow you more." His eyes dipped to the parchment in Baccha's hand.

Baccha held up three fingers in a rude gesture and Aketo grinned. "I need more time, and I'm sure you can *soothe* the Princess's . . . anxieties."

Aketo flushed, but lifted his chin. "How much time, Hunter?"

Baccha didn't answer, spinning his horn bracelet around his wrist. His mind wasn't on Aketo anymore, but on his next few weeks and how he would explain her to the Tribe. *I've disobeyed your orders, yes, but only because I knew our hope, our salvation lies within this girl, who is terribly powerful, but wants nothing more than to be free—who deserves nothing more than that.*

He pulled a knife from his sleeve. Steel flashed as he turned it over and under his knuckles, calming himself.

Aketo repeated his question and Baccha considered every option before landing on the truth. "I won't be traveling with the Princess. I need you to protect her, and I need you to give this to her." Baccha held up the bracelet. He couldn't afford to be followed. "I can only leave if I know she has it. Do you understand?"

"How can you leave after everything?"

Gods, he was going to regret this. He rolled up his sleeve to reveal the tattoo there. Despite its age, it had never faded—a red crown, a black staff, and a narrow dagger. "There is a legend, Prince—a hope—but very few khimaer let themselves believe in it. Do you know of what I speak?"

Aketo's mouth fell open. "The Tribe? You—you've been with the Tribe?" the Prince asked. "The Tribe still lives?"

"Yes." Even that one word sent a spike of pain through the base of his skull. The Tribe was a secret buried deep within a legend, and a fair amount of magick. Their secrecy was thrice sworn by all who learned of the Tribe. But in the centuries since leaving Myre to work for the them after the Great War, Baccha had learned a few ways around the prohibition.

Before Eva, he'd thought previous knowledge was the only one. Even though he'd all but spilled their every secret, he didn't worry about Eva finding out more. This was buried too deep for a girl who was raised human to have ever caught wind of. Now he knew that finding a way to share thoughts with someone would do it, though Baccha would not again risk coalescence. It had tied him to the Princess too tightly, making it impossible to follow his orders completely.

The old woman had ordered him to learn everything about the Killeen line and shatter their dynasty if he could. Well, he had learned—and he'd found a way to break them. But he didn't think the Tribe would consider putting a Killeen Princess on the throne drastic enough.

"And *you*? Why would *you* be with them?" Aketo's spine straightened, every inch the Prince.

"I may not be khimaer, but everything I am, I owe to them." Baccha wasn't going to explain that he would die without them—that he almost *had* faded when he tried to run during the Great War. There was no need to sound even more self-serving. "I must return, because I am sworn to, but also because I must find someone to teach Eva. The magick inside of her . . . There is only one person I know who can teach her to use it, and it is not me."

The girl had true Queen's magick. Khimaerani's magick.

"Why won't you just tell her you have to leave?" Aketo's fists were clenched. "If you go without seeing her, she won't forgive you."

"I can't." She would lock him away, and dungeon escapes were always tricky.

"Mother's cup, Baccha." He rubbed a hand over his face. "She can't take this, not now. After everything, how you could even consider it is beyond me."

"I know you want to protect her, but there is strength in her. Eva will endure what she must, and even if she never forgives me, I must do this. I don't have time to explain it all to her—or to you."

"How long, Hunter? How long will you be gone?"

"I'm not certain." He hoped the trip would be short, but

he had no way of knowing. "Protect her in my absence—and keep her sharp. Tell her I will miss her, and I will return as soon as I can. If she needs me, tell her to look to the bond. That may offer some comfort."

Baccha saw the disappointment on the boy's face. Luckily he was used to such reactions. He was trapped between an oath that couldn't be broken and his own desires. That rarely made for good company. "Just . . . be what she needs, as much as you can. I will find both of you as soon as I am able. By then I expect you'll have told her why you truly came here— and what her choices will mean for you."

Aketo winced. "I can't. Not yet."

"Your choice, Prince. Your risk." Baccha shrugged. He nearly warned the Prince that Eva's reaction to his departure might be unpleasant, but thought better of it. "Now go."

Before he could say anything else, Baccha gave the Prince a knife for himself, and the bracelet for the Princess.

After he left, the Hunter set to collecting his things.

It was time to make a Princess into a Queen.

ACKNOWLEDGMENTS

THIS BOOK WAS born of so many things, but the foremost among them was the love of my family and friends. This book would not exist without you. Thank you.

To my super agents, Taylor Haggerty and Holly Root, whose belief in me and this book—and Baccha—changed my world two years ago. Thank you for always having my back, for your sage advice, and for fielding my panicky emails. We will have those I HEART BACCHA T-shirts one day, I promise!

To my editor, Stacey Barney, whose wit, vision, and insight are sharp enough to stand against the many blades wielded in these pages. From the first time we spoke and laughed together, I knew Eva couldn't be in more capable hands. Thank you for your patience and relentless pursuit of my best. I've grown so much as a writer because of you and I am beyond grateful. I can't wait to go on this journey again.

To the incredible team at Putnam and Penguin Teen. Thank you for your passion and kindness and help in making this book-shaped dream a reality. I look forward to getting to know more of you, but for now, special thanks to Caitlin Tutterow, Felicity Vallence, and Lindsay Boggs.

To my brilliant cover artist, Alexxander Dovelin, and designer, Samira Iravani. Thank you for bringing Eva and Isadore to life, with all the beauty and fierce energy I dreamed of. It still takes my breath away.

Six years ago, I moved to New York for graduate school, and I am so grateful for the community I met and made there. A thousand thanks to my New School professors, Caron Levis and Sarah Weeks, and especially to David Levithan, my thesis advisor, who saw an early, frightful draft of this book and did not run screaming. Thank you also to my Writing for Children cohort, and especially P. G. Kain, whose advice still rings in my head daily: write the book.

To two of my closest friends, Laura Silverman and Anna Meriano. I could not have navigated this year without you. Thank you, Anna, for answering all my grammar questions, and thank you, Laura, for all your email advice. Thank you for keeping me hopeful. Thank you for making me a better writer.

To my dear friend and critique partner, Kyriaki Chatzopolou. Kiki the Impaler to my Amanda the Great. Simply put, I could never have done this without you. Your heart for story inspires me always. Thank you. Thank you. Thank you. All my love, always.

To my third-grade English teacher, Mrs. Zorns, who when I misbehaved placed the first Harry Potter book in my hands. You first taught me the joy of writing and I am so thankful.

To my brothers, Daniel and Jordan. Dan, your love of